A TOP TEN PICK O

O, The Oprah Magazine

"A mesmerizing read."
—*Seattle Times*

"Perkins-Valdez manages to shed a poetic light
on one of the ugliest chapters in American history."
—*Essence*

"Positively riveting. There will be obvious
comparisons to classics like *Beloved* and *Dessa Rose*, obvious
but deserved. *Wench* is risky, rich, confounding, maddening,
satisfying, illuminating, and downright fascinating."
—RANDALL KENAN, author of *Let the Dead Bury Their Dead*

"A finely wrought story that explores the
emotional lives of four slave women caught in
the web of the Peculiar Institution."
—LALITA TADEMY, author of *Cane River* and *Red River*

"Perkins-Valdez eloquently plunges into a dark
period of American history. . . . Heart-wrenching,
intriguing, original, and suspenseful."
—*Publishers Weekly*

"Absolutely phenomenal. . . . An excellent novel. . . .
Dolen Perkins-Valdez has crafted a historical
narrative that shouldn't be missed."
—*Sacramento Book Review*

WENCH

WENCH

A Novel

DOLEN PERKINS-VALDEZ

AMISTAD

An Imprint of HarperCollins *Publishers*

A hardcover edition of this book was published in 2010 by Amistad, an imprint of HarperCollins Publishers.

PS.™ is a trademark of HarperCollins Publishers.

Illustration of Tawawa House used courtesy of the Ohio Historical Society.

FIRST AMISTAD PAPERBACK PUBLISHED 2011.

The Library of Congress has cataloged the hardcover edition as follows:

Perkins-Valdez, Dolen.
Wench : a novel / Dolen-Perkins Valdez.—1st ed.
    293 p. ; 24 cm.
ISBN 978-0-06-170654-7
1. Women slaves—Ohio—Social conditions—Fiction. 2. Resorts—Ohio—19th century—Fiction. 3. Fugitive slaves—Fiction. 4. Ohio—History—1787–1865. I. Title.
PS3616.E7484 W46 2010
813'.6—dc22   2010277174

ISBN 978-0-06-170656-1 (pbk)

11 12 13 14 15 OV/RRD 10 9 8 7 6 5 4 3 2

DEDICATED TO MY PARENTS:
BARBARA AND JAMES PERKINS
FOR BELIEF, SUPPORT, AND LOVE.

WENCH:

(c. 1290): A girl, maid, young woman; a female child.

(1362): A wanton woman; a mistress.

United States:

(1812; 1832): A black or colored female servant; a negress.

(1848): A colored woman of any age; a negress or mulattress, especially one in service.

Her beauty was notorious through all that part of the country; and colonel Moore had been frequently tempted to sell her by the offer of very high prices. All such offers however, he had steadily rejected; for he especially prided himself upon owning the swiftest horse, the handsomest wench, and the finest pack of hounds in all Virginia.

—THE SLAVE: OR MEMOIRS OF ARCHY MOORE (1836)

PART I

1852

ONE

Six slaves sat in a triangle, three women, three men, the men half nestled in the sticky heat of thighs, straining their heads away from the pain of the tightly woven ropes. The six chatted softly among themselves, about the Ohio weather, about how they didn't mind it because they all felt they were better suited to this climate. They were guarded in their speech, as if the long stretch between them and the resort property were just a Juba dance away.

The men nibbled and sucked at yellow flowers, spitting the seeds into the water tins beside them, offerings they would make to the women when they were done. The women parted the hair with their fingertips, meticulously straightened lines crisscrossed like checkerboards. They warmed a waxy substance in their hands and spread it onto the hair. Two of the men had silky coils that stretched long. The other one had hair so short the plaits stuck out like quills.

They watched as the stranger approached. She balanced a basket on her head, the way they had in the old country. They could tell from the way the woman's skirt moved the fabric was a good one. But what was most striking about her was the bush of red hair that sprayed out from beneath the basket like a mane. None of them had ever seen hair so red on a colored woman.

Reenie, the oldest of the group, spoke first. "You staying at Tawawa?"

"Yeah." The red-headed woman took a careful survey of the group. Two of the women looked to be about her age. The oldest of them, the one questioning her, had yellowed, rheumy eyes that still maintained a sharpness. The men—twins and a third one with a flickering cheek—looked well fed and healthy. "Mawu."

"What?" said the old woman.

"That be my name. Mawu."

"I ain't never heard a name like that," Lizzie said. "How do you spell it?" Lizzie was proud of the fact that she could spell.

Mawu did not answer. She pulled at her left earring.

The slaves examined the red-headed woman as if she had just dropped from another world. They were unashamed in their curiosity, boldly eyeing the freckled hands, the unruly hair, and the two small earrings that bent the sunlight.

The stranger let them look, accustomed to such invasions.

Sweet spoke up. "Us can plait your hair."

Lizzie instantly wished she had thought first to ask. She wanted this creature with the strange name to be trapped in the curve of her own strong thighs.

Yet Mawu only regarded Sweet and her swollen stomach with a pitying look. She lifted a hand to her crotch, as if to warn off the misfortune that had resulted in Sweet's circumstance.

"No," said Mawu. "Tip wouldn't like it." She gathered the skirt and waved it about, boasting that the fabric was the result of keeping this "Tip" happy. But the three slave women responded with a tacit acknowledgment that this Tip was no different from theirs.

"Sit with us for a spell," one of the twins offered, pointing to the thickest patch of grass.

Lizzie was certain Mawu would decline the invitation, so she was surprised when the woman set down her basket, pulled up her skirt, and gathered her legs beneath her.

"They call me Philip," said the man between Lizzie's legs. He liked the looks of this one. He also liked the way she talked—a melodic accent that pulled at the corners of her mouth. He hadn't taken a woman in months, and hadn't had a woman of his own in years. But something about her—maybe it was the hair—warned Philip that his interest shouldn't be of the permanent kind. "And this here is Henry and this is George. They brothers. I suppose these here women can introduce theyselves, but I can save them the trouble. This here is Reenie, they call this one Sweet, and the one here behind me is Lizzie. Me and Lizzie from the same plantation down in Tennessee."

Mawu added, "I come from Louisiana," although no one had asked.

Reenie nodded briefly and the other two women took that as a sign to go back to their work. The men tilted their heads again and popped the flowers into their mouths. Lizzie's hands were working on Philip, but her eyes were working on the lioness. She watched as Mawu looked off into nowhere, and so was the first to see Mawu's lips pucker and begin to hum something light. It sounded like it had some spirit in it, but it was no tune Lizzie had ever heard.

Mawu adjusted her melody, stringing together short rhythmic phrases here and there, the way the conjuring man had taught her. The mustard seeds plunked into the tin cups like drumbeats beneath her voice. When the seeds were all spent, she ended with a flourish. An appreciative silence followed.

"How long y'all gone be up here this summer?" Reenie asked, resuming their lazy conversation.

"Drayle says he wants to stay four weeks," Lizzie answered for her and Philip. "The missus says she wants Philip back so he can train this new hand they're buying."

"Us too," Reenie said. "Four weeks."

This was the second summer at the vacation resort for the six slaves. Three of the Southern men brought their slave women with them, first on ships and then riding in separate train cars after they entered free territory and boarded the Little Miami Railroad in Cincinnati. None of the Southern men brought their wives. Reenie's master had brought his wife up close to the end of the previous summer, and Sweet's mistress was dead. Lizzie's master, Drayle, had never mentioned the possibility of bringing his wife.

It was no secret many of the Northern whites who stayed at the resort disliked slavery. Even more, they disapproved of the slave women staying in the cottages with the white men. The resort was set in an area populated by Quakers and Methodists who declared themselves antislavery. West of Columbus, east of Dayton, sixty-four miles north of Cincinnati, the resort cast together an unlikely association of white Southern planters, white Northerners, free coloreds, and slaves. So the six slaves stuck close together, even avoiding the free black servants who worked in the hotel.

Now there would be one more, upsetting the easy balance of six. Lizzie guessed that Mawu was staying in a cottage like the rest of them. Surely Mawu's man wouldn't put her in the hot hotel attic with the rest of the servants and male slaves. She wanted Mawu to be in a cottage near hers. Even with Reenie and Sweet, Lizzie sometimes got lonely at this place. Reenie was always working, and Sweet was always tired. They all speculated on whether the woman was pregnant with twins, big as she was.

The twin named George switched positions so that Reenie could finish the other side of his head. "I hear tell of this place nearby. Colored folk. Free and fancy colored folk."

"What you talking about, George?" Philip faced him.

"I heard them talking. It's a place on the other side of them woods. It's where the free folk go to have summertime. Just like this place, excepting it's for us'n. All you got to do is walk right through them there woods."

"Well, I ain't never heard of such," Lizzie said. "Free colored folk having summertime!"

Mawu edged so close Lizzie could smell her. "Well, Miss . . . what you say your name was?"

"Lizzie."

"Miss Lizzie, you must not ever been off your place before. It's plenty of free colored folk. Rich, too."

"I know it's free colored folk," Lizzie snapped. "I am just saying I ain't never heard of them having summer in the country the way the white folks do."

"George is right," Reenie said. "I hear the white folks talking, too. Say they can't understand why they build this place so close to that one."

Everyone was quiet for a moment. They knew that Reenie, the oldest of the women, didn't lie. If she said she heard it, there wasn't a truer fact.

"Just how far is it?" Philip asked as Lizzie braided the next to last plait.

"Close enough to walk. Yessir it is." George rocked back and forth.

"Shh . . ." Reenie said. "Calm yourself. You know these trees got ears."

They all looked around as if Reenie had actually seen the trees lean forward. Except for Mawu. She looked right at George.

"So when us going?" Mawu asked.

Sweet stopped plaiting. "Us? Go? Ain't no womenfolks going nowhere."

"Well, you sho ain't going seeing as to your condition and all. But I want to see these rich colored folks." Mawu challenged them all with her voice. Lizzie tried to picture this Mawu's master, what kind of man *Tip* might be, what kind of place she lived on down in Louisiana.

"All right," Lizzie said and patted Philip on the shoulder.

"Your hair look real nice," Sweet said. "That ought to keep for as long as you here."

"It'll help with the heat. This sun is hot for sho," Philip said. He stood and stretched his legs and caught Mawu admiring his body as he did so. He knew he was something to look at. He knew it from the comments of slave owners and slave traders. He stole a peek at the new woman.

Lizzie sensed something between them. He cast his eyes back at the ground, but Lizzie thought there might be a secret meeting later. She had known Philip since she was a girl.

George stood, too, as Sweet gave him a final pat.

"I don't know why you don't want us to plait your hair," Reenie said to Mawu. Any of the other women would have heard and obeyed the command in Reenie's voice, but Mawu just shook her head.

"Come on, Miss Lizzie." Sweet beckoned her over. "Let me do your head." Lizzie planted herself on the ground and leaned forward so Sweet could start in the back.

Reenie pushed Henry out from her legs so he could follow the other two men who were already walking off. There was nothing left for her to do, so Reenie sat there glaring at Mawu as if her sudden uselessness were all her fault.

"You even know how to plait," Reenie said in what didn't even try to pass as an asking tone.

"Course I do. What kind of woman you think I is?" Mawu folded her arms across her chest.

"That's what we're trying to figure out," Lizzie said, rising to the defense of Reenie. That woman had been too good to her to allow this red-headed, slow-talking woman to insult her.

"Well, I can sho see what kind of womens y'all is."

Sweet let out a high-pitched belch. "What?"

"You heard me. Y'all ain't talking about nothing, ain't doing nothing. You probably run behind your mens all day sweeping up they dirt."

Reenie calmed Lizzie with a touch of her toe on her friend's calf.

Instead of words, instead of a tongue lashing she would remember until she left the camp, they gave Mawu silence. They rewarded the arrival of this seventh slave with a cold, thick wall of disregard. Treated her as if she weren't there. Treated her as if she were an unfamiliar white woman sitting among them to whom they had no obligation. Sweet braided, Lizzie closed her eyes, and Reenie picked through the seeds the men had left.

Mawu sat there for a moment, waiting. Then she picked up her basket, perched it on her head, and walked stiff backed toward the resort.

TWO

~

Mawu waved her hands when she talked. She fluttered them about as if rearranging the air around her. There was a fluidity about the woman that made Lizzie take notice. At that very moment, she was stroking her bare chest right above her left breast, and Lizzie couldn't stop following the movement.

Lizzie compared her own dark brownness to Mawu's lighter hue. In her mind, she lined the two of them up side-by-side: legs, arms, waists, shoulders. Drayle had told Lizzie countless times she was pretty, but she'd never really believed it about herself. The shape of Lizzie's face was squarish and strong. Someone had once commented that her thick eyebrows were becoming, but she'd always thought of herself as too hairy—it covered her legs and arms in a soft down, and instead of freckles like Mawu, she had been cursed with moles—fleshy ones, large and small across her chest and back. A particularly juicy one lay tucked in the corner above her left nostril, a final unfair flourish to her mannish face.

Mawu was freckled red, specks dotting her face like rain. She was petite with a short torso and long, thin legs. Her neck stretched long and seemed to be the only part of her body left unmarked. She had one pointed pinky nail that made Lizzie wonder how she worked with such a thing.

Lizzie had finally caught sight of Tip, Mawu's master, and she couldn't help but think he didn't deserve to feel the tender scratch of that fingernail along his back.

"You listening?"

Lizzie nodded her head yes and looked back into the skillet.

"My mammy taught me how to make this. She said—"

"Your birth mammy?" interrupted Lizzie.

"Course my birth mammy. Ain't you got a mammy?"

Lizzie shook her head. "She died before I remember. But I've got other ones. Aunt Lu raised me before I came to the Drayle place. Then after I was sold, Big Mama became my mammy. But when I moved into the big house . . ."

The unfinished sentence did not hover. They both knew what moving into "the big house" meant. They both knew the way it affected relationships in the slave quarters. This understanding was the main reason Lizzie liked coming to Tawawa. She didn't have to always explain herself. And sometimes that was a good thing since she didn't always have the words for it.

"Well, you take this here lesson on how to fix this stew back to your Big Mama. She gone love you for it. No reason why they can't eat like this in Tennessee."

Mawu tossed a careless smile in her direction. Lizzie didn't say that Big Mama was dead.

Instead, Lizzie looked off at the circle of twelve cottages that flanked the hotel, arcing around a pond. Most of the guests stayed in the main hotel, but the Southern men preferred to rent the cottages for the privacy. The hotel was a lofty white structure, three stories high, with twenty-four pane windows. Rocking chairs sat in groups of two on a wide porch verandah that ran across the front of the building. Six columns lined the verandah, forming a colonnade. In the middle of the pond, a wooden water wheel turned slowly, patiently, as if to signal that the days at the resort would turn just as steadily and would be in no hurry to cease. Drayle had described to Lizzie how the encompassing forest had not been decimated, only thinned, so that the most majestic trees remained. Meandering paths throughout the property led to the main building from various directions. The hotel sank into the hills, hugging the curve of the earth. An American flag topped a small carousel that perched above the hotel's highest point. When Lizzie first laid eyes on the resort, she thought it was a plantation, the grandest plantation she had ever seen.

Mawu explained how she had chosen the spot because the wind was coming from the east and "that big old tree blocked the wind like a giant woman." She said she figured her fire would stay lit long enough for the stew to simmer for a couple of hours.

Lizzie had been taking down laundry behind her master's cottage when Mawu came up from behind and put her arms around Lizzie's thick waist.

"Come help me cook these here birds."

Lizzie turned around, trying to hide her pleasure at the first sign of Mawu's interest in her. "A stew?"

"Yeah."

"I make a real good stew. Beef stew, mostly. Or pork."

"Yeah. Bet you don't make no stew like this."

Lizzie trailed after Mawu as they weaved between the cottages. "Wait, girl. These shoes are too small."

But Mawu didn't wait. She hurried on, never once turning around to see if Lizzie was keeping up. She just called back over her shoulder, "Your man ain't gave you no proper shoes?"

Lizzie slipped out of the shoes and continued on, her bare feet slick against the grass.

When they got to the spot Mawu had chosen, the bird pieces were spread out on a fresh cloth, already cut and partially cooked. Mawu had built a small fire out of six pieces of wood.

But as she stood watching and listening to Mawu's instructions, Lizzie could barely concentrate. Mawu looked down into the pot, and the taller Lizzie stood just behind her. There was something different about this one. Something about the way she set her shoulders, placed her lips, slit her eyes, planted her feet, swayed her hips. As if something bubbled beneath her surface just like the flesh simmering beneath the thick soup in the iron pot beside them. Lizzie started to ask her if she ever got beat. But what she really wanted to know was why this girl was so carefree in a world full of nothing if not care.

Mawu poured oil into the flour and stirred until it thickened into a gravy.

"I make my gravy with water," Lizzie said.

"Girl, that be your problem right there."

"What?"

"You don't half listen. Here I is, teaching you how to make my ma's stew and you still talking about what y'all do back in Tennessee."

Lizzie worked on being quiet.

"Now while I is making this here, you get them thangs over there ready."

"Your mammy was a white woman?"

"What?"

Lizzie inched closer. "Your mammy. Was she a white woman?"

"Why you ask that?"

"Cause I ain't never seen hair that color." Lizzie finally got close enough to touch it.

Mawu pulled her head back. "No, my mammy wasn't no white woman."

"Oh." Lizzie studied Mawu's light freckles that seemed to shift colors. One moment they were dark and the next they disappeared into the blush of her skin.

"But hers was a white woman. My granny. Can you believe that? A white woman fooling with a slave man. She disappeared."

"Your mammy did?"

"No, my granny. Ain't you listening? After she birthed my mammy, she disappeared two days later, they say. Left the baby behind." Mawu put the skillet aside and settled a deep cast-iron pot onto the fire.

"They killed her?" Long forgotten names came back to Lizzie, names of ones who had disappeared.

Mawu stopped and looked at her. "Girl, you got gizzards for brains? No, she just went away. She a white woman. She somewhere living but not somewhere where no slave daughter can find her."

"But ain't the baby free if the mammy is white?"

Mawu motioned toward the pot. "Put those carrots and thangs in this here pot. Us got to let them boil a bit. Then when us get everything in here, us gone add this here."

Lizzie did as she was told while Mawu cut up a big chunk of ham and dropped the pieces into the pot.

"I ain't never heard no such thing. Sides. That baby was rightful property," Mawu said.

The smell was making Lizzie sick with hunger. It didn't smell like her stew at all. And the bird wasn't even in there yet.

Mawu scooped up some in a spoon and fed Lizzie from it. Lizzie blew on it and sipped.

"This here the secret," Mawu said. She took a tiny sack from inside her dress and opened it. She poured what looked like ground-up herbs into the stew.

"What's that?" Lizzie asked.

"This what can soften the white man."

"Does it work?"

Mawu stirred.

"What'd you put in there?"

Mawu kept stirring and didn't answer.

Soften the white man. Lizzie turned the words over in her head as she waited for Mawu to tell her what to do next.

Once they had dropped the pieces of bird into the pot and Mawu had poked the fire down a bit, they lay beside each other on the ground and Mawu stroked between her teeth with a blade of grass. The wind had slowed to a crawl and the humid air beaded on their skin.

Lizzie raised up on her elbows and thought vaguely of the laundry still hanging. Then she turned back to Mawu and studied her again, wondering if she was some kind of witch. *Soften the white man?*

"You talk different." Mawu tossed the blade of grass aside. "Like the white folk."

"I can read," Lizzie said, as if that explained it.

Mawu stared at her for a few minutes. "You like coming here?"

"I like having a vacation like the white folks. And I like getting to spend time with my man." Lizzie had never met a witch before. But she'd heard about them. Mawu didn't look like any witch she'd ever dreamed up.

"He not your man, you know."

"Course I know that. But I don't mind spending time with him."

Lizzie figured that Mawu understood what she meant when she said *spending time* with him. Drayle said he brought Lizzie to tend his cooking. Sweet's master said he brought her to mend his clothes. Reenie's man didn't offer a reason. Lizzie wondered what lie Tip, Mawu's master, had told the wife he left behind.

"You don't?" Mawu tossed the grass away and sat up. She

looked Lizzie full in the face as if seeing her for the first time. "You think you love him?"

Lizzie felt the "course" rise in her throat, but stopped herself as she registered Mawu's disapproving tone. She felt if she answered no, she would be betraying Drayle. If she answered yes, she would be betraying something else.

"What is love?" Lizzie decided to say instead.

"How old you is?"

"Twenty-three." Lizzie didn't know her birthdate exactly. But she had always been told her age by Big Mama who had overheard Drayle telling it to his wife when they first bought Lizzie. Ever since, Lizzie had carved each year in the wall of Big Mama's cabin.

"You gone learn when you get to be a little older."

"How old are you?"

Mawu shrugged. "I don't know. Twenty-five maybe."

"That ain't so old. You've just got two years on me." Lizzie was quick to display her figuring abilities.

Mawu's face looked confused for a moment, and Lizzie guessed she didn't know how to figure numbers. She immediately resolved to teach her.

"Two years is a lifetime when you a slave."

Ain't that the truth, thought Lizzie.

"I ain't never loved Tip."

Lizzie nodded. Reenie and Sweet had said just about the same thing.

"So why are you with him?"

Mawu looked at her as if she were plain stupid. "Cause I belongs to him."

They sat beside the pot until after dark, Lizzie asking Mawu about life in Louisiana and Mawu asking questions of her own. When they saw the first of the white men walking back to his cottage, sweaty with fatigue and drink, they knew it was time to pack up. They split the stew between them and went their separate ways.

Lizzie held the hot pot out in front of her, hurrying back to her cottage so she could bring in the laundry before Drayle returned.

THREE

Inside the cottage, Lizzie felt human. She could lift her eyes and speak the English Drayle had taught her. She could run her hands along the edges of things in the parlor—two chairs, a sofa, a wooden table, a tall oil lamp with a milkglass base, a cast-iron stove—as if they were hers. And she could sit.

When she cleaned, she could do so with the satisfaction of knowing it was for her own enjoyment. After sweeping the floor, she could slide her feet along the smoothness of it. And she made sure every soup bowl was unsoiled because it would be her lips and her mouth that drank from it.

She heard Drayle remove his boots on the porch and listened to the familiar scrape as he lined them up, leaned his fishing pole against the side of the house. Then the swish of clothes as he stripped off what he did not want to bring inside, shedding them like a second skin. Without seeing, she knew he would fold them over the porch rail, neither touching the other.

"What's that smell, girl?"

"Stew." She accepted his kiss. He smelled of pine and dirt. A piece of cottonweed had folded itself into his hair like a patch of gray. She plucked it out and slid it into the pocket of her dress.

"I don't reckon that's a stew I've ever smelled."

She smiled. "Tip's woman taught me how to make it. Say it's Louisiana style."

"Who?"

"Tip—I mean Mr. Taylor's girl."

He laughed. "Oh yeah? Tip. That new fellow. He sure caught a big one today. And he didn't share it at all. I suppose his gal will have a hell of a time cleaning it and cooking it up this evening."

This evening? After spending hours over her mama's stew, Lizzie thought. She imagined Tip being true to his name, "tipping" over the bowl set before him until its contents ran red over the tablecloth, then shoving a pail of stinking fish meat into Mawu's arms. She could see Mawu standing behind the cottages near the creek, slitting the fish under its gill, tossing the guts into the water.

While Drayle went and washed up, Lizzie finished setting the table. Each time she did this, she felt the presence of the other slave women scattered among the cottages. All of the dishes in the little white houses were alike. Rumor had it that the wife of the owner had chosen them, and while she had been frugal with the furniture, she had splurged on the dishes. It seemed silly to Lizzie because so many of the dishes were broken that first summer. In this kind of place, the men grew careless with their living—fell asleep in their plates, belched freely, pissed close enough to the house to be seen, took their slaves on the tables. Even Drayle, who was the most orderly of men, sometimes took her in odd places. No. Dishes didn't have a chance.

Gold writing on the bottom of each dish curled into itself, too small for Lizzie to read even if she squinted. But she knew they were from some place special. Europe, maybe. The only thing

Lizzie knew of Europe was that it was another land where white men ruled.

Drayle's wife, Miss Fran, said slaves should eat with their hands because that was the way they did it in Africa. She said slaves didn't need dishes and such. Some slaves back on Lizzie's place had fashioned plates and spoons out of metal or wood. But many of them still ate with their hands.

Lizzie arranged the dishes just so, striving for perfection in the table. Drayle expected it. Even though she measured the distances between everything, he would sit down and rearrange everything one more time. He would judge her table with his eyes. This evening, she was especially aware of how important the table was. They had not had this talk in a while. It was time again. And she wanted nothing to distract him.

Wait till he has just finished the first bowl and is about to ask for the second. Stand, take his bowl and comment on how intelligent and well dressed the children are. Neat and respectful. Tell him to picture his beautiful children as slaves, sold off after his death to some mean old buzzard (not like him, nossir!) who would likely put them in rags and take away their books. Drop a dollop of cream on top of his stew and rub his shoulders. Remind him of that lawyer who always comes in the fall. Kiss him behind both ears . . . Be quiet and wait . . .

This was the plan, a variation of the script in her head she had repeated to herself all day. On the boat ride up, she had decided she would use time with him this summer to speak about her children once more. It was her second time crossing the Ohio River into free territory, and she felt the burning in her chest stronger than ever. Something in her moved as she thought of her children back on the place, unprotected by their mother, left to the whims of Drayle's wife who sometimes favored them and sometimes didn't.

And then there was this Mawu's stew. *Soften the white man.* Lizzie usually didn't trouble herself too much with religion,

let alone superstition, but she was counting on this stew. She'd
tasted it, and it was some of the best stew she'd ever had. It was so
good she'd made gurgling sounds as she sloshed it down, spread
it across her lips, stained them tomato-red. She wiped her mouth
on the rag she used to lift the pot. Then she ladled some more. It
tasted good, even cooled. The cottage was too hot to eat the soup
too warm. The spices awakened her tongue in unfamiliar places.

Final touch: daylilies in a cup on the table.

All she had to do was get him to talk with that lawyer so she
could make sure her children would be free. She would need to
see the papers herself, of course. He would have to show them to
her because she had heard stories of owners lying to their slave
women about their fates should their masters die, and then when
the time came, the women ending up on the auction blocks just
like the others, removed of their favored status, stripped of their
illusions.

Drayle drank the first bowl of stew faster than she could get
her nerve up. She walked right up behind him and refilled the
bowl, reminding herself to mention the beauty of their children.
She counted four deep breaths.

"You know, Drayle. We've got these two beautiful children that
look just like you. Your only son bearing your Christian name."

"No doubt about that."

"Our little Rabbit is so white, one day she could just up and
disappear into the white race altogether."

Drayle paused his spoon in midair for a second as if this
thought had never occurred to him. Lizzie was glad she had
named her son after him. Nathaniel Drayle, just like his daddy.
Fran had opposed it, of course. At first, she had refused to call
Drayle's son anything at all, simply referring to him as boy. *Get
that boy a rag and wipe his nose. Put that boy outside, he's mussing
up my parlor.*

Lizzie went on. "Just think. Our beautiful children sold off to some mean old slaveholder who doesn't realize how precious they are. Nate beat till he has forgotten all of his catechism. Rabbit picking cotton. Your grandchildren slaves forever."

"Oh, Lizzie," he said, cleaning his lips with his tongue. "You imagine too much. I never should have taught you to read. Slavery won't last forever, what with all this abolitionist talk going on. Shoot, I reckon by the time my grandchildren are born, they'll be free as a bird. They'll be little schoolteachers helping lift up all the other nigger children."

Lizzie dropped the spoon.

"I'm sorry, Lizzie. I'm sorry. I don't mean to upset you."

Lizzie forgot all about her carefully constructed plan.

"Drayle, free the children," she whined. "For God's sake, what kind of man lets his children be property? They are too soft for slavery. You have done nothing but protect us, but what'll happen when you're dead? What'll happen if that old witch Francesca outlives you?"

"Watch your mouth."

She stared into her cold stew.

He wiped the bowl with his finger, then stuck it in his mouth and sucked. He froze just as he was pulling the finger out of his mouth, as if remembering his manners. He rose, came around to her chair, and lifted her by the sides of her torso. She felt a bit of panic. She was supposed to have stood behind him, working on his shoulders. Maybe the spell had worked on her and not him.

"Come on, Lizzie. Haven't I done right by you? Haven't I always treated you like you were my very own wife?"

He kissed her behind her right ear, whispered the word *wife* as if it had a magical property all its own. Although he had washed up in the basin set up for him, he still smelled like the outdoors. She closed her eyes, searching behind her eyelids for the script she had practiced.

He pulled her up and led her into the other room, standing behind her, fitting his body into hers. Then he pushed her onto the bed. She lay flat on her stomach and waited.

He drowned her thoughts by saying: *don't you know how special you are? Don't you know I picked you out of all the slave women? Don't you know you're the first slave girl I've ever brought into my house? Don't you know you're the mother of my firstborn?*

The words came faster, sinking into her kinks. He touched the back of her neck along the edge of her hair with his lips and rubbed his face down her loose-fitting dress. As he talked, he stuck it inside of her and she did what she always did: clung to the words, wrapped them up inside, let them work her over. It was mainly this, his careful voicing of loving things that kept her in this place of uncertainty about her children.

When he was finished, he did not turn her over. She waited for him to start up again. When she heard heavy breathing, she lifted her head.

She slipped from beneath him. The breeze from the open window cooled her face. She stood up gingerly, so as not to wake him, and went back to clean up the dishes.

Soften the white man. Hmph. Some stew. It occurred to her he had not even noticed her new hairstyle, the careful plaits that had taken Sweet the better part of an afternoon to complete.

When all of the dishes were stacked, she went out and sat on the porch. She thought of her children back at the place, already working and doing chores around the big house. It had begun with pulling weeds in the garden patch, but soon that would amount to something more. Full work days were just over the horizon for her son, the older of the two.

The sound of Drayle's snores drifted through the window. He would sleep through the night. She observed the windows of the eleven other cottages that curved around the lake. Perhaps in those rooms, stifled with the nighttime heat, the other white men were all sleeping, too. And their slave women, all slumbering in the same dreamland.

A trio of ducks slept on the bank, their heads turned around and tucked under their wings. A nearby creek bubbled, and she let a mosquito whine in her ear until it stung her. She clapped it in her hand and studied the smear of blood in her palm.

FOUR

They had been given that Sunday off with one condition. Sweet would stay at the resort. If any members of the group were so much as a few minutes late for evening chores, she would be beaten, pregnant or not. It was a cruel bargain—one harsh enough to make them sit around the camp for three hours that morning wondering if they should venture off anywhere at all. It was a promise layered on top of other unspoken threats, hinting at violence to their children, parents, siblings back at the plantations should they overestimate the men's pity for a pregnant woman. This was a most trusted group of slaves, so none of the white men actually believed their slaves would run off. But they were in free territory and had to take precautions. Lizzie tried not to think about Drayle's silence that morning as the slaves had lined up before the men, waiting to receive their gift of a day's rest.

That morning, they'd discussed making their way to Xenia. The omnibus that had brought them from the railroad depot in town had taken almost thirty minutes on the turnpike, but they weren't allowed to use it without the presence of their white masters. Reenie and Lizzie suggested they stay close to the resort out of loyalty to Sweet. None of them wanted to separate. None of them wanted to be the first to suggest the colored resort. So they sat around the camp that morning behind a curtain of indecision.

It was Mawu who finally pushed them. "I is going."

They all knew where she meant. Her cheeks were slightly burned by the sun. She folded her arms across her chest, pressed her knotted fists into the creases of her arms. She started off, and the rest of them followed. Reenie stumbled over a rock in her haste. Philip picked up a rag and ripped it. He tied the pieces to the low branches of trees as they walked.

"But you don't even know how to get there," Lizzie said.

"I'll find it. These ain't the first woods I done worked my way through. Just follow the path. Bound to lead somewhere." The path was so faint it threatened to disappear, too narrow to have been sliced through the forest by horse hooves. Insect clouds broke before them.

The voice approached from behind, breathless, as if trying to catch up. "*I know how to get there.*"

They heard, but kept on walking. The instinct of the men at the sound of what was obviously a white woman's voice was to keep moving. Only Lizzie turned her head.

It was the white woman who delivered the eggs and dairy. Her husband was a local farmer who provided necessities to the hotel and each morning this woman could be seen wheeling a cart to the meeting place where two black servants would unload her bundle and take it from her. Lizzie studied the woman's calm face and watched as she pointed to the rag ends poking from Philip's hand.

"You won't be needing those." The woman relaxed into an expression that said *don't be afraid of me*. She worked to slow her breaths, her colossal bosom heaved, rising and falling in short bursts.

The slaves had not admitted this to one another, but each had memorized her features. Eyes the color of grit. Hair the color of wheat. Lips a thin line of pink. There was something about the way in which she shared the air with them. As if it belonged to all of them and was not hers alone.

These slaves had been around Northern whites long enough to recognize one who didn't understand the rules. But they were all bred in the South, which said they did not go up to strange white women with whom they had no business and strike up a conversation. So it was up to this young woman who moved as if she knew exactly where she was going.

The white woman had approached Lizzie just days before when Lizzie was alone, picking flowers for the cottage. Lizzie guessed it had taken the woman a full year's span between summers to get up the nerve. It was just the two of them that day. "There are some pretty flowers over thataway. The color of sunset," the woman had said to Lizzie.

Lizzie turned, but decided against looking the woman in the eye.

"Come on. I'll show you."

Lizzie hesitated, but the woman touched her arm. The contact was enough to quell the tension.

So she followed her. From the way she stepped, Lizzie had been certain this white woman knew these woods as well as she knew the ones back on her place in Tennessee.

The woman looked back at her and Lizzie finally returned the look. A smile pleated the woman's face, and Lizzie struggled to determine if it was a real one.

"Thisaway."

Lizzie rushed behind her, carefully holding her cloth sack of flowers away from her hips so the flowers would not get crushed.

They came to a round grove. The woman had told the truth. The flowers were the color of sunset. And not the yellowish tinge of a lazy sun either, but the intense orange of a sun refusing to set on anyone else's terms. The flowers were at their full height, their stems as straight as backs, the petals at full blossom.

"I love flowers. I've probably got more on my land than you've ever seen in one place," the woman said. She stooped over and picked the flowers one by one. Lizzie didn't move. She wasn't sure what was expected of her. So she just stood there and watched. The woman picked until the folds of her dress were full. Lizzie watched her meticulously choose where she broke off a flower, careful not to disturb the ones she left. Then she dumped the flowers out of her dress into a sack on the ground. She pushed the sack into Lizzie's hand.

"You take them," she said.

Lizzie felt trapped. She looked around to see if she could find her way back to the resort on her own. Once she determined that she could, she clutched the bag of flowers to her chest and took off running.

She had not seen the white woman since. But she had told Mawu about it. Now Mawu was watching her watch the white woman, as if to see what Lizzie would do.

"My name is Glory. I'm a friend."

"We just taking a walk," Philip said after several moments of silence. The slaves had all stopped. Glory now blocked the path in front of them, the sun facing her back and casting her wide body in silhouette so that her face appeared darkened. They squinted at her.

"No, you aren't," said the woman who called herself Glory. "I know exactly where you're going. And I don't blame you, either."

Mawu studied the face beneath the bonnet. Then she said, "Take us then, why don't you?"

Glory led them, her long skirt sweeping the ground as she

ambled along. Lizzie watched it gather dirt. Philip stopped now and again to tie a rag to a tree. The other slaves patiently slowed for him, sharing in his mistrust.

Lizzie's ears tingled, and she wondered if the others might be feeling the same unease. She imagined her Rabbit walking beside her, and she knew she would gladly leave her at this colored place and risk her own flogging and Sweet's too for the chance that a well-to-do colored family might raise her.

The woods were bisected by a long ravine east of the resort, and Glory led them along the edge of it to a place where they could safely descend into it. The men went first; then they reached up their arms and helped the women down. They waded through a shallow creek, hopping from one stone to the next. The sides of the ravine were high, and they searched for a vine to pull themselves out of it on the other side.

The heat caressed them, opened their pores, greased their faces with exertion. They walked in a line, shawdowless beneath the midday sun, the women ahead of the men, George and Henry bringing up the rear. The fauna gradually changed the farther they got from the resort. Lizzie's feet registered one hour. Her thoughts shuffled between a pack of images—her children, Drayle, the place, the cottage.

Oh, if she could just set eyes upon this place—this oasis that would confirm for her the glory of free colored people, the limitlessness of her children once Drayle set them free. Her left foot began to ache and she knew it was rubbing against her shoe's hard sole. Her feet had always been delicate for a slave woman, perhaps a sign of her relatively light workload. She felt a limp coming on. But she had to see this dream for herself so she could pass it on to Rabbit and Nate. She had to know if there really was such a thing as free and fancy colored folk.

The sunlight guttered through the trees. And then a flat sketch of land spread itself out before them like a readied banquet table.

Glory stopped and the rest of them formed a semicircle about her at the edge of the clearing. Lizzie pushed her way between George and Philip who had rushed ahead.

They took it in amidst a prayerful silence. The feeling in their hearts made it easy for them to overlook the discrepancy between the place of their imaginings and the place that appeared before them. Unlike Tawawa House, there were no individual cottages edged around a pond with a grand, white hotel at its head. There was only one structure, a gray saltbox house with a sloping gabled roof. Lizzie counted five windows along the top floor and four along the bottom, each framed by black shutters. For a moment everything appeared still, lifeless, unreal. Then they saw a small body bound through the door, and from the sweep of her dress, they could see it was the figure of a pale-skinned colored girl.

Lizzie almost dropped to her knees. Nate's catechism with the handwriting of four different white children. Rabbit's roughened feet. Nate's insolent defiance of his father. Rabbit's trembling lip when she was scared. Nate's memory. Rabbit's natural tendency to play the fiddle. Lizzie wove these thoughts together like chicken wire.

"This is it," Glory said. "Lewis House. Around here, white folks call it Dumawa House. Mimicking Tawawa House, they say, even though the colored place was built first. I'll take you just a bit closer, but we can't get too close. This is slave-catcher territory, and I wouldn't want you to be mistaken for the wrong runaway slave."

"What about the free mens who stay here?" Philip asked. "How they tell who free and who ain't?"

No one spoke.

"They come here for the water," Glory said.

"The water?" Lizzie repeated.

"Yeah. Don't you know why the Southern white men come so far to this place? It's said that if you take the water, it'll cure you.

It'll get rid of diseases and cure mental states and things like that. Some folks think the water around here is magic. Colored folks included."

"What you mean 'take' the water?" Mawu asked.

"Bathe in it. Drink it," Glory answered.

Lizzie sniffed and caught the scent of a nearby spring pulsing through the air. She put a hand to her damp forehead and patted. Drayle had never told her this. Was he sick? She remembered the water she'd drunk earlier that morning. From the pump. Had it been special water? It hadn't tasted any differently than the water back at the place. It had made her urinate more. In fact, the summer before, she had urinated so much she thought she might be pregnant. But this Glory was saying the white men bathed in it, too. Some of the water smelled rotten. Surely that water couldn't be good for you.

Glory went on to explain that the hotel was even named after this water. "Tawawa" was the Shawnee Indian word for "clear water," she said.

"Sometimes you can see them on the back lawn playing games or their fiddles," Glory said in a way that made the others think she was a regular spy on the colored vacationers.

A woman came out of the main door and said something to the girl. It looked like a mild scolding. It was strange for Lizzie to see a colored woman and child using the front door of what looked to be a white man's house.

Mawu stretched and popped her neck. "Well, I is going over to introduce myself to that there lady." She sprang up and ran off.

"Mawu!" Lizzie rose up.

Reenie grabbed Lizzie's dress. "Don't you run after that fool woman."

Philip had run after her, though. The rest of them watched as Mawu gained speed, surprisingly quick on her short legs. Philip eventually caught up with her and grabbed her arm. Mawu jerked free and ran off. Philip took off after her again. By the time he caught up with her, they had been spotted by the woman on the porch. She disappeared into the door, and returned a few seconds later with a tall, dark man wearing bright trousers. The woman pushed the child back into the house and pointed at the two running slaves.

"Get back, get back behind the trees so they don't see us." Glory waved her arm, a flap of bare skin swinging like a signpost. The slaves obeyed and stepped back into the cover of the woods. Lizzie and Reenie shared the refuge of an oak tree.

"Would he turn us over to the slave catchers?" George asked.

Glory shrugged. "You never know."

They peeked through the trees and caught the tail end of Mawu's dress as she disappeared inside the big door of the house. Philip was nowhere to be seen.

"They went inside the house," Henry said, his voice high and scared.

Lizzie turned on Reenie. "Why did you hold me back?"

"That girl done turned you crazy. Have you forgot about Sweet? Us gots to get back. I say us head on back, with or without them."

"I ain't going back without Philip," Lizzie said, knowing that what she really meant was she wasn't going back without Mawu. The throbbing sore on the bottom of her foot reminded her that she didn't have much choice in the matter. She had to get back to tend to it.

"We'll give them a few minutes," Glory said. "If they don't come out before we leave, they'll just have to follow those rags back."

They sat in the prickly grass, shooing bugs. Several times, people came in and out of the house, but none of them was Philip or Mawu. To these slaves, these free colored people were different from the free servants working at Tawawa House. Those were working people. These were free coloreds on free territory having vacation. Lizzie tried to wrap her mind around what it would feel like not to have to work. Even though they were having a free day, there was really no such thing. Work was always just around the corner. These free coloreds probably didn't think of themselves as a free slave at all, she thought. They probably thought of themselves as a free free. It tickled her to think of it, and once or twice a little laugh escaped her, attracting concerned looks from Reenie and Glory.

When they caught the first sign of the sun dipping in the sky overhead, Glory rose and leaned on a walking stick she had scavenged halfway there. "We better get back," she said.

Reenie stood and looked down at Lizzie who had not moved or taken her eyes off the sight of the two young children playing tag while their mother looked on from the porch. From time to time, the woman looked right into the trees where the four slaves and one white woman were hiding.

"Sweet," was all Reenie had to say to prod Lizzie.

Lizzie gave Lewis House one last look before turning around and following Glory and the others back through the brush. Each time they passed a rag, Lizzie looked at it and thought of Mawu, picturing the world of treasures she was surely seeing inside that house.

FIVE

The slaves had been back at Tawawa House for only a short time before Mawu was spotted sweeping her cottage porch as if she'd never left. As they passed one another, they gave the silent signal to meet at the stables that night: eye contact, a glance in the direction of the stables, and brushed fingertips down the forearm to signal dusk.

At the appointed hour, while the white men were having their dinner in the hotel, the slaves gathered at the edge of the resort grounds. The light was orange and cast a glow over everything around them. One thin cloud sat high and alone above them like a raised eyebrow. Horses whinnied softly from within the building.

Mawu and Philip shared a tree stump, back to back, his legs out long and her skirt spread like a fan. The twins lay sprawling on the grass. Reenie shook out a blanket for the three women. Sweet rearranged herself over and over again so she could get comfortable enough to listen without interruption.

"Tell us," Sweet said when she had finally settled. "Tell us."

Mawu hunched her shoulders, licked her lips, and leaned in.

"The dining room table must've been built out the largest tree you ever did see," she said. "I imagine it was big and long enough to seat at least thirty white folks. All shiny and dark. So shiny, you could eat right off it with nary a splinter. The womens was sitting around sewing, but they put it away soon as us come in the house."

Philip nodded as if to confirm the truth of her words.

"One of the childrens was playing the piano when us come in and another boy was reading a book."

"A piano." Lizzie had dreamed of such a thing for Rabbit.

"That's what I said, Miss Lizzie. He played that thang like he was an angel and the other one carried that book around as if it was a bag of money. I couldn't have grabbed it from him if I'd tried."

Philip looked as if he were about to say something, but Mawu only paused long enough to catch her breath.

"There was a big old bowl of fresh peaches, and I saw one of the menfolks walk by and pick one right up and take a bite out of it. And they was walking on this fancy rug that felt like a bed of cotton right beneath your feet."

Philip's words tripped over Mawu's. "And two men smoking."

"The womenfolks was just sitting about," Mawu continued. "They had servants serving them just like rich white ladies. And a big wide staircase. You could hear people moving about. It was families all up in that house just minding they own business."

Lizzie stopped listening. *Families.* The word aroused her.

". . . they sho acted like they was scared when us walked up to that door, snatched us right in, they did. Said it's slavecatchers all over here and us had every bit the mark of a slave," Mawu was saying.

"They feed you?" George asked.

"You bet they did!" Philip slid off the stump and wiped his hands on the backs of his pants. He gesticulated wildly, as if the table of food were right there before him. "They fed us till we couldn't move. Seem like they think slaves ain't used to getting a bellyful, so they all sit around watching us while we eat. Even the childrens."

Lizzie pictured them sitting at a long table with platters of food before them: wild duck, stuffed potatoes, loaves of bread, bowls of greens, mash, cornmeal cakes. She could taste mounds of cranberries on her tongue, as if she'd just smeared it across her mouth with the back of a spoon.

"But what were the people like?" Lizzie asked.

"They was fine, Miss Lizzie," Mawu said. "They minded they manners better than the whitefolks. And I didn't even mind the stares. The children wanted to play in my hair, and the mens asked Philip a lot of questions about his place back in Tennessee."

Philip sat back down on the stump.

Mawu scratched her foot in the dirt. "They wanted to know if I could read, and they seem real sad when I say I can't."

Lizzie sucked her lip. She had not known that Mawu couldn't read.

Philip shook his head and chuckled. "I knew it was time to go, but I tell you after my belly got full, I just wanted to stay there forever. I wanted to go to sleep and never wake up."

"You think if y'all was escaped slaves they would of took you in?" George asked.

The ensuing silence held their feelings in check, and none dared speak.

"Well . . ." Mawu began. "Let me put it this way—they sho know where to send us if'n they don't."

"Yessir," Philip said. "Whitefolks burn that house down to the ground if they even 'spected they was hiding runaway slaves. But I is pretty sho it's some slaves hiding hereabouts in these woods."

Quiet again.

"I just don't understand y'all," Mawu said. "Us is here in free territory and ain't nobody thinking about making a run for it?"

"Shhh!" Reenie put a finger to her lips.

Mawu's eyes narrowed into fissures of shiny black rock. "I is tired, Miss Reenie. I is real, real tired."

Lizzie turned on Mawu. "Don't even think about it. If you get caught, that'll be the end of all of us. Won't none of us be able to return."

"Us on free land. This here is free land. Folks die trying to cross that river and here us is done crossed it." Mawu was talking quickly now.

"Yeah," George said in a questioning tone, as if he'd already thought of this and now wanted to know where Mawu was headed with it.

"So what's stopping us? Why not break and run for it?" Mawu pressed on.

"I don't know what's stopping you," Sweet said. "But I got childrens. Four of them. We all got childrens or folks back at the place. If we run for it, what'll happen to them? Don't you got little ones, too?"

Mawu rolled her eyes at Sweet. "Who don't got childrens? But what I'm gone do for my child as a slave woman? I need to run off so as I can try to get my boy out. As long as I is a slave, ain't nothing gone change."

"What ideas you got, girl?" George asked in an almost-whisper.

Mawu's words hummed in Lizzie's ears as she murmured her plan. But even more disturbing was the penetrating concentration of the others, the rapt attention of their bodies and barely audible breaths. Even Reenie. Only Lizzie looked from face to face.

"I figure us can get that white woman to help us get a letter to the high yellow woman I met at that there resort." Mawu looked around. "But I can't read nor write."

George spoke again: "Lizzie know how to write the best."

Lizzie's throat narrowed and she had to open her mouth to breathe. Once, when she'd first been bought by Drayle, she and another child had sneaked off to the woods to play. They'd witnessed a line of slaves whose ankles and feet were chained, led by a young white boy with a rifle almost bigger than he was propped on his shoulder. Lizzie had just been a child, her hair still in pigtails, but the memory had never left her. The girl hiding behind the bush with her had pointed to the group and whispered "runaways." As the slaves walked by, Lizzie could smell something like fresh feces. One of the men was wearing a shirt and no pants, and she caught a glimpse of an oozing scar tucked into his thigh as he walked by. Flies flew around the limp hand of a woman that was blackened with the dried blood of what looked like fresh bite marks.

Drayle rarely beat his slaves. He preferred to sell what he called a bad slave rather than break him. The fear of being sold off what they figured was a good plantation to a lowdown slave trader was enough to keep them in line. Most of the time. Since he sold off the rebellious ones, Lizzie could not remember a slave trying to escape the Drayle plantation.

"How we find that woman when she the one what find us?" George asked.

Mawu turned to look at Lizzie once more, and this time the others followed her eyes. Lizzie looked down at her hands. They were soft and smooth, not work-worn like field hands. Her nails were a bit yellowed, but they were strong, not peeling and withered like those of the women who lived down in the quarters. She could feel Nate's soft curls stretched between her fingers.

"She know." Mawu said it quietly, so quietly that Lizzie could barely hear. Lizzie tried to shift her eyes around to the others, still not believing they were serious. There was a canyon to cross—as wide as the Ohio River—and Lizzie was being told to take the first leap.

SIX

~

Mawu was from a plantation in Louisiana about twenty miles west of the Mississippi border. Her master, Tip, owned a modest thirty-six adult slaves—twenty-five men and nine women. Of the eighteen children living in the slave quarters, more than a dozen were tan-colored.

Tip's wife had died years before and it was agreed among the slaves that the man had gotten meaner each passing year since her death. Mawu had been a child when her mistress died, but she remembered that the death had been a slow one. Many moons had passed as the woman lay there wasting away until her frame was covered by a thin layer of yellowed skin.

Tip didn't believe in hiring an overseer. He said he could oversee his own farm. He'd sit astride a giant horse and watch the slaves as they plowed, hoed, and tilled the crops. If someone failed to work or lagged behind, he beat them himself. When he didn't feel like doing the beating—which was rarely—he had a young slave do it for him.

Tip visited the women in the slave quarters even before his wife was dead. After the mistress was gone, his visits increased. He barely waited for the young girls to stain their pallets red before he took them. Mawu held him off longer than most. The first time he came for her, she bit him and kicked him in the leg. The second time, she dropped an iron on his foot that broke a toe. After that, he brought her down to the barn for her first beating. When he told her to strip off her clothes, she refused. Even though he was smaller than the average man, she was even smaller. He took her afterwards while she was still sick in bed healing from the lashes. The more Mawu fought, the more determined he became to have her over and over again. He had her strapped to the bed on more than one occasion.

She'd given Tip four children, but he'd sold three of them outright. The last child left was a four-year-old boy with a lazy blue eye. He'd been dropped as a child—fallen out of the cloth tying him to Mawu's back while she worked in the fields. The ground might have served as a cushion as it was still soggy from the previous night's rain, but the baby had the bad fortune of hitting his head on a rock hiding amid the cornstalks. When he finally started talking at three years old, he had difficulty answering straightaway and often gave a blank stare when he was told what to do. His mind wasn't right, they said. Tip denied that the "slow blue-eyed nigger" was his.

Once Mawu's third child was sold, she told Lizzie that she just stopped loving. She knew she couldn't bear losing another child, so she figured it was better not to think of her youngest as her youngest anymore. Now he was a pickaninny just like any other pickaninny. She didn't allow him to suckle like she had the others. She had loved them so—light skin, silky hair, and all—but now, she told Lizzie and Sweet and Reenie that she knew all her children had been born of evil spirits.

After the sale of her three children she took the name Mawu

and started spending time with an old conjuring man the slaves called Doctor who lived back of the plantation. Even though Tip owned the elderly slave, he left him alone. Some said Tip was scared of him. Mawu took the Doctor his meals, and soon began asking him questions about the sacks hanging around his neck. The old man did not answer at first, but once he was convinced of her belief he emptied out some of the sprinkling powder and demonstrated Mawu's first conjuring trick. It was a spell to keep the bad spirits away from her boy. Mawu was surprised that the Doctor even knew she had a son. It wasn't long before she was asking him how she could keep Tip away. The Doctor gave her a bag of herbs that she tied inside her skirt. It worked for a while. Then Tip started up again. The old man gave her a bitter root to chew that made her breath so foul it was difficult for anyone to be within five feet of her. Whenever Tip got close, she spat on the ground near his feet. That worked for a while, too. But Tip just took her from behind. She continued to go to the Doctor's cabin, begging for new tricks, paying him with stolen food from the big house, learning as much as she could about his magic. He taught her to mix her Christian religion with the spells, neither upsetting the other. It turned out that she liked the spells better than Jesus.

When Tip announced he was going to Ohio for the summer, he chose Mawu as his companion. She had been as surprised as the others. She had never performed her duty like the rest of them— quietly and without complaint. And she wasn't considered his favorite by any means although they all admitted that she stood out from the rest of them, both in looks and spirit.

Tip's cousin would run the plantation while he was away. They did not know how this cousin would treat them, they said. They feared Tip would not return. Ohio seemed like another country. Someone said it was God's country. Another called it Canaan. Mawu did not know what they meant.

It was only after she reached the train depot in Cincinnati and overheard two white men referring to Ohio as a "free state" that she understood. She'd tried to calm the new feelings in her chest.

Mawu told all this and more to the women as they went through their daily chores. She talked about laying tricks and mixing powders, claiming she knew how to ward off evil spirits and put somebody in a good humor.

Reenie dismissed Mawu's conjuring talk as superstition. But Lizzie pressed Mawu to keep talking. Sweet listened, too.

Mawu told them she was telling her story so they would know why she couldn't go back to Louisiana, why she didn't feel the same pull they felt toward their children. She didn't live in the big house like Lizzie. Her children had not had special favors like Sweet's. She hadn't had a cabin built for her like Reenie. She was just a slave like any other—beaten, used, and made to feel no different than a cow or a goat or a chicken.

Each day she spoke of yet another violation, another wrong committed by Tip over the years. As each memory sprang forth, she shared it with them.

Next she pointed out how their own men were no different: Sweet's master worked her despite her pregnancy; Reenie's master never looked her in the face; Drayle refused to free the children he claimed to love. Mawu worked on them in the days following their visit to Lewis House—nudging, cajoling, infusing them with thoughts of escape. She asked them: *How can you stand being a slave? Don't you want to claim that arm? That leg? That breast?* She declared that no one would suckle her titty again—man or child.

Lizzie felt each defense of Drayle die in her throat. At night, she felt safe and certain, protected in his arms. In the day, she felt unsure of anything.

Then Mawu said she'd caught Drayle staring at her breasts.

Even though the thought of his betrayal made her want to vomit, Lizzie believed the newcomer.

The four women stacked the preserved fruit against the wall of the ice house. The ice house was thirteen feet long and twelve feet wide, a nearly perfect square. A ten-foot-deep hole was dug into the ground and filled with ice from the pond during the winter. After the ice was buried, the hole was covered with straw. The house remained cool throughout the summer. The resort used it for storing various foods such as fruit and eggs. Barrels of whiskey sat in the corner.

Sweet leaned against the wall. "Y'all mind if I rest a bit? My back ain't holding up too well."

"Naw, you go on and rest yourself," Reenie said.

"This ground sho is cold," Sweet said.

Mawu stooped and touched the ground. "This ice house wouldn't last a Louisiana summer. Ain't cold enough."

"Louisiana ain't no hotter than Tennessee," Lizzie said.

"Hmph. You ain't seen one of our summers." Mawu's voice was quiet. "You write it yet?"

Lizzie could make out the shapes of the women. Sweet formed an r. Her baby face—the origin of her name—led into a thick neck, wide bust, and sloping belly. Reenie's older, thinner form was ramrod straight, her boniness cutting a sharp edge in the dim light of the ice house. Mawu's hair was tied back into an uncharacteristic bun and covered with a yellow cotton handkerchief. Lizzie traced the woman's body with her eyes: the small high breasts that had caught Drayle's attention.

"You write it yet girl?" Mawu repeated.

Reenie and Lizzie stood side-by-side, stacking the jars in six neat rows: peaches, nectarines, plums, cherries.

"I ain't sure I want to," Lizzie said. She could feel the cool air creep through the folds of her dress. She cleared her throat.

"Do it," Sweet said.

Both Lizzie and Reenie stopped working and looked down at the pregnant woman.

"I had a man once," Sweet said. "He escape and leave me behind. I keep thinking he gone come back and get me. I wait and I wait. But he don't never come."

Lizzie wondered why Sweet had never told them this.

"I ain't going nowhere," Sweet went on. "Got too many childrens back home. I reckon I ain't gone never leave Master. But the ones that wants to go oughts to be able to go."

"Who exactly are the ones that want to go?" Lizzie pursed her lips until the words came out in a whistle. "I ain't leaving my children neither. Nobody but Mawu wants to go." Lizzie looked at Reenie when she said it. Surely the woman was too old to start over.

"I is still collecting my thoughts," Reenie said.

"Collecting your thoughts?" Lizzie repeated.

Mawu walked over and grabbed Lizzie's arm. She bit down into the flesh with her nails. Lizzie tried to pull away, but Mawu's grip was firm.

"You write that letter, you hear?"

The salted carcass of a pig swung in the side vision of Lizzie's eye, its broad back as purple as a bruise.

SEVEN

It began with a flurry of excitement over wearing a new dress. The news they would be dining in the main hotel with the men was strange, but welcome. The four couples—along with a Northern businessman—were to dine in the library on the top floor of the hotel. The Northerner's presence would be as unusual as that of the women. The Southerners and Northerners did not interact often at the resort, particularly when the slave women were around.

A colored woman with a wooden foot and a cane traveled nineteen miles from Dayton to bring nine dresses. She took them out of a trunk and spread them out in the main room of Lizzie's cottage. Then she leaned on the carved head of a duck and studied the four slaves as she waited. The promise of business kept her from commenting, but a mean-spirited little "bah" escaped her lips every few seconds.

The four women eyed the dresses with the knowledge that they only had two days to sew. Some of the dresses were ripped, torn. Others had holes still bearing the cracked, empty shells of moth cocoons. But they were a far cry from the "negro cloth" some of the slaves wore back on the plantations. Negro cloth was just another name for a coarse cotton, and when they wore it, it scratched their skin.

Lizzie chose one that the woman said was made of something called batiste and the color of a tangerine. Mawu commented that the dress was the perfect color for Lizzie's dark skin and black hair. Mawu took a liking to a blue dress. It was not often that she got to wear color, and she didn't believe she had ever worn anything blue.

For Sweet, it was docility unleashed. She chose the only empire waistline dress of the bunch and ripped the sleeves off because they were too tight on her arms. Even after she had let the dress out, the constricted bodice would push her breasts into two engorged maternal mounds.

Although they insisted that she choose first, Reenie chose an unbecoming dress. She was the only one of the four who did not plan a complete transformation. The dress she chose was out of season and would surely be too hot for a summer evening. It had a long train and high neckline. There were so many buttons down the back that it took two women to secure it. Some of the buttons were tight, and they decided they would need to let out an inch so the buttons wouldn't bulge and pop. Sweet said it looked like Reenie was going to a funeral.

On the night of the dinner, when the dresses had been sewn and they had oiled their hair and faces and Mawu had rubbed aloe onto an unexplained fresh scar on her right cheek and Lizzie had darkened each woman's eyes with a smudge of shadow, they walked to the hotel, unescorted by the men, holding each other through the arms, coupled two by two, excited about being ladies for a change. Reenie walked in front with Sweet, and Lizzie and

Mawu walked just far enough behind so they wouldn't trip on Reenie's train.

The servants did not hide their curiosity as the slave women walked through the kitchen. Each woman had experienced a range of reactions from the slaves back home: jealousy, pride, pity. Here in Ohio, they had not spoken much about what the free colored people thought of women like them. This was partly because they did not care. They had each other, unlike down south. There, it was a lonely battle.

They stepped carefully because the servants' stairs were steep. At the top of the stairs, another servant met them and pointed the way to the library that had been set up as a dining room so as to spare the other guests the sight of white men and slave women eating together.

They could hear the voices of the men as they approached the door. Once they were inside, the doors were closed behind them with a firm click of the lock. Each of them took in the room: the soft glow of the lamps casting an amber light, the smell of the leather-bound books, the white tablecloth and delicate dishes, the freshly cleaned floors. The room had no windows, and this fact along with the low ceiling made the room, despite its spaciousness, feel intimate.

A trio of colored musicians filed into the room from a door within the bookcase and collected themselves in the corner. Sweet admired their clothing. She knew firsthand the difficulty of sewing the ruffles that streamed down the front of their white shirts. Their pants were black and tight like riding pants. Faces greased to a shine, they moved as if one body, silent and practiced. Once they had set up, one of them lifted his head and when he lowered it, they all hit the first note together.

The music was light. It made Lizzie feel as if she would rise up off the floor. Even though there wasn't even a hint of religiosity in the music, Lizzie couldn't help but be moved by the unfettered talent of the freedman. She tried not to stare at the musicians as she took her place beside her Master. She did not want him to think she found them attractive.

Lizzie knew for a fact that Drayle had suggested an evening such as this the summer before. The other men had protested, and it had never happened. Imagine, they'd said, if their wives knew they were letting these slave women dress up like ladies and dine with them at a full-service dinner table! This summer, the men had finally agreed to Drayle's suggestion. It made Lizzie proud to know her Master had been so thoughtful.

Drayle held out his hand. She reached out for him. He wore a thin summer suit and his sun-chapped face was freshly shaven. In her eyes, he was as handsome as a preacher. She touched his face. His cheek was cool in her palm.

"Would you care to dance?"

She answered in a voice that didn't quite sound like her own. "Why thank you, Nathan." She called him by the name that only Fran used. It was not lost on him. Three lines appeared in his forehead, and then relaxed into faint etchings.

Lizzie sneaked a quick peek at the others. Mawu was standing next to Tip looking bored. From the looks of him, he was already drunk. Reenie was filling Sir's pipe with tobacco as he engaged in a conversation with a man sitting in a high-backed leather chair beside him. Reenie tapped the edge of the pipe bowl against a nearby bookcase to settle the tobacco. She performed her chore methodically, as if she had done it countless times. Sweet's man had plunged his face into her cleavage and Lizzie could hear her tinny laugh.

"That's some dress."

"Tangerine," Lizzie said.

"What?"

"The lady that brought it said it is tangerine."

"Ah," he said.

Drayle moved her hips back and forth, and once they had set-tled into a comfortable rhythm, he rested the tip of his chin on her head.

The lighting in the room was dim, so dim Reenie had trou-ble filling the pipe. It was as if the white men were afraid that if it were too bright in the room, they might remember they were about to dine with a group of well-dressed colored women.

The hotel manager entered and stood in the corner, survey-ing the room. His eyes kept returning to the women. When the manager's eyes found Lizzie, she tried to steer Drayle around so she could put her back to the manager, but Drayle was leaning too heavily on her. She knew that look in the manager's eyes, and she did not want to be the object of it. She turned her head into Drayle's chest and when she took another peek, she saw he was now focused on Reenie. Reenie's high-necked stance had stiffened. The bag of tobacco dangled from her fingers as if forgotten.

Someone rang a glass dinner bell and the couples took their places at the table. Mawu maneuvered Tip around to Lizzie's side and slipped into the seat next to her. The Northern guest sat on one side of the table, unaccompanied. No introductions of any kind were made.

"They gone serve us?" Mawu whispered.

"I reckon so," Lizzie answered.

A servant with bumps covering his chin and neck unfolded Mawu's napkin and spread it across her lap with a flourish.

"Ain't this something?" Mawu fingered the cloth.

Lizzie was fascinated by the free servants. They floated into the room like angels and held the dishes aloft like sacrificial of-ferings, announcing each dish as if they were presenting a guest. Lizzie tucked the display into her mind so she could try to emu-late it later. She wanted to serve dinner back at the place like free colored folk did it. She wanted to slide the spoons onto the table with crisp, little movements, pour wine with a flourish at the end, shake out a napkin with a soft pop of the fabric. The servants announced a turtle soup. Lizzie could smell it as the bowl came her way. She did not wait for the others to be served, plunging her spoon into the thick, red soup. She tried to separate the flavors in her mouth: onion, tomato, cayenne. The turtle meat was a bit chewy, but well flavored.

"I can make a real good turtle soup," Mawu whispered to Lizzie, leaning over Tip. "This ain't nothing."

"You mentioned this morning that you might have a horse for sale?" asked Sweet's Master.

"Yes, yes," answered Drayle. "He's only got one eye, but he's fast as lightning."

"Good with children?"

Drayle put down his spoon. "What age are we talking?"

Sweet's master pawed her hand. She rested the other hand on the lid of her stomach. "For Sweet's oldest boy," he said.

Drayle picked his spoon back up. He did not look at Lizzie who was watching him and waiting for his response. Surely he would be honest about the horse, she thought.

"A horse with only one good eye? That doesn't sound like a deal," said the Northerner. He had a thick mustache that he kept licking with quick darts of his tongue. He obviously had not caught that Sweet's master was intending to buy the horse for his slave son. "How much you want for it?"

Drayle laughed. "We're old friends. We can talk price later. I'll make it worth the trip out to my farm, I can promise—"

"Horses won't do you no good if we go to war." Sir sniffed.

"Nobody's going to war," Tip said, belching loudly. "I'll be damned if I let some Yankee take away my hard-earned property."

The Northerner laughed nervously as if to assure them that although he was a Northerner, he was no Yankee. "What would the country do with a bunch of freed niggers anyway?"

The servant announced a beef dish.

Mawu spoke. "Master Taylor say if us go to war, he gone free me first. Say he'll be damned if the Yankees get me."

"Shut up, Betsy. I never said nothing like that."

This caught the attention of the other three women. Betsy? That was her given name?

"Yeah, you did."

Tip pinched her on the arm, and although it looked playful, Mawu rubbed the flesh he had grabbed.

The manager of the hotel entered the room again. He said something to one of the servants who came and leaned down beside Sir and whispered in his ear. Sir excused himself and followed the manager into the corridor.

"Let's talk about more pleasant things," said the Northerner. He rested his small hands on each side of his plate and licked his mustache. "How is the new Fugitive Slave Law working, do you think?"

Drayle pulled at the lapels of his dinner jacket. "I'm proud to say that I don't have such problems. My slaves are all trustworthy and docile. They would rather live on my farm any day than try to come up North and deal with these cold northern winters. Isn't that right, Lizzie?"

"Yessir," she said in a soft voice.

"If the federal government keeps sticking their nose in places it doesn't belong," said Tip, "then the Fugitive Slave Law won't make any difference whatsoever. We've got to protect our own interests. Who are they to tell me, a God-fearing man, how to run my business affairs?"

Lizzie had heard about this law. That was one reason she was scared of Mawu's plan. She had tried to explain that to the other slaves, but they didn't seem to care. They were used to slave patrols, they said. A Northern dog was no different than a Southern dog, they said.

"All you got to do is make the reward money high enough. That'll catch a slave, for sure," Tip continued.

"I'm not worried about anybody ending slavery anytime soon." Drayle stared directly at the Northerner. "This country has been built by men like us."

The bumpy-faced servant refilled the men's glasses with wine.

Sir returned and Reenie searched his face.

The manager beckoned to Sir from the doorway again, and he stood once more. They discussed something heatedly for a moment. Then Sir called Reenie over.

Reenie's napkin fell to the floor as she got up from the table. Sir took her by the elbow and a loud "no" erupted from her.

"What's going on?" Mawu asked no one in particular.

The dessert plates sat untouched. Reenie and Sir's voices drifted over to the table.

"Naw, naw, naw."

"Shut up woman and do as I say."

"I ain't doing it. Sir, please!"

Lizzie pushed back her chair, but Drayle grabbed the loose fabric of her dress.

Sir pushed Reenie into the hallway, and she pushed back. The manager stood looking up at her, for now that she was standing next to him, it was clear she was the taller of the two.

Mawu managed to escape Tip and made her way over to the struggling couple.

"Let her go." Mawu grabbed Reenie's other arm.

"You stay out of this and mind your business," the manager said. When he turned his head and the light caught his profile, Lizzie and Sweet could see that he was sweating.

"Let her go, let her go, let her go," Mawu said, pulling and breathing heavily.

"Drayle," Lizzie whispered. Drayle took a sip of his wine.

Sweet whimpered and started to cry. Her master rubbed her back.

Lizzie watched as Reenie's body went limp, as if breathing out its last bit of energy into the darkened room. The soft sound of her false teeth clicking together ebbed until there was silence. Sir and Mawu let go of her.

The manager raised his head. "There, there now," he said to Reenie. Lizzie could see Reenie's face clearly now. She had the look. The look of a woman who is done fighting. The look of a woman months after her children have been sold from her. The look of a slave who has decided it is better not to feel. All three of the women recognized what they saw on her face.

Reenie followed the manager into the corridor and they disappeared. Lizzie watched the gaping hole, the space where Reenie had just stood.

"How could you?" Mawu said to Sir.

He cracked his hand across her cheek.

"Don't you ever come between me and my slave woman again, you hear me?"

Tip rose out of his seat. "Goddamnit, that's my property!"

Mawu felt her face where the still-fresh scar had just been opened up again. She examined the blood on her fingers as if it weren't her own. Sir returned to the table and a servant slipped through the side door and passed him a wet cloth to wipe the blood from his hands.

"Now, what's this y'all are saying about a one-eyed horse?" Sir curled his lips into a grin. The servant returned with a bottle of wine. Sir took it from him and drank a long swallow directly from the lip of the bottle.

Lizzie looked at the light twisting through her empty glass. She couldn't drink or eat another bite. The music and the sound of the men's voices faded. She let the silence take her. When she finally looked up, the seat beside her was empty and Mawu was nowhere to be seen. Her master Tip was gone also.

But across from Lizzie, in the place where Reenie was supposed to be sitting, was a yellow-haired white woman with red-rouged cheeks. Sir had his face in her neck.

EIGHT

Reenie and Lizzie were told to pluck and prepare the birds the men brought back from their hunting trip. The two women sat on the ground and spread the dozen or so birds out. The evening sun was behind them and the half moons in their armpits had dried. Each woman took a bird, dipped it in a washtub of hot water, and pulled out the feathers in handfuls, their hands slick against the warmed skin. Once they had established an easy, quiet rhythm, they spoke in hushed tones.

"Tell me your story, Reenie."

Reenie looked up at her younger friend sharply. Stories didn't get told unless they had to. Stories were for remembering, and none of the women wanted to tell how they had gotten there. When they told their stories, they preferred to tell the ones about that faraway place. They preferred to tell ones they had patched together in their heads, hundreds of oral remnants whispered in dark slave cabins.

This was what Lizzie knew about Reenie: She lived on a plan-

tation not far from Lizzie in Tennessee. They hadn't known each
other before visiting Tawawa, but when they spoke about it, they
thought they might be kin. Two of Reenie's cousins had been
hired out the previous winter to work where Lizzie lived, and she
had gotten to know them well. The first summer at Tawawa, Lizzie
and Reenie had spent hours exchanging names, searching for a
real connection and the fact that they hadn't discovered any blood
didn't lessen the affection between them.

Reenie had an extended family on her plantation, and though
some had been sold off over the years, they were remarkable for
the numbers that remained. In fact, her plantation was made up
of several families. The way Reenie told it, each of these families
did their work together, and if one member fell ill, the others took
up the slack. If a new slave was bought, the families would meet
to decide which "family" he would join. Sometimes, according
to Reenie, there was even a bit of friendly competition between
families. This was different from Lizzie's plantation, where the
slaves toiled each for himself, suffering their individual punish-
ments if they failed to complete a day's work.

"Why you asking?"

Lizzie shrugged. "Wondering is all." She did not say she had
been worried about Reenie ever since the older woman had begun
her nightly visits to the manager's suite in the hotel.

Reenie stuck her finger in a hole on the bare skin and dug out
the bird shot. She tossed it to the side and continued to pull feathers, more slowly and deliberately than before.

"He my brother," she said, her voice low and flat.

Lizzie almost dropped the bird she was dipping into the tub.
"Who's your brother?"

She wiped at her runny eye with the back of her arm. "Sir."

Lizzie tried to digest the news. She had heard about such
things.

"So your daughter, the one that got sold off . . ."

"Sho. She my daughter and my niece." Now Reenie was yanking the feathers out, one by one. Her dark forehead shone in the red dusk.

"So I fixed myself," Reenie said. "I fixed myself so he couldn't make no more childrens. My family helped me. All the womens and mens gathered round me and prayed over me. All night, they went right on praying. Then right before the sun started to gather herself up, us fixed it so it wouldn't happen no more."

Lizzie heard the crack of a rifle in the distance.

"Wasn't the first time the womens had done it. But I was a youngun. Fourteen and my baby was still nursing. I was still peering in her face near about every day wondering when God was gone strike his fury on her." The dead bird lay limp, belly up in her lap, its head cradled in the crook of her groin. "But didn't nothing happen. She just got prettier and prettier. And smaaaaaart, too. No sooner than her teeth start to growed, and she was walking and talking."

"Did he . . . did he still mess with you?"

Reenie grinned, her false teeth eerily large and white. "Sho, honey. Ain't nothing change. Ain't nothing gone ever change about that, I reckon."

So different from what she had with Drayle. She loved him. He loved her. And even more, he was good to her. Hadn't he fixed the leaky cabin roof that was dripping on his children's heads? Hadn't he given the slaves Sunday mornings off when she told him about their secret worship meetings? Hadn't he rubbed her feet countless times when she was tired from cooking all day? Hadn't he protected her after she was attacked on the ship?

"Sir's daddy took my own mammy before she got her first blood. She give him three childrens before he died. He weren't yet cold in the ground when the missus had my ma whipped in front of everybody. As a punishment for her sins, she called it. Not long after, my ma disappeared. Just up and disappeared while we was working in the fields one day. None of us knowed what happened. Maybe she run off. Maybe she was sold off by the missus in the middle of the night. Maybe she dead."

Lizzie tried to picture Reenie's mammy. Such things were possible. A proud woman, tall with Reenie's stiff back and long neck, rose in Lizzie's mind. Like Reenie, she would be so strong that even a beating couldn't break her. Some folks couldn't be broken. Lizzie didn't believe a woman in her right mind would just "up and leave" her children.

"Us wasn't treated right, but the missus kept us on. Me and my two brothers still live in the same cabin Sir's daddy built for my ma. When the missus got married again, her new husband decent enough. At least he ain't go messing off in the slave cabins, and I reckon she would shoot him dead if he did."

"But his son . . ."

"Made us call him Sir when he was still a boy right after his daddy died. Only took one beating for the whole lot of us to get the hang of it. I been calling him Sir ever since."

Reenie picked up the bird in her lap and stretched out a wing. She pulled at the feathers along its edge.

But Lizzie didn't feel like pulling feathers anymore. She took one of the birds that had already been plucked and cut through its neck with a small, sharp knife. She removed its head and pulled out the bloody gullet and the windpipe. She kept digging, and she was only satisfied when she had hooked her fingers into the lungs, pulled them out, and tossed them into the dust beside her.

NINE

～

Nearly a week after the dinner, more than ten days into the collective breath holding that had been gathering pressure since Mawu issued her challenge, the colored barber arrived to line the white men up in chairs along the porch of the hotel. The barber visited the resort once or twice a week. Some of the men wore beards, and would have the barber trim them after their haircuts. Others such as Drayle preferred a more clean-shaven look, and the barber would use a straight razor over their faces. This barber had a sterling reputation for keeping his razors sharp.

The barber's daughter typically helped him. She worked as a maid in the hotel, but whenever her father visited she would come outside to assist. She'd wheel a tray onto the porch and open the leather carrying case holding his tools. Straight steel razors. Brushes. Scissors. Two leather strops. Cup and soap. She would moisten the bar of soap in the bowl of hot water so the lather

would be ready to spread. Or she would hold the brass shaving
bowl at the man's neck if her father requested it.

She was a prettier and fatter version of her father, with softly
rounded cheeks and light brown eyes. She had the kind of skin
that came alive in the heat, glowed like a smooth dark stone. She
kept her hair bound in a dirty rag, as if to diminish her beauty so
the white men would not notice.

The white women had left early that morning to go bathe in
one of the resort's five mineral springs. The men stayed behind to
be trimmed and shaved, and those who were not patiently waiting
for the barber to service them had ventured out on the fifty-four-
acre property to hunt for passenger pigeons. Except for the steady
toil of the servants inside, the hotel was quiet.

Sweet was in her cottage repairing pants. Back on her plantation, she was considered a wizard with a needle and thread. So
her master had given her several pants belonging to men staying
at the resort. Reenie was in the private room of the hotel's manager, waiting for him to return as he had ordered her to do.

Lizzie and Mawu stood at the well near the hotel pumping
water into pails. Every few minutes, a hotel servant came out
with two empty pails and carried two more full ones inside. His
task was to empty and refill the washbasin in each room with
fresh water. The two slave women had been instructed to help.
Even among the most free-thinking of whites at the resort, no
one seemed to relish the sight of the colored visitors idling. It was
recognized that their primary duty was to their rightful owners,
so the slaves tried to appear busy at all times. Lizzie and Mawu
had been caught sitting under the tree in the shade, trying to escape the heat, when the manager ordered them to the well.

The two women could hear Drayle and Sir chatting on the
porch. They had seen the ritual enough to know what was happening. The daughter was lathering the soap. The barber was
stroking the razor across the strop. Back and forth in long even

strokes, they could hear the whisking sound. Then silence. Then metal against leather again as he worked to keep the razor sharp.

"Sho, Mr. Drayle. I bought a slave before. They learn under me the barbering business." The gray-haired barber was speaking exaggeratedly, as if he were not accustomed to the southern way of speaking but was making every effort to imitate it. They could tell when he was talking because air slipped through his teeth with a whistling sound.

Lizzie and Mawu strained to hear what they could. Mawu kept edging closer to the porch until she was crouched just beneath it. Lizzie continued to pump. It was hard to hear over the squeak of the pump, and she did not want to get in trouble. But Mawu changed the air around Lizzie, made her do things she normally wouldn't. She stopped pumping.

"How do I know you're going to treat my Philip right? He's a right good hand, and I treat him better than most. What are you going to do with him? He doesn't know anything about city living," Drayle was saying. "He's a horse man."

Lizzie heard the words, but she was not sure she believed them. Was it possible the barber was trying to buy Philip? Mawu waved at her, then crouched down and disappeared beneath the porch. Lizzie looked at the back door, and ran over to the dark space beneath the porch to join Mawu. She crawled under it and followed. She looked behind her and saw the hotel servant come out of the back door. He put his hand to his eyes. He set down the empty pails and grabbed the remaining full ones. Then he went back into the hotel.

The ground was hard and dry against Lizzie's knees. She placed a palm against it to steady herself. Sunlight peeked through the cracks of the porch. She looked up. She could just make out their silhouettes.

"You right, Mr. Drayle. I couldn't never treat him good as you. I ain't rich and powerful like you—"

Lizzie and Mawu waited tensely, listening to the dull scrape of the razor gliding across a face.

"Well, how can you afford his price? I don't get how you can afford to just throw away that kind of money and get nothing in return," Sir said.

"Oh, he's getting something," Drayle said. "Philip is a first-class nigger."

"That nigger is liable to run off and leave you," Sir added, ignoring Drayle's comment. The last couple of words were muffled as if the barber working on him had placed a hot towel over his mouth.

"You right, you right. I can't afford it. Your man is gone have to pay me back," the barber said.

"Philip is one of my best hands. I just don't think I can let go of him."

"I understand, Mr. Drayle. I do understand."

The girl coughed. She placed the strop back into its carrying case. The barber tipped Sir up and brushed the clipped hair off his shoulders.

Hard-soled shoes dragged across the wood porch and stopped with a thud right above their heads.

There was silence for a few long minutes. Lizzie frowned. True, Philip was a hard worker and a good slave, but Drayle could buy another horse man. And it sounded as if this barber had offered Drayle a fair price. It wasn't like they were haggling over price. Drayle could easily buy a new slave the next time the trader came through. If Drayle wouldn't let Philip have a fair shake, then . . . She couldn't complete the thought.

"Well, what you say?" It was Sir's voice. "You gone sell the nigger or what?"

"That's my final answer, I'm afraid," Drayle said, so softly they almost didn't hear him. "I just couldn't let go of Philip. Francesca—that's my wife—would never forgive me."

"I understand, Mr. Drayle. I do understand," the barber said.

Even though the bargain had not been struck, Lizzie couldn't help but be proud of Drayle. He had discussed the matter with the barber as if he were a white man. Most slave owners wouldn't even have entertained the discussion, particularly with a free colored. They would have dismissed him outright. They might have even dealt him a blow just to remind him that his papers meant nothing, that he was only a train ride away from washing a white man's feet, sharing his woman's bed, toting bales of hay across his striped back.

Mawu motioned to her. It was time for them to leave. In a few minutes, the men would be up and moving quickly and the house servant would be returning for the next buckets.

"What you think about that girl?" Mawu asked. "The barber daughter."

"What?"

"She clean rooms in the hotel."

Lizzie thought it was an odd question. Why was Mawu asking her about the barber's daughter? What did she have to do with this? Didn't Mawu understand the significance of what they'd just heard?

"You don't know?" Mawu looked at her.

"Know what?"

"The barber' daughter and Philip. Them two got something going on."

"Since when?"

"Hell, I don't know girl. Ain't this your second summer?"

So that was how Philip had gotten the barber to make an offer for him. "And the daddy is already trying to buy him?"

"I reckon so."

"What kind of love is that?"

Mawu looked at her. "The real kind, I reckon."

Something had definitely been going on with Philip. Lizzie

and Philip were as close as brother and sister, and Lizzie knew when his mind was occupied. She had thought he might have a thing for Mawu. Why hadn't he told her? Lizzie squinted at the sun as they pumped.

"Girl, it's only one way out of slavery," Mawu said once the hotel servant came out and told them these were the final two buckets of water. They splashed water onto their faces and dried their hands on their dresses. Lizzie fingered her mole, and Mawu walked toward the cottages. Lizzie tried to catch up.

"What do you mean?" Lizzie asked.

They spotted Philip helping a white man load large sacks onto a cart. He looked over at them. Mawu sped up without giving Philip a second look and without answering Lizzie's question. And Lizzie realized she would be the one giving him the bad news.

TEN

"How many?" he asked her.

She had heard that some rivers flowed upstream, but she did not believe it. A slave had once told her that some insects and animals did not need a mate to have a baby. She did not believe that either. She'd once watched two flies, one hump-backed on the other, as if hitching a ride.

"How many?" He grabbed her by the shoulders and started to shake her.

Recently, Lizzie had stared into Massie's Creek and understood with a surprising clarity that life did not imitate its peaceful ripples. Her own experiences had always been as rutted as a rotting log. Even now things seemed to move without any kind of structure. She could see Drayle throwing things about, spit sliding down his chin.

And far away, she could hear her own voice murmuring inside her head.

". . . And you were a part of this plot as well?" he demanded.

"No, no," she protested, wondering how long she had been silent. "There weren't any others. It was just Mawu's idea. She's the one who planned to run."

"Should've known, should've known better."

"What are you talking about? Any slave with half a mind would try it, Drayle."

"So you're saying you did think about running?" He grabbed her by the shoulders again.

Lizzie squeezed her eyes shut, trying to figure out how to lessen his anger. He was reacting worse than she had anticipated. His face was red. They weren't back on the plantation. And it wasn't like she had told him that Philip was plotting to escape. It was Philip who had every reason to run. Mawu wasn't even his slave.

But Lizzie understood the anger even if she hadn't expected it. She forgave him for it. He loved her, and he was afraid she would leave him, too. That was what made him so upset. Her leaving. His beloved Lizzie. The mother of his children.

"Don't let him hurt her, Drayle. I just told you so you'd stop her."

"I've got to tell Tip, Lizzie. I wouldn't be a man if I didn't."

Lizzie kissed him. "I'm just saying. Talk to him and don't let him beat her hard. Just enough to keep her from—"

In the past week or so, after telling Philip that Drayle had refused to sell him to the free colored barber, she had noticed something new between the slaves. Tremors in their hands, unusually meek mock-smiles, glib "yessirs" and "thank yuhs." Their movements were slack, tame, sluggish. She recognized the overextended supplications. And between the words, there was a quiet.

Lizzie did not believe Reenie would really try to escape. Reenie had family back at her place. But the forced nights with the manager could make any woman reckless. And George might follow her, if given a plausible chance. Maybe Henry. Philip was more distant than she'd ever seen him, so she was counting him as a possible runaway, too.

She would have to warn Mawu, caution her to lay a trick on Tip so he wouldn't beat her too hard. Lizzie didn't believe in spells, but since Mawu did it ought to work. She began to think of ways to sneak out to Mawu's cabin before the night was over.

Drayle planted both hands on her shoulders. "What am I thinking, my sweet Lizzie. Of course you wouldn't leave me. Why would you come tell me about these plans if you were going to go with this woman? Come here."

Lizzie walked willingly into the trap of his arms.

Y'all need to know one thang and one thang only. These here United States will *never* be free for you. Y'all are slaves today and you will be slaves tomorrow. Your children will be slaves. And your children's children will be slaves."

He wielded the riding crop onto Mawu's back. He was the only white man present. The others had excused themselves. Lizzie stood among the slave men and women. Even Sweet, with her protruding belly, was made to stand witness. Two white women sat on chairs fanning themselves and watching intently from a distance.

The whip was small, a thin riding crop that barely broke the skin. But just as Lizzie congratulated herself on Drayle keeping his promise by making sure that the whipping would not be so severe, Tip showed them who he really was. He stripped off Mawu's clothes, tearing her dress into shreds until she was lying flat naked.

"Look at her! Look at her!" Tip prodded Mawu between her butt cheeks with the whip. "I won't stop until every eye is on me."

They all turned in Tip's direction, but Lizzie knew they had each carefully shuttered their eyes to keep from seeing. From the look of Mawu's limp body, it appeared the girl had passed out. Lizzie thought she herself would pass out, too. She could not pick up her feet, move her arms. She had only told on Mawu because she cared about the woman, admired her.

Tip undid his pants and mounted Mawu from behind, pulled her up onto her knees. With the first thrust into her, Lizzie knew Mawu was still conscious. Mawu yelled like an animal, a shriek so cold and shrill that Lizzie knew that he had done something unnatural. And he had done it in front of all of them.

One of the white women uttered a high-pitched "oh" and placed a handkerchief to her mouth. But neither of them stopped looking. A line of blood trailed down Mawu's thigh.

When he was done, he said in a hoarse whisper that carried above the wind as he turned toward them: "If I hear word that any of you other niggers is thinking about escaping, I swear as God is my witness I will do that and worst to every last one of you. I will make you *wish* you was in the fields under the lash. I will make you *wish* you was dead. And I won't leave a mark."

Lizzie tried to stop the pain in her head. The resort had lulled her into feeling human again. Had she glanced around at the others, she would know it had done the same to them. They had forgotten to protect themselves.

"Don't touch her. Don't nobody touch her," Tip said, stumbling back to his cottage.

The slaves started to move off, heading back to their unfinished tasks as if nothing had happened. Only Lizzie stood rooted. Her eyes clung to the ground a few feet away from Mawu's still body. She put her forearm into her mouth and bit down until she tasted blood. She wanted to hurt herself.

She sucked at the blood until it no longer flowed, until she felt dizzyingly empty.

ELEVEN

Somewhere between Mawu's beating and Philip's disappointment and Reenie's long walks to the hotel each evening, their spirits buckled one by one. Sweet allowed her pregnancy to get the better of her and simply sat down. Reenie's lips set into a straight, emotionless line. Mawu no longer talked back, the words she did speak taking on an air of vapidity. Philip was chained at night, no longer trusted. So it was no wonder that Lizzie sought out the white woman then.

Although they never said it outright, it was clear to Lizzie the women were upset that she had told. Yet even their anger could not compete with her guilt. She was the one who took tense breaths each time she saw Mawu's bruised face. She was the one who recoiled when one of them turned a stiff, humped shoulder in her direction.

Shame stretched Lizzie's face into false smiles, placed a kind word here and there on her lips, extended a ready helping hand.

She imagined them talking about her in the quiet when she wasn't around.

She had been dreaming of the path to Glory's farm, so she found it without a problem. After catching sight of the lone figure in the field and glancing around for watchful eyes, Lizzie rapped on the door. Glory answered and stared at her evenly, either unsurprised or hiding it. Only when the two women had settled comfortably in the main room of the cabin near the window where Glory could keep an eye out for her husband did Lizzie shake off her head scarf, swat at the fly that had been nagging her since she entered, and relax her hands in her lap.

Thin, faded quilts sagged across the backs of each chair. Out of respect, Lizzie tried not to lean back into the one on her chair. In the corner, a pot-bellied stove sat rusted, still full of the ash of the winter, as a reminder the hot, sultry summer would soon end and snow would fill the cabin doorstep once more. Three hooks on the wall, two holding overalls for a smallish man, freshly washed, as if each morning Glory's man stepped into his slops, laced up his boots, spooned up his meal, and walked out the door.

"Thirsty?"

Lizzie nodded and started to get up, but Glory beat her outside and returned in a moment with a tin of cold water.

"Best thing about living around here."

"What?" Lizzie patted her neck dry with her scarf. The air in the room felt oily.

"The water."

Lizzie took the cup, announced a clear distinct thank you. She felt she was mimicking somebody else's manners. It was odd, having this waxy-faced white woman serve her. The cup might even be the same one Glory's husband drank out of. Northern white folks were something else entirely.

"Something bothering you?"

Lizzie hadn't known it until that very moment, but something was bothering her. Her feet. The blister on her left thumb. Her stuff down there, worn sore by the endless nighttime activity. She fumbled with embarrassment, tried to forget she was sitting before a strange white woman, groped with the knowledge that Glory could not understand her. The gulf was too deep, too wide.

Lizzie, wake up! Come quick!"

Lizzie heard the sibilant whisper through her window. It was loud enough to wake her but not Drayle. She hurried out of bed, knowing the nighttime call could only mean one thing. Sweet was ready to deliver. By the time she got outside her cottage, the servant was gone, returned to her room, her errand complete. A light flickering in one of the cottage windows beckoned Lizzie like a finger.

Lizzie got to work before they had a chance to ignore her. Reenie sat beside Sweet drying her forehead with a cloth. Mawu dipped a pile of rags into a pot of boiling water. Lizzie gathered a stack of blankets, linens, some moth-eaten, others torn, stained. In the quarters back at her plantation, the women used a birthing chair. Here, Sweet would deliver on the bed. Lizzie shook out the blankets and layered them, one on top of the other, so they would provide a barrier between Sweet's labor fluids and the hard bed below. Momentarily disturbed, dust swirled and hovered in the moist air like stars.

Lizzie gave Reenie the signal everything was ready. Reenie spoke softly to Sweet who lay there, wet with exhaustion, her eyes slits of discomfort.

"I need for you to stand."

As soon as she said it, a labor pain racked Sweet's body and she heaved herself up, the bones in her neck jutting out like cords. She moaned, low and vicious, more like a growl. She was a mean birthing woman and spit venom at Reenie. As the pain gathered strength, Sweet grew louder. Even though the cottage was already so hot the walls were damp with moisture, Lizzie closed the windows. It would do none of them any good if Sweet's swearing woke the men. She slid a pasteboard square from beneath the stove, shook off the loose soot, and fanned Sweet with it.

"Get up, now. Get up," Reenie urged when Sweet's pains had subsided.

"I can't."

"Yes, you can. You got to get up and walk so you can bust your bag of waters."

Reenie helped to lift her up. She and Mawu walked Sweet around the room for over an hour, supported her when she had a pain so strong it made her collapse. Lizzie sat and watched.

"I can't walk no more," Sweet said.

They got her back onto the bed. Lizzie sat behind her and cradled Sweet's head between her legs. She remembered her own labors. Reenie reached into Sweet's womb and worked her hand around. They waited, hoping Reenie would be able to find the bag quickly.

When the pain started up again, Reenie drew her hand out. Sweet had several more labor motions while Mawu rubbed her feet and Reenie talked her through it.

Reenie was as good as anybody at birthing a baby. But Sweet didn't look good. No birthing woman ever looked good in Lizzie's opinion. She had seen what looked to be easy, quiet, and simple turn into a death scene. She had seen woman and child survive large amounts of blood while another woman and child died in the clean of a warm blanket.

So the bloody patch that spread like a flower on the linens beneath Sweet's womb only mildly stirred them. Mawu rearranged the blankets to keep her dry. Reenie said "somebody take hold of a leg" and reached her long fingers into Sweet's womb once again, working furiously. Sweet let out an open and full scream from the middle of her belly, and it lasted so long that she wore herself out.

"I think us need to go fetch her man," Mawu said.

Lizzie pictured the man sleeping soundly in one of the rooms in the hotel. He was far from being a worried father. His celebration would be less over a newborn child and more over a newly acquired piece of property. She was pretty sure he hoped for a son. Sweet did, too. Three of her four children were girls. Tomorrow, he would sit with the other men and debate over when would be too soon to put the child to work. They would argue over whether it was better to put him in the fields or treat him like the halfway son, halfway human they believed he was and allow him to work and live in the house.

"Yeah, maybe he wants to be here," Lizzie said.

"I ain't talking to you," Mawu snapped.

"Shut up, both of you," Reenie said. "You thinks her man gone appreciate you waking him up in the middle of the night? Us can catch this baby our own selves."

So they waited. And after some time had passed, Sweet's bag of waters finally burst.

Me too," Glory said.

"You too what?"

"I'm lonely out here too. I don't really have too many friends."

"What makes you think I'm lonely? I've got the other women-folks." Lizzie finished her water and aligned her feet beneath the rough-hewn table. She placed her features exactly where she wanted them. She didn't want this white woman figuring her thoughts anymore.

"That's right. So why else would you come here? You know me and you both could get in trouble."

"Tell me something. Why do you and your man live out here all by yourself? Why don't you live around the rest of society?"

"My husband, he likes it. He likes living out here."

"How come?"

"This is where he's from. The country."

"He owns all this land?"

"No. He just farms it."

Lizzie considered that.

"You like it out here, too?"

"I suppose it's all right. I ran away from my family to marry him. They didn't approve."

"Were you rich and he poor?" Lizzie thought of Fran and Drayle and how her family had disapproved of him. The only thing that had saved him was his talent with horses. He had been little more than a horse trainer, a hired hand, a mouthy charmer when she met him.

"Naw. Simpler than that. They just didn't like the looks of him. Said it was something about him they didn't trust."

"Were your parents like you?"

"What do you mean?"

"You know." Lizzie couldn't express what she meant in words. *Were they like you, a white woman that doesn't mind us*, she wanted to say. *A white woman that doesn't mind sharing her cup with a slave-woman.*

"Huh uh. I suppose that's what made it so easy for me and him to become religified. Being disowned makes you change a lot of things about yourself."

Lizzie studied Glory with a freedom she had never exercised with a white woman. She wanted to ask about her religion, why she dressed the way she did—the gray dress, bonnet, long hair—but instead, she said: "How do you feel about him?"

"What do you mean? He's my husband."

"You feel something in your insides for him?"

Glory paused. "I suppose he's all right." Lizzie noted that she spoke of him in the same voice she'd spoken of living in the country. "Yeah. I do love him."

Lizzie smiled. At least they had that in common.

The baby would not come.

They did everything they could to get the baby out. Mawu stretched Sweet's leg out wide while Lizzie lay across her belly and pushed down as hard as she could. As the labor pains came closer together, Reenie rubbed more oil onto Sweet's perineum. They all had sense enough to know that if the baby didn't come soon, as fast as the labor pains were coming, both Sweet and the baby would be in trouble. When Lizzie wasn't bearing down, she was praying, sometimes in her head, sometimes out loud.

Sweet's cursing had progressed from them to their mammies, and she was now working on cursing God. Her palms were scratched where she had balled her fists hard enough to break the skin with her fingernails.

Sweet's man came by after the sun was up, the smell of coffee and whiskey on his breath, and ordered somebody to fetch the doctor. He struck Reenie across the back of the head with a rolled-up newspaper for allowing Sweet to suffer through the night. He swore that if his baby died, he would blame them all. Lizzie smiled. He shouldered his rifle and left.

"Told you," Mawu couldn't resist saying.

Reenie looked up. "Don't you know nothing? If us had of woke him, he would of struck me for disturbing his sleep. Ain't no way to win, child."

When Lizzie had given birth to her second child, Drayle hadn't slept the entire night. She had learned this firsthand from one of the house slaves who waited on him while he sat in the parlor drinking. He had been determined that the medicine woman who was called upon to help birthing slaves in trouble would not maim his child with her herbs so Lizzie had been given nothing for her pain. There were a couple of white doctors in the area of the plantation whose main duty was to tend animals. But rarely was a doctor in that part of Tennessee sent for a laboring woman, white or colored.

This Ohio doctor arrived more rapidly than they would have expected. He was a young man who would have looked older had he worn a mustache. His bearing was not a convincing one for someone who was supposed to possess a secret knowledge. He carried a wide, thin box and placed it on the table beside the bed. His first words were to order them to open the windows, and he hadn't been there five minutes before he requested a bowl of cold water. Lizzie brought it in, thinking he would use it to douse Sweet. Instead, he dipped his hands into it and splashed the water onto his own face. Lizzie handed him a dry cloth.

"How long has she been laboring?" he asked.

"All night, sir," Reenie said.

"Hmph," he said. He sat in Reenie's chair and after a few minutes seemed to nod off into his own thoughts.

"She doesn't appear to want to open up," Lizzie said, trying to rouse him.

"Huh? Where is her husband?" he asked.

The women halted in their places. He had not asked, and they had assumed that he knew that Sweet was negro. Sweet was pale with clear gray eyes and a wide flat face. Her top lip was smaller than her bottom, and her thick hair was pulled back off her face. They could see how he made the mistake even if she did appear plainly colored to them. But hadn't the person who fetched the doctor told him that a slave woman was having a baby? It wasn't unusual that colored women would be attending a white laboring woman, especially one from the South. Lizzie felt disoriented by northern ways. What would he do if he knew? Perhaps he was a kind man. On the other hand, perhaps he would feel misled by their unintentional dishonesty. Sweet was almost unconscious with pain. They couldn't let him leave just yet.

"He went hunting," Reenie said.

A half-truth. Yes, he had gone hunting. No, he was not her legal husband and never would be.

"Well, he should know that his wife and the child are in grave danger," the doctor said.

He opened a box and selected a metal tool with handles like scissors and two long arms. Mawu opened her mouth as if about to say something, but then closed it.

"Get some more dry cloths," he told them.

Lizzie did as she was told. When she returned, the doctor had taken hold of the baby with the ends of his clamp and was pulling the baby out by the head.

"It's coming, it's coming," Reenie told Sweet who was too weak to push any longer.

A head full of black curly hair. It entered Lizzie's mind for only a moment that the doctor might soon understand the true "nature" of his patient, but she forgot all about it as she marveled at the instrument he was using to pull the baby out. She had never seen anything like it. He wasn't as ignorant as he looked after all. She couldn't wait to go back to the plantation and tell. He stretched Sweet with one hand while he tugged with his clamp with the other.

"Lay across her belly," he instructed Reenie. Reenie bore down on Sweet's belly and pushed while the doctor pulled and Lizzie stood by ready to swaddle the baby.

⁓

And now I got a question for you," Glory said.

Before she asked, Lizzie knew that Glory's question would mirror her own. It was a question many people thought about—slaves who watched as they went around in their better, but not quite good clothes and softer, but not quite soft feet, northern whites as they sat at the dining table and chose decorum over curiosity, wives who pretended to be asleep when their husband rose from their beds or never came to bed at all.

Did they love them? She couldn't speak for the others. She could only speak for herself. And she could say, without reservation, that she did. During his last days, she knew she would care for him. And upon his death, she knew she would grieve like a widow although she could make no such claims.

Glory listened to this and something rose between the women. Lizzie couldn't tell if it was mistrust or understanding, a rift or a tenderness. All she knew was something grew between the two women sitting at the oak table, sipping on empty cups, ignoring the fly buzzing around them. It grew between them like a tree trunk planted firmly in their wake. It mounted into a quiet that Lizzie would often think about when she remembered Glory years later.

Then he walked in.

Sweet gave birth to a dead thing. Dead in that it did not cry, did not move except to wave its nubbed hands and feet as if still scrambling in the womb. Reenie smacked it good and hard and it showed life by jerking in recoil. A day later it would be dead in the earthly sense. But for now, the doctor pronounced it healthy despite its hands and turned Sweet over to make her expel the afterbirth while Lizzie cleaned it off and tried to suck out whatever might be blocking its windpipe with her mouth.

The baby was a girl, her tiny body wrinkled with newborn worry.

The doctor did not wait for them to finish swaddling the baby. He left his bill on the table and told the women to bid the manager hello.

Lizzie believed there were only three ways to act when in the company of strange white men:

Don't look them in the eye. In fact, pretend they're not there. Walk a wide circle around them unless your master tells you otherwise.

Don't look them in the eye, but wait on them without being asked. Get their water before they even know they're thirsty.

Don't look them in the eye, but answer. And if your eyes should meet theirs, give them a stern look that lets them know you are not available for their whims.

When Glory's husband walked into his house, Lizzie went through the three choices in her mind. She couldn't choose number two as his wife was right there. So it was either number one or three. She considered the choices before her and chose the first one. As soon as he entered, she sprang up from the table as if she had been caught looking through his personal things. But she had already caught a glimpse of him. He was older than Glory.

"Relax, Lizzie. We've had your kind in our house before," Glory said.

Lizzie stuck to her choice and retreated to stand next to the wall behind her. Roosters cackled outside of the open window. She was aware that Glory's man was home earlier than sunset, and she tried to guess why he might have returned. He placed his hat on the table.

"Glory, I hope you didn't bring one of them girls home from Tawawa."

"No, sir. She came here on her own."

Lizzie could feel him studying her.

"Well, what does she want? Don't go making me lose my work. That's good money we make from Dr. Silsbee."

"Nobody saw her."

He addressed Lizzie directly. "Anybody see you walk out here?"

Since Lizzie had chosen rule number one, she didn't answer. She would only answer if Glory encouraged it.

"What's wrong with her?" he asked. "Is she dumb?"

"Naw, she's not dumb. You're scaring her is all."

"Get her out of here, Glory. We don't need any trouble."

He stooped and dragged a box from under the table.

"And you call yourself a Quaker," Glory said quietly.

He hoisted the box up and tucked it beneath his arm before tossing his hat back onto his head and leaving out again without another word. Lizzie watched him from the corner of her eye.

"You better get going," Glory said in a flat tone that was neither rude nor friendly.

The swath of familiarity they had cut minutes earlier dissolved. Lizzie retied her scarf and hurried through the still-open door.

Morning sunlight peeked into the cottage. The spirited whistles of sparrows did not move the melancholy resting on the women's faces. Sweet's too-quiet baby suckled at her breast. The mother rested peacefully. Mawu washed the birthing cloths with a steady brushing sound against the washboard in the yard behind the cottage. Sweet's man believed that dirty birthing linens were diseased, and he had instructed them to wash and hang the linens as soon as the child was born.

Lizzie found solace working with the women to clean the cottage and prepare it for the return of Sweet's master. She wanted the time she was spending with them to last for just a little while longer. Despite the doctor's intrusion, Sweet's labor had been women's time. And cleaning, yet another form of labor, was also women's time.

But she knew that this time would end and the others would remember her betrayal. Lizzie was of two minds. She wished she had not told. But if she hadn't, Mawu might be dead. If she had run and been caught, there was no doubt in Lizzie's mind that her friend wouldn't have allowed herself to be taken alive. And what if the others had followed? Drayle had done the right thing. So had she. She wished they could understand why.

For now, she just kept in step with the chorus of chores.

The next morning, while Sweet was still asleep and her master had not yet returned to the cottage as he waited for the "air to clear," the women discovered the baby dead in her arms. They wrapped it in layers of cloth and took it to Philip who summoned the other men to help him prepare a small grave. Then they returned to Sweet's doorstep and lingered outside as they searched for the plainest words of compassion. The sound of her voice from inside broke their trance and quickened them into action.

"The baby? Where my baby? Where my girl?"

Reenie, in her usual manner, delivered the news. "Her Father took her."

"Her father?" Sweet's voice was hopeful, but in less time than it took to blink twice she understood, knew in her heart that Reenie meant Father and not father. And her face did not crack.

She lay back, silent, as if all the wailing of childbirth had sucked her clean of any more sounds. And the trio of women who had known their own share of this kind of grief left her there, not coldly or callously, but with the understanding that she needed to be alone. Later, they would return to clean and dress her labor wound. But for now, they filed out, heads up, eyes as dry as they could muster.

Lizzie returned to her cottage to find Drayle just rousing from his sleep. He took the news quietly and asked if she wanted to kneel in prayer and she said yes. She whispered a fierce prayer, a tangled mess of biblical verses and cries of "have mercy, have mercy."

When she was finished, he placed his hand on her head reverently, devoutly, as if he were a preacher anointing her. Something in his touch flowed through her and helped her to make peace with the loss, which for some reason felt like her own. Then he left her kneeling there in her own thoughts, just as they had left Sweet. And she stayed there for a moment, disoriented, alone.

Then she walked out of the cottage, down the worn path that led between the houses toward the woods. There was a post where Glory delivered eggs and freshly slaughtered chickens or hogs to the hotel each morning. It was a white post and on it was painted: TAWAWA HOUSE ➡ Each morning, two servants, colored women from the hotel, met Glory there and took her bundle. Sometimes they were late, and often Lizzie had walked by and seen Glory standing there, waiting patiently with her bundle on the ground beside her.

It was early, and Lizzie was almost certain that Glory had not yet arrived for her daily delivery. She spied the white post in the blue light of the morning, its natural wood already beginning to etch through the paint.

She sat on the ground and waited for Glory, her legs tucked

beneath her. She wondered if Glory knew the pain of a dead child. The woman did not have children even though she had long been of childbearing age. Surely she did, Lizzie thought. Surely she had her own heft of memories.

Lizzie watched the sun break over the tops of the trees and listened to the gurgle of a nearby creek. She witnessed two sparrows play catch-and-kiss. She waited patiently for the white woman.

PART II

1842–1849

TWELVE

The first night he went to Lizzie, she was soaked with a sticky wetness that clung to her. The door was more than cracked, but it hadn't done much to relieve her in the small storeroom. She had extinguished her candle because even its flame sent off more heat than she could bear. One arm rested above her head on the moss-filled pallet and a foot was planted against the shelf, her legs propped wide. Looking back, she reckoned she must have looked as if she were waiting for him.

She had been owned by the Drayles for six full crop cycles before her master finally followed up on his incessant staring and came to her. Before she moved into the big house, she lived in a cabin with the blind woman they called Big Mama. Big Mama was known for her soap made from lye and crackling. It was good enough to sell to nearby plantations, and had turned a pretty good profit over the years. But the woman had been blinded when a vat of lye sputtered into both eyes. Lizzie spent the early years in the workyard with her. An area of the quarters sectioned off by chicken wire, the workyard was where clothes were sewn, mended, and boiled, slave food prepared, candles made, sausage ground, and butter churned. It also contained a small vegetable patch. At one end of the yard sat a long trough where the children ate their midday meal, sometimes scooping up the mush with long-handled wooden spoons but mostly using their fingers since there weren't enough spoons to go around. Those who didn't work in the fields stayed in the workyard most of the day. Lizzie had never been ordered to the fields. She stayed close by Big Mama's side, filling in for the old woman's eyes.

According to Big Mama, the Drayle plantation had originally belonged to Miss Fran's family. Big Mama had nursed Fran as a baby. That's how long she had lived there. Although the slave cabins remained the same, Drayle had added a kitchen onto the original house, ignoring his father-in-law's fears of a kitchen fire. The main house was larger on the inside than it appeared from the outside. But the grounds were impressive. A long dirt drive-way wound through two acres of flat manicured land and ended at the red brick colonial. Behind the main house, the slave cabins lined up in three neat rows. The fronts of the cabins all faced the back of the main house, as if Fran's father had wanted his slaves to keep an eye on his back, or as if to keep them from looking out beyond the property and envisioning escape.

When Fran married the horse breeder, her parents took off to live in Mississippi, leaving the house in Shelby County for good. They did not approve of the marriage mainly because Drayle had no wealth.

Gradually, however, they came to accept Drayle's marriage to their daughter even though he did not give them the grandchil-dren they craved. Their son-in-law managed to turn a steady profit from the hundred and twenty acres of mostly soybean and cotton fields. And even though his horse breeding had never amounted to more than a hobby, Drayle had attained a certain status in the surrounding community due to his equine knowledge.

Later Lizzie would reason that perhaps Drayle really was just passing through the kitchen and noticed her door open and only meant to close it. Perhaps he did think he heard a disturbing noise and came to check it out. And it was certainly possible he didn't even know that the house girl slept in the storeroom off the kitchen. It was closer to dawn than dusk when she removed most of her clothes and propped the door open. If someone came in the kitchen, they would have to light a lantern, giving her time to cover herself.

But there was no warning light and he appeared in the doorway like an apparition, a sudden whistle of breath, a book tucked beneath his arm, a glass in his hand.

"It's terribly hot in here," he said.

She didn't have time for a "yessir," rolling over until her body was safely wrapped in the pallet, the muslin shirt too far to reach without exposing even more than she already had. What had moments before seemed like utter darkness now looked like blue light, and she could easily make out his form. She hoped her dark skin offered some cover.

Once, she had fancied a slave called Baby on account of his round, boyish face. The most tender moment of their relationship had been when he brought her a dead squirrel for supper. She'd fried it in bacon fat and they'd picked the meat off the scrawny animal with their fingers. Grease smeared over his face while he ate and when he smiled at her she'd wanted to lick it right off. The relationship had never gone beyond their awkward groping.

"I'm very sorry," her master said.

"Yessir." She wasn't sure what he was talking about or what to answer. Big Mama had taught her when these moments happened to just say "sho" or "yessir."

There were so many things to remember. It had taken a full week to remember to answer to her new name. The first change after she moved into the main house was that her mistress renamed her. She had been Eliza, but she became Lizzie because Miss Fran felt it was easier to say. The second change was that she was told to forget the slave cooking ways she'd learned down in the workyard. At her previous plantation, the cooking had been done in a cabin separate from the big house. It had been a larger plantation, and there had been much more to prepare. The location of the kitchen within the big house at the Drayle plantation threw Lizzie into closer proximity to whites than she had ever been.

"Here," he said. "Take my water."

She stared at his outstretched arm. Her eyes adjusted to the dark, but she still couldn't see his expression well enough to tell if he was setting a trap for her. *Sometimes they set traps for you*, Big Mama had said. *You got to be awares at all times. Ain't no such thing as a truth-telling nigger. They's only a dead nigger and a live one.*

"Oh, no sir." Then a pause. "Do you needs something?"

"Please." He moved into the storeroom, so close his toe touched the edge of her pallet. "I won't leave until you drink every bit of this here water."

She sat up and pressed her back to the wall. She stared at the cup as if it contained poison. *What do I do, Big Mama? Lord knows I is thirsty.*

"Please," he repeated. He set it on the floor in front of him as if he knew she would not take it from his hand.

Something about the way he said it the second time made her think for a moment that he was being kind. She looked down at her hand as it made its way across the bare mattress and finally closed around the cold, sweating glass. She touched it to her lips and drank it down. When the glass was almost empty, she stopped.

"Go on," he said. "Drink it all, now."

She felt done, but she drank the rest of it, hoping it would make him leave.

"You get some rest now," he said.

For the next week or so, he brought her cold water in the middle of the night, and each time, she took it more and more willingly until she was waiting expectantly, her body tense with restlessness and thirst while she anticipated his low rumbling voice. He changed glasses twice, until finally he brought a large jar she couldn't finish off at once. Now he sat down to wait.

And with each visit, he moved closer and closer to her on the pallet, until finally he was lying beside her, his smooth skin slick against hers as he touched the cold glass to her face.

THIRTEEN

He brought her books. The first word she learned to read and write was "she" and it delighted her so much she wrote it everywhere she could. She wrote it in the biscuit batter with her spoon. She dug it in the dirt out back with a stick. She sketched it in the steamy windows when it rained. When she pricked her palm with a kitchen knife, she squeezed the skin until she could write her new word out with blood on a scrap of cloth. She traced the word with her fingers on the smooth parts of his body while they lay together in the storeroom at night.

She was afraid of him, but with each reading lesson she allowed him to take one more step with her. At first, he told her he just wanted to touch her tiny breast. Then he said he just wanted to place his hand on her hip. At first, he *asked* to touch her. Later, he did not. Each touch was like a payment for his kindnesses.

She waited for him without clothes because he liked her that way. He said he wanted to drink her. He stared as if her thirteen-year-old body held a great secret, a miracle milk that would cure him if he drank of it only once. He seemed to savor each night, the anticipation arousing him to a point that stretched his penis as taut as a pig's belly.

She gathered a stockpile of books, precious gifts from him, and hid them behind the flour sacks in the storeroom. She couldn't read most of them yet, but she enjoyed turning the pages, fingering each book's binding, making out the page numbers as she learned how to count and figure.

He told her to call him Drayle, his last name only. Most of the slaves called him Master. He asked her to drop the title. At first she couldn't bring herself to do it. She felt if she dropped it he would take the final step and hurt her in the way she hoped he wouldn't.

Big Mama had once told her she had to prepare for a life in which she would be violated: *it hurt the first time*, she'd said, *but you get used to it*. It was that first time that frightened her, and Lizzie hoped that for him, looking and touching would be enough. It had been for Baby.

He asked her if she had a wish and taught her the word *genie*. She said she'd once heard she had a sister. Somewhere close by. Her only living blood relation that she knew of. Could he find her? He promised with a serious face. She believed him and permitted him an extra touch.

He said he enjoyed teaching her to read because she had a keen intellect. She liked the word *keen* and turned it over in her mouth. She realized her phonetic ability to sound out words. He appeared to have endless patience as she mouthed the words on the page with her lips before saying them. He only interrupted to remind her to lower her voice. The nights were quiet, and they remained undisturbed in their secret meetings. He had been educated in the North and she admired his knowledge.

When she had no more room to store her books, he brought her food. She enjoyed the food more than she had thought she would. She already ate better than the field slaves, but he showed her there was even more food to discover. He brought her cocoa, which she mixed with hot milk and sugar in the dark kitchen. They drank it together, sucking its thick sweetness with their tongues. He brought her johnnycakes from town, and she made a gravy to go with them. They devoured them, licking the gravy from their lips.

When he learned how much she craved sugar, he used it to tease her. When he didn't have any more sweets, she stole sugar cubes from the kitchen and sucked on them while she worked.

Finally, she dropped the Master and called him Drayle.

These were the things that happened in the night. In the day, she had to hide that she now looked at the other slave women through new eyes. Before, she had felt like a child among them. But she was no longer the timid girl they'd given a bucket of potatoes and ordered to peel on her first day in the house kitchen. She felt she was something else. Her skin had begun to clear, her shoulders broadened, and even though she still did not believe in her beauty, she was aroused by this new awareness of her body.

She moved quickly around Miss Fran, Drayle's wife, certain that if the woman looked her in the eye, she would know her newest house slave was betraying her. Fran's eyes were never the same. Sometimes, they were listless and empty, staring down at her needlework as if wondering how it had appeared in her hands. Other times, they were alert and watchful. At these moments, they looked as though they could see right through Lizzie.

As Lizzie learned the meanings of new words and what the letters looked like on the page, it became more difficult to hide the fact that she could read. She wanted to read everything. She scanned the spines of books along the shelves in Drayle's library. She looked over Fran's shoulder as she cleaned around her, straining to make out the handwriting of Fran's mother. She wanted to read to the slaves in the cabins. There was only one man among them who could read the newspaper, and Lizzie thought she might be able to read as well as he could. She wanted to show him up, prove that women could learn, have everyone's eyes hungry for her mouth to open and turn the piece of pulp in her hands into hope.

The summer stretched into August, and work around the farm picked up as the season for cotton harvesting began. Drayle came to the storeroom less and less, and gave fewer gifts. Lizzie was relieved she had escaped unharmed. She believed she had been like a toy to Drayle, and he was now tired of playing with her. He gave no explanation as to why he stopped coming, but she saw how hard he was working. It was the first time she'd examined the great muscles in his back and the texture of his face. He was built like a slave, only white. She did not know how old he was, but his hair was a vibrant blond color and his skin reddened in the sun. She thought his face might have been perfect were it not for his slightly long nose. She was enchanted by the color of his eyes.

And then she discovered something she had never before seen in her life: a mirror. She had seen her reflection in the nearby pond many times, but this piece of glass was magical. It was in Fran's bedroom, and each time she passed it she found herself pausing to get a good look at herself.

She stole a brush from Fran's drawer, stripped the hairs from it, and boiled it. She tried to brush out her knots. It took her three days of brushing and cutting the tangles. But when she was finished, she discovered she had a mound of hair that hung in frazzled coils around her face. She made excuses to be in Fran's room every chance she got.

There was only one other slave woman who lived in the house. Lizzie sensed the older woman's demeanor begin to change toward her a few weeks after Drayle began visiting her at night. Not long after his visits subsided, Lizzie found Dessie in the storeroom, holding the brush in her hand as if it were a giant vermin. Lizzie tried to figure out how she could have forgotten to put it away.

"Where you get this from, 'liza?"

"My name be Lizzie," she said.

Dessie had lived in the house attic for years. Lizzie knew her from the shape of her back; it was a form she was used to seeing bent over a tub or the fire in the kitchen. Her face looked as if it had been pretty once.

"Give it," Lizzie said, her lip twitching.

"Not unlessen you tell me where you got it. Is you a plum fool, girl?"

She started toward her but something in Dessie's posture stopped her. Lizzie was certain that had she been within arm's reach, the woman would have knocked her in the head with the brush.

"You don't know what you done brung in this house," Dessie said, setting the brush on the shelf with a loud clap.

Lizzie moved to the side as the older woman, stooped again, walked past her. "You don't know what you done brung in here," she repeated as she scooted through the kitchen.

Lizzie was too frightened to move. Dessie knew. She was sure of it. She wanted to tell her that she hadn't asked Drayle to come in the first place. And he had stopped coming anyway. Not altogether, but mostly. She wanted to tell her that. She wanted to say more than "give it." She wanted to ask her what she meant about bringing something into the house.

Two nights later, Lizzie knew. Two nights later, when Drayle finally took what he had been lusting after for so long, Lizzie understood the something that had been brought into the house was her.

FOURTEEN

They entered the woods behind the slave cabins, the one-eyed horse following a barely cleared trail. Fat spiders rested in opalescent traps. Drayle brushed at his face, cleared the webs for her. Lizzie reached out to pull at a strand of web lingering in his hair and stretched it out, stronger than she'd expected, tensile.

"This here is what they call a smooth-gaited horse."

Lizzie wanted to laugh. Smooth-gaited? She was certain she would tumble off at any moment. If this was smooth, she didn't want to ride the others. She held on.

After a few minutes of walking, she felt him squeeze his legs and they took off into the woods at a slow trot. She bounced in the saddle. She clenched Drayle's waist, feeling for hardness beneath the fat of his stomach. When the trail split, Drayle merely looked the way he wanted to go and the horse followed.

She felt sore in her saddle area and asked Drayle to slow down. He responded after she had repeated her request twice.

When Drayle had told her that morning they would be taking a ride, she tried to hide her fear. As friendly as she knew the horse to be, it was massive, the haunches of the beast taller than her shoulders. She followed Drayle, praying the horse would recognize her as the girl who sometimes stopped and gave him a bit of sugar or a pat on the head. Until recently, she had been afraid to do even that, the mouth of the horse a giant hole threatening to swallow her up.

Philip had walked the one-eyed horse down to the woods from the barn. Drayle mounted first, and Philip gave her a hand while she stepped into the stirrup. After trying to gain her balance for a few moments, she felt comfortable enough to let Philip go. She tied a cloth around her hair.

"Hold on tight now," Drayle said.

"Where we going?"

"Where *are* we going?"

"Where *are* we going," she repeated.

"You'll see," he answered.

Now they were stopped in the middle of a trail and the horse had begun to empty its bladder. Lizzie felt the urge to empty hers.

"Drayle?"

He turned around to look at her.

"I got to do it, too."

He eased himself off the horse before helping her down.

Lizzie looked behind her at the stretch of trees. She'd only left the place two or three times in recent memory. Drayle had bought her when she was seven years old. In the years since, his farm had become her most familiar place.

He pointed to an area behind a bush, and she went behind it grateful for the privacy. It occurred to her that some white men wouldn't think enough to point to a bush. Modesty was for ladies. When she'd been brought to the auction block, she'd been chained to a line of slave women, ready to board the trader's wagon. As the smallest, Lizzie had led, but she'd felt the jingle of metal when two of the women in the back kneeled down so the very last woman could squat right there in the middle of the road. Her skirt was the only privacy she had, and Lizzie had noticed the woman's eyes close as if to shut out her audience.

When Lizzie was done, she came back to him. She listened to him breathing in the air, his nostrils flaring like the horse's. His tall form cast a shadow over her, and she felt safe in the cool of it. They walked along for a bit. He did not hold her hand as she had seen some slaves in love do from time to time, but she felt his nearness. She looked over at the horse to see if it was watching her as it had so many times before, but its good eye was focused straight ahead. After a while, they climbed back onto the horse.

A barn peeked over the crest of the hill and she shaded her eyes with her hands. They reached a small house. Drayle whistled and a slave girl of about ten years old came out onto the porch. Lizzie took off her cloth to better show her face.

"You belong to Leo Nesbitt?"

The girl nodded.

"I'm looking for his slave Polly."

"Which one?" the girl said. "They's two."

Drayle shrugged. "How the hell should I know?" He pointed back at Lizzie. "Is there one that looks like this one?"

Lizzie was sweating beneath her dress. She did not like that he referred to her as "this one" although she was not sure why.

The girl came off the porch to get a closer look. "I'll be right back, sir." She ran off, leaving a cloud of dust behind her.

It took the girl a while. Drayle got off the horse and helped Lizzie down.

"What you up to?" Lizzie asked.

"Didn't you tell me you heard you had a sister around these parts?"

Lizzie was finding it hard to breathe. She shook her head back and forth and patted down her hair.

"Didn't I tell you I'd do anything for you?" he said.

The girl returned with a woman following her. The woman carried a basket.

"Polly?" Drayle called out.

The woman stopped about five yards away. She was staring at Lizzie.

"Yessir?"

"I believe that this here is your sister. Come here. Let me get a closer look at you," he said.

The woman didn't move, but Lizzie did. She closed the distance between them until she was standing right in front of the woman. Although the slave was older than Lizzie, they were the same height, the same shade of mud brown. And even more, both were covered with a spattering of moles that ringed their necks like precious stones. Lizzie did not know how to feel. It was as if she had been locked in a closet all her life, and someone had just opened the door to reveal her first bit of light.

"You my sister?" Lizzie asked.

The woman studied her. "Maybe you wants the other Polly. I don't know nothing bout no sister."

"My mammy died when I was young. But they say I got an older sister who lives in Shelby County. Where were you born?"

The woman's face lit up as if this would solve the mystery. "Weakley."

Lizzie's hand flew to her mouth. She turned back to Drayle. He nodded.

Polly put down the basket. Then she stretched back up, as if ready to examine this stranger who might not be a stranger after all.

"What your name is?" she said.

"Lizzie. I mean, Eliza. But they call me Lizzie."

She touched Lizzie's face and ran her fingers along Lizzie's jawbone. Then she took Lizzie's hand and turned it over in her own, as if the lines would reveal the truth.

"You my sister?" Polly said, finally.

Lizzie blew out a yes.

Polly reached out and slowly folded Lizzie in her arms. Their embrace was awkward. Neither seemed to know what to do. The slave girl who had fetched Polly sat on the edge of the porch, legs dangling, watching them.

"That's enough," Drayle said after a few minutes. "You can come back to visit her, Lizzie."

Lizzie held fast to the woman, not believing him. Polly kissed her on the eyelids. Her lips were wet. She smelled like peaches, and Lizzie sucked the scent through her mouth. For the first time in months, Drayle did not exist. This was her blood, her real blood kin. But Polly felt fragile, light, as if she would disappear. She was thinner than Lizzie, not as well fed. Lizzie had a strange thought. If she could crush this woman, crumble her into dust and take her back to Drayle's plantation, she would.

"I promise," he said. "I'll write you a pass. Long as you don't try to run off. I'll write you all the passes you need."

He walked over and pulled Lizzie by the hand. He helped her onto the horse. He turned the horse, but Lizzie did not take her eyes off the woman. She turned almost completely around in the saddle as they rode off. Polly waved and Lizzie tried to memorize her face. The barn disappeared behind the hill.

When they arrived back at the edge of Drayle's place, he told her to get off the horse. Then he rode on up through the cabins without her. He did not have to tell her it would not look good if they returned together. He did not have to tell her to hang back and wait until she thought he'd had a chance to dismount and hand the horse over to Philip.

That night, she thanked him by giving him what he wanted.

~

When it was almost morning, she thought she heard something in the kitchen. Drayle never stayed all night, but they had both fallen asleep. When she saw the lantern light up in the kitchen, she shoved Drayle awake. He jumped up while she pulled the shirt over her head. He leaned to peek through the door, but whoever it was must have been headed straight for the storeroom because before he could open it, the door pushed toward him.

Fran. Matter-of-fact. Unsurprised. As if she had not just caught him in the room where the slave girl slept.

"Nathan? I thought I heard something. Did you hear something?"

Drayle shielded Lizzie with his body. "I didn't hear anything," he said. "Go back to bed, dear."

Lizzie could not see Fran's face, but she imagined it wore a quizzical expression. She wanted to shrink into the corner until she became another lump in the blanket Drayle had given her.

He closed the door behind his wife and returned to her. She didn't realize she was shivering until he touched her.

After a while, she said: "She might sell me."

"Oh hush, Lizzie. Besides, I reckon Fran doesn't mind. She's a Southern woman. She expects a man to do certain things."

Lizzie didn't believe him, but he kissed her and she convinced herself his words were enough. Nothing would come between them. Drayle was the man of the house.

He reached beneath the blanket and pinched her nipple until it hurt. She had told him that she did not like her nipples pinched, but he did it anyway. He trailed his fingertips down the front of her stomach, dipped into her navel, and circled it.

"I want you to have my child, Lizzie," he said between his lips and her skin. "Can you do that for me?"

Lizzie went soft. "Your child?" she repeated.

"I gave you your sister. Now you give me a son. Can you do that for me?"

He pressed against her.

Lizzie tried to think straight. Tried to keep her mind and body separate. She had never been drunk before, but she imagined this was what it felt like.

Drayle didn't stop. "A son, Lizzie. My first son."

She had not thought of this. She did not feel ready to be a mother. She knew Fran hadn't given him a child, and she tried to think of what it would mean for her to do this for him.

He entered her forcefully while she was still muddled in her thoughts. And then she could think no more except to understand that his desire for her was all she had. He moved on top of her, and it was as if a world moved on top of her, its weight at once delightful and burdensome.

When he was done, when they were done, she fell asleep.

FIFTEEN

Drayle did something that astounded his wife. Tired of sleeping on the storeroom floor with his new lover, he moved her into the guest bedroom across from his own. That was when Fran began to pinch Lizzie.

The pinches were hard enough to bruise. Fran did it secretly—in the kitchen, on the stairs, in the hallway, in the yard. She searched for new places, beginning with Lizzie's cheek. Then an arm. Thigh. Side. Shoulder. She seemed to relish discovering each new point of hurt. Sometimes Lizzie even caught the woman examining her body, as if searching for a new place. Lizzie tried to stay out of her way. Tried to bypass her in the familiar layout of rooms.

At night, Drayle came to her, but Lizzie didn't tell him about Fran's game. Instead, she made excuses for the bruises. She told him that colored people bruise easier than whites. This explanation seemed to satisfy him and he took care not to touch her in those places.

After two weeks, Fran grew tired of her pinches and left Lizzie alone. Lizzie was grateful and went out of her way to make Fran pleased. She cleaned the woman's room without being asked, ironed her clothes, and put extra sausage on the breakfast trays delivered to Fran in the mornings.

The house slaves had accepted Lizzie as Drayle's woman, and they now looked to her to convince him of favors. If someone was sick down in the quarters, they asked Lizzie to whisper the news to him so the person would be granted a reprieve. Another time, Lizzie convinced Drayle to let the slaves have extra rations of meat. Each time Lizzie was able to redeem a request, the field slaves accepted her position a bit more.

Now that she could read, Drayle gave her the leftover weekly newspaper. She asked him questions about current events. She wanted to know about these fights over expanding United States territory. She had read about it aloud to the slaves in the quarters. She repeated Drayle's words and told them any fight over new land was connected to their fate. The more slave states acquired, the greater the chance of slavery enduring. They wanted to believe in the whispers of abolitionism that came their way, stories of slaves freed up North, of rebellious uprisings, promises that there were white men out there who wanted to do away with this system of human bondage. But their everyday reality was bleak. Their work days were too predictable for them to imagine any other way of living. They did not know where this Texas was or what it had to do with them. A couple of the older slaves remembered the Missouri Compromise, and they expected some other kind of compromise this time, too.

She was in the quarters reading to the slaves when she first learned Drayle planned to sell the one-eyed horse they'd taken to meet her sister the first time. She had learned the horse's name was Mr. Goodfellow. Each time she walked past Mr. Goodfellow, it turned its human-like eye and studied her. She felt an affection for him that she did not feel for the other horses.

"But why are you selling him? Ain't he a good horse?"

She stood up straight. She had been picking herbs out of the garden, folding them into the front of her shirt. The rosemary had finally rewarded her efforts, stretching long and elegant across the garden bed. It was an herb she had only recently discovered. Her sister Polly had given her a bit to chew on when she'd visited last. She'd planted it, hoping the seeds would take root. They had.

"Yes, he's a good horse. But I just got word on another horse I've been wanting, and I've got to make a trade."

"Don't sell him, Drayle."

"Lizzie, there are better horses on this farm. Besides, he only has one eye."

"One *good* eye," she said. "The other eye is there underneath that patch."

"Say your goodbyes," he said.

When she reached the pasture, she found Mr. Goodfellow grazing. Four horses stood off to one side, as if they had no time for a one-eyed horse. She tried calling out to the horse, but it only lifted its head for a moment and then went back to eating.

She went to find Philip. He was in the barn shoeing the Saddlebred. She told him she wanted to ride the one-eyed horse. She knew Philip as a quiet man who didn't smile much. In the long stretches of silence that he made no effort to fill, one could hear him making a low clucking noise in the back of his throat from time to time.

He put down his tools and took a saddle off the wall. They walked out to the field together. When he whistled, the horse came. He saddled the horse, and helped her up onto it. She tried to steady herself. It was her first time on a horse alone.

"I'll lead you," he said. He led her around the field once and she stroked the horse's mane. When she was done, she patted it on the face and whispered in its ear while Philip untied the saddle. Then he slapped the horse on its hindquarters and it moved back out into the field.

She circled the barn and slave cabins and made her way to the back entrance of the house. The women were scuttling around the kitchen with their heads bowed. Their movements were mindful, and Lizzie guessed there were guests in the house. She tied on an apron.

Fran appeared in the doorway, rubbing a sweaty forehead with the back of her hand.

"Lizzie, I have someone I'd like for you to meet," she said. She stared at Lizzie's equally tall but more youthful figure. Then she narrowed her eyes at Lizzie and sniffed, as if she could smell the reek of the horse sweat between Lizzie's legs. "But clean yourself up first."

SIXTEEN

He was tall and wore a crisp black hat that he did not take off even though he was standing inside the house. He sucked on something that smelled like tobacco, a hard lump in his lower right jaw, and Lizzie waited anxiously for him to spit on the clean wood floors. His shirt was wrinkled and loosely tucked into pants that bulged across his distended belly. He didn't look like family and was dressed too shabbily to be a reverend.

Fran watched his expression so intently that a blue vein stretched taut against the white skin of her neck.

"So?"

Lizzie looked at the floor and grabbed both sides of her dress with her hands. She waited for the person who Fran wanted her to meet to jump out of the shadows. Surely it was not this tall, strange white man with whom she could have no business. He pulled his pants up.

"You say she can cook?"

"Of course."

"You say she ain't got no pickaninnies?"

"Not a one." Fran looked over at her.

"Clean?"

"As a whistle."

The lines of the hardwood floor converged in front of Lizzie.

"Healthy?"

"As a horse."

"What's the catch?"

"There's no catch, Mr. Simpson."

He paused and pulled up his pants again. Lizzie lifted her eyes to look at him. The light outside had turned dusky red and he squinted in the dim light of the hallway, as if trying to ascertain if there were certain things wrong with her that were invisible to the naked eye. Reading his face, Fran lit another lamp and the foyer brightened a bit.

Lizzie could taste her last meal on her tongue, and she tried to separate out each flavor in her throat. As the knowledge of what was happening to her rose fully in her mind, she tried to remember the last time a trader had entered their place. She vaguely remembered a slave who had tried to escape three times, the last time taking his bow-legged woman with him. She remembered they had spoken some other language, a bastardized echo of what their mothers had taught them, and she remembered the two had been cousins. The slave patrollers returned with the bow-legged woman but without her cousin. No one knew what happened to him, but soon it was clear the woman was big with a child. She gave birth soon thereafter, early, to a tiny baby that didn't look quite ready for the world. The baby lived, but the woman never knew that because she was sold off to a trader who had stood outside in the swirling dust and eyed her just as this man was now eyeing Lizzie. Lizzie remembered that day. She had been a young girl, only a year on Drayle's place, but old enough to hear and understand the whispers circling through the slave cabins and the dead expression on the woman's face as she climbed into the back of the wagon.

Now here Lizzie stood in the same space, searching inside herself for her own response, wondering if the nothing she was feeling was the same nothing the bow-legged woman had felt.

He ordered her to open her mouth. She did. He poked around inside her mouth with his finger. Then he squeezed a breast. She flinched. He ordered her to take off her apron. She dropped it to the floor. While he ran his hand down the front of her dress, she saw Fran look nervously toward the window.

"What's it going to be?" Fran looked as if she were ready to be done with the whole thing.

"I'll take her." He picked up something from the floor beside him and undid the piece of cord around it. He unfolded a musty blanket, and it coughed up dust as he wrapped it around her shoulders.

Lizzie didn't protest, allowing him to lay the blanket across her shoulders like a shawl. She didn't protest when he opened the front door and she followed him out to a horse tied to a ramshackle cart. He pushed her onto the cart and tied her hands and ankles. He tightened the rope around her ankles and she felt it cut into her skin. She bit her lip until it bled. He turned to Fran and exchanged the money with her wordlessly.

The evening was quiet, save for the bowing wings of crickets. Dessie was in the kitchen working, and the rest of the slaves were still in the fields. There was no one around to witness Fran's betrayal. Lizzie did not know where Drayle was, and she figured that to protest would be futile. A passivity settled upon her along with the blanket. This resignation was a feeling she would not soon forget.

The man in the hat climbed onto the horse and picked up the reins. As soon as the cart lurched forward, Lizzie put her hand over her mouth and vomited through her fingers. It went down the front of her dress. Everything in her stomach came up until she was heaving air.

"What the devil?" The man in the hat stopped the horse and turned around to look at her.

"What's wrong with her?" he shouted at Fran.

"Nothing, nothing," Fran waved him on. "Just scared. She'll get over it."

"I asked you if she was healthy."

"She is. I'm telling you she is."

"Well, why'd you rush me? And why is she getting sick all over the place?"

"I'm not rushing and I'm not deceiving you."

"Well, what is it?"

Now that Lizzie's belly was empty, she found her voice and began to cry.

"May I remind you, Mr. Simpson, that I am a lady."

"Well, lady, you best give me my money back."

"I'll do no such thing."

"Oh, yes you will."

"What's going on here?" Drayle walked around from the back of the house, clapping the dirt off his hands.

Lizzie shook off the blanket.

"I want my money back. I got to head to Missouri tomorrow morning and I don't need to add no sick slave to my bunch, infecting everybody else."

"Fran, what are you doing?" Drayle turned to his wife.

"I'm selling her, Drayle. She's no good," Fran said. But the look in her eyes said she knew that her chance had passed.

"What do you mean? We didn't talk about selling any of the slaves."

"Well, we need the money."

"For what?"

"I don't care to discuss our financial matters in front of strangers."

"Lizzie, get down off that cart," Drayle said.

The man untied her, and Lizzie gathered her stained dress and hopped off the cart. She wobbled on her feet. She saw Fran reach into the front of her dress and pull out the crumpled wad of bills. She handed the money back to Mr. Simpson without counting it out.

Lizzie didn't stay around to see what happened next. She headed straight for the slave quarters. For now, it seemed safer to be there than anywhere else.

SEVENTEEN

Word made it back to the quarters that Fran had tried to sell Lizzie, and it made the rest of them nervous the mistress might bring a trader around for one of them next. The Drayles weren't known for selling off hard-working, peaceful slaves, but someone said the Drayles might be in financial trouble. First, talk of selling a horse and now talk of selling a slave. If creditors came, they might pick off slaves, animals, property, and anything else that would satisfy the debt. The women shot questions at Lizzie about what had happened, what the man looked like, what Fran said. Lizzie did not tell them the real reason Fran wanted to get rid of her.

For the first few nights, Lizzie shared a pallet in a small cabin with four other slave women. They did not like Lizzie staying there in the cramped one-room cabin, but they felt a temporary pity since the mistress had tried to sell her.

Lizzie was too frightened to go back to work and sleep in the big house, and no one came for her over the next couple of days.

Instead, she helped the women with their chores in the workyard. The women were kind to her, grateful for the extra help. But on the third morning, she was too tired to get out of bed. She was so exhausted that each time she moved to rise up, a headache forced her to lie back down.

Philip carried her all the way to Big Mama's cabin himself. The old woman knelt beside her.

"What's wrong with you, child?"

"I don't feel well, Big Mama. I think I might be sick."

"Too sick to work?"

Lizzie nodded.

Big Mama rose and went outside. She returned with a dipper full of water. "Sit up and take a drank so as I can look at you."

When Lizzie tried to pull herself up, her head split into three daggers of pain. She sipped the water. For Big Mama, taking a look meant feeling her forehead and putting her ear to Lizzie's chest.

"What's wrong with me, Big Mama? I ain't never felt so bad in my life."

Big Mama rolled out a pallet for Lizzie to lay down. When she was done, she took out her sewing and felt around for the stitches. She sat on a chair with a cowhide bottom and rocked back and forth. Lizzie waited.

"Big Mama?"

The old woman turned her way. She put down her sewing and said: "He done finally done it. Nobody thought he could."

As soon as Big Mama told Drayle that Lizzie was pregnant, he ordered her back into the house. The first three months were difficult for her. She almost fell asleep while cutting up onions and shelling peas. The only thing she felt like doing was lying down. The vomiting stopped, but the unsettled feeling in her stomach did not. She couldn't help but wonder how the women in the quarters continued to work in the fields while they were carrying a child.

The slave women commented on her spreading nose. They checked her neck to see if it had darkened. Dessie stuck a bucket under her chin when she had to vomit and no sooner than Lizzie was done did Dessie push the bucket into the younger girl's chest so she could empty her own mess.

Fran took the news with what appeared to be a debilitating sadness. She stayed in her room all day and slept. She ceased going into town. As the Christmas holidays neared, she did nothing to prepare. It was as if Christmas was not coming that year in the Drayle household, except for in the slave quarters where the slaves were preparing to take off a few days.

Fran ordered Lizzie to come into her room and rub her feet. Lizzie rubbed the white woman's feet with liniment oil until she fell asleep. Each night Lizzie went to Fran's room, lifted the blanket, and rubbed the oil onto Fran's feet until the woman dozed off. Eventually, Fran moved the two of them to the front parlor. Lizzie would massage while Fran urged her on. That first morning, as she tried to stifle the taste of vomit in her throat, the smell of the liniment rising through her nostrils like gas, the slave women going about their duties around her, her face growing hot, eyes burning, she had thought to herself that if Fran offered up one word of criticism, one negative comment, she would surely grab a knife and hold it to the woman's throat.

Since she'd moved back into the house, Drayle spent most evenings in his library reading. He still visited Lizzie in the bedroom across the hall, sometimes only to caress her belly and talk about what he was certain would be a son.

As the early sickness subsided, Lizzie started to enjoy the changes in her body. Her tender nipples were puckered and swollen, her breasts bigger than they had ever been. Her figure was rounding out a bit, and she felt more womanly. The slave men noticed as well, and she was aware they had begun to look at her in a new way. She frequently caught them watching her.

She took sugar to the one-eyed horse one day and found Philip brushing him. If Lizzie was the closest female slave to Drayle on the plantation, then Philip was the closest male slave to him. He was the most trusted hand with Drayle's precious horses. Philip had grown up around horses and there wasn't a wild one he couldn't break and bring under his spell. He was a powerfully built man with a big head of hair that stuck out of his head like raw cotton. In return for his loyalty, Philip was trusted enough to have a permanent pass allowing him to ride off the plantation. He also had been given the materials to build his own cabin.

Lizzie stood outside the fence, patting Mr. Goodfellow with one hand. The horse poked his nose through the fence and nuzzled against her.

"You likes that horse, don't you?" Philip said.

"Yeah."

"He a good horse even if he do just got one eye. I'm sho glad Marsuh didn't sell him off."

Lizzie smiled. That had been her doing, a reward for the baby she was about to give him. It hadn't been exactly a fair trade in her opinion, but it had been a small way for Drayle to show his satisfaction with her.

Her stomach wasn't big yet, but she thought Philip might have noticed the other changes. She shook the corners of her dress off her shoulders so he could see her neck and the way it curved down into her ripening chest.

"Everybody got some good in them," she said.

They stood easily in the silence that followed. She listened for the sound, and after a few minutes she heard it. Cluck. Cluck.

He spoke again: "Hey, when you gone read to us on Sundays again? That Jessie can't read half as good as you."

Lizzie was flattered. She'd never known they missed her. They didn't know it, but sometimes Jessie made things up when he didn't know a word exactly. She didn't do that. She hadn't been there lately because Drayle had been keeping a close watch on her.

"I was awful sorry when I heard they tried to sell you off."

His words touched her, and before she knew it, she was reaching out for his hand which rested on the other side of the fence. She placed her fingers on top of his.

He jerked back as if she had burned him.

"What?"

"Why you touching me?"

"I-I-don't know."

He stepped back.

"I ain't for sale."

"What?"

"Ain't that white man good enough for you? Gone back to him."

He walked away and the horse followed him obediently. Then it threw a look back as if it, too, stood in judgment of her.

EIGHTEEN

⁓

Her pregnancy changed. From the moment his eyes caught the hilly landscape dimpling her thighs and the bumpy terrain of her buttocks, Drayle retreated. Each time he moved to take her, his penis got soft. He told her he was afraid he would hurt the baby. She became terrified by thoughts of him with other women. A whisper reached her that he had taken up with another woman down in the quarters. She felt a pain in her stomach during those months that she feared had nothing to do with the baby's strengthening kicks.

And that wasn't all. Drayle had never asked her to put her mouth down there, and she never would have thought of such a thing. But in the final weeks of her pregnancy, that was what he wanted. Each time he made her do it, stroking the curls around the nape of her neck, he told her she would grow to like it. But she never did. When her feet became too swollen to fit into her shoes, Drayle had a new pair made for her. He thought this would be enough to change her mind about the thing he wanted her to do.

She gave birth to a boy that winter and the first thing she did when they lay the baby on her chest was count out the toes and fingers. As a house slave, she wasn't allowed to nurse, so she sent him down to a woman in the quarters who'd been nursing babies for the past seven years straight. Drayle resumed his regular visits soon after the baby was born. She wasn't ready, but he didn't appear to care. The only good thing was that he no longer asked her to do that other thing.

Before she could get used to the idea of being a new mother, she was pregnant again. By the time she came into her sixteenth year, she had two children, a boy and a girl. When her daughter was born, Lizzie examined the skin around her nails and waited anxiously for it to darken. The child had smooth pale skin with watery blue eyes and a bald head. She had expected the baby to be light in color but she was whiter than Drayle. After nine months, the girl baby still had not darkened. The only change was a new sprout of yellow curls on her head. Lizzie kept the baby covered as much as she could, both to protect her from the sun and because she was ashamed of her appearance.

She named the boy Nate after his father and the girl May because that was the month she was born. But one day, when the child was hopping around the workyard, Big Mama called the girl Rabbit and it stuck.

As the years passed, Lizzie learned to use her new status as the mother of Drayle's children more and more. But she was unable to help the field slaves out of a situation that all started when the overseer Roberts fell out of a tree. Roberts had been on the plantation for over two years, but was still widely mistrusted. Over-working or beating was not what they feared most about him. He fancied himself a doctor of sorts. Whenever a slave complained they could not work or that they weren't feeling well, he would examine them. He had a wooden table in his cabin expressly for this purpose. Whatever the injury—stubbed toes, broken fingers, stiff wrists, sprained ankles, knee pain—it required a full-body examination. The possibility of an exam had the same effect as overworking the slaves since no one wanted to complain they weren't feeling well. Rather than mention whatever was bothering them, they worked through it.

Roberts usually sat in a big hickory nut tree, cracking nuts between his teeth as he watched the slaves work. One day he dozed off and fell out of the tree, breaking his leg. A doctor was called who set the leg, but Roberts did not heal. He stayed in bed and sent his wife to watch over the slaves. She was a tall woman covered in a thin coat of white hair, a fair amount of it grazing her upper lip and chin. She assumed the same position in the tree as her husband. When someone slowed, she called out to them in a great booming voice that sounded so much like her husband's a few of the slaves forgot it was a woman in a dress straddled across the largest branch.

She began to walk between the slave cabins and peer through open windows and doors in the evenings after work hours. Up until this time she had mostly kept to her cabin, but her curiosity seemed to get the better of her as she strode down the lane shamelessly staring at children playing and women preparing the evening's supper. For those first few days, she didn't say much but after a while she called out a short greeting here and there. The slaves did not raise their eyes when they spoke back.

But one of the slaves did not like the overseer's wife at all. Jeremiah wasn't known to speak much, but the longer folks were around him, the more they got to know his way of communicating. His right eyelid jumped twice when he was angry. He shook his knee when he was impatient. He'd had a nervous way about him since he was a child.

But that Sunday, after prayer meeting, Jeremiah had something to say.

"Ain't right, I tell you," he said.

"What's that?" mumbled one of the men. The women had gone back to the quarters. Four men sat around chewing leaves, whittling, resting for a few minutes before returning to the labor that never ceased.

"A woman bossing us round, that's what. Woman ain't sposed to boss a man." Jeremiah's right shoulder flinched.

"That ain't just any old lady. That's the bossman wife. We got to do right by her till he get well." Young Joe sat next to his daddy who would be too old to work in the fields within the year, leaving Drayle with the decision of what to do with him. The old man's hand shook and Young Joe placed his own on top of it.

"That don't make it right," Jeremiah said.

"At least she don't doctor on us," Young Joe added.

"You does have a good point," said the one they'd always called Baby.

"Well what do you plan on doing about it?" Young Joe said. "March your nappy-headed self on up to Marsuh's house and tell him you ain't working for no woman?"

"I aims to do just that," Jeremiah said.

"Y'all hush up," Old Joe said. "Ain't nobody marching up to Marsuh house. Bossman'll be back in no time and won't nobody have to work under no woman no more."

Baby rested a hand on his wide thigh. "It ain't right for no nigger to work under no white man and it sho ain't right for no man to work under no woman. I say we all sits down in the fields tomorrow and don't start working till Bossman Roberts come back out here."

"The man can't walk," Young Joe said. "How he gone come back out here?"

"He can pick up a stick and use it, same as everybody. Remember that time I broke my leg?" Jeremiah said. "I was made to hop right back out in that there field, cripple and all. Ain't nobody care. And I did it, too. Roberts don't want to work. He just trying to shame us by sending his woman out here."

The men weighed Jeremiah's words as he shook his knee. Somebody rang the supper bell in the slave quarters and the men stirred. Young Joe held on to his father. Jeremiah had to hold onto the tree for support as he helped pull Baby to his feet. They walked slowly to the quarters.

By the time the slaves heard about Jeremiah's visit to the big house, it was dusk. Bellies were as full as they were going to get, and the children had finished the final chores of washing plates and cups. A group of women sat around the workyard mending shirts.

The word passed with the speed of most rumors on a plantation. Jeremiah had gone to the house and their master was coming down to see about Roberts. From the cracks of their cabin doors, women watched the path leading from the Big House. One woman sat her five-year-old out in the yard to keep watch. They figured they would not know the outcome of it all until the next morning when they had to report to the fields again.

As the night grew dark and they sank into the thin soft of their pallets, they slept lightly, anticipating the crowing of the cock so they would know if they would have to work under the white-haired woman again.

In the morning, the slave women rose earlier than usual to begin breakfast. They looked to their tow sacks for the grain they used to round out their meals, but found that the sacks were empty. The women went from cabin to cabin to see if the same was true for everyone. And then the slow realization sank in that the food had been rationed.

Master Drayle had taken their food in order to punish them for complaining about the woman overseer. They were certain of it. When they reported to the fields that morning, there perched the hefty, white-haired white woman high in the tree, the heavy folds of her dress snapping off tips of branches.

"Get to work!" she yelled, fiercer than usual.

The slaves began their toil, their stomachs rumbling with emptiness. No one spoke to Jeremiah, even those who had encouraged him. He was back to his usual silent self. A sack of nuts made its way from slave to slave, and the sound of shells being crunched between teeth rumbled among them. That night, the women barely spoke to their men, blaming the lot of them for the empty sacks hanging slack by their doors.

NINETEEN

On Fran's fortieth birthday that year, the slaves cooked a celebration dinner. Fran's best childhood friend, Yancy Butterfield, arrived in a sea of green. Taffeta, earrings, necklace,
jingling bracelets. Green shoes peeking from beneath her dress.
All set against a skin so translucently white that Lizzie had to force
herself not to stare. Mr. Butterfield and Drayle retired to the library
where they defied Fran's wishes by having a before-dinner cigar.

The two women settled in the parlor and waited for Lizzie to
stoke the fire.

They began their visit by taking turns admiring each other's
jewels. Lizzie couldn't help but notice that Yancy's were more ex-
quisite. Fran seemed to note it, too.

"What a lovely dress, Yancy. You outdo me on my own birthday."

"It's all in the fabric, dear. That's why I brought you something
special." She lifted her chin toward Lizzie. "Miss Dessie. Would
you mind fetching that box out of my carriage?"

Lizzie forgave Yancy for calling her the wrong name. All because she said "miss." Because she said "would you mind."

"Yes, ma'am."

"Wash up first," Fran added.

"Yes, ma'am."

Lizzie knew that the women had grown up together and were closer than Fran was to her own sister, but the two friends seemed different to Lizzie. Whereas Fran was moody and subject to extreme changes in temperament, Yancy exhibited a mild steadiness. There was a genuine pleasantness to her that Lizzie sensed to be more than a public offering, and when Lizzie saw the woman sitting next to her husband in the parlor, she observed a tenderness between them that she had never seen between Drayle and Fran. At one point, the man had even fondled the bracelets on her arm. Lizzie felt that if she lived with the Butterfields, she would not be so guiltless in her betrayal of the mistress. In a way, Fran's spite made it easier.

Lizzie was transfixed by the Butterfield carriage. She had never seen one so fine. Leaves swirled around it, its dark fabric a stark contrast to the fall foliage. She poked her head inside and inhaled. Lilac sweet, just like Yancy Butterfield. Lizzie climbed into the carriage and closed the door behind her. She shut her eyes and pictured her and Drayle, riding along, his head on her shoulder, her hand on his knee.

She leaned back into the seat and felt a soft package dig into her back. She pulled it from beneath her, hoping it wasn't ruined. She perched it on her shoulder and went into the house where she carefully deposited it in front of their guest.

"Thank you, dear."

Yancy placed the package in Fran's lap. "Why don't you open your present now? The men don't have much interest in these things, and I can hardly wait."

"Why not?" said Fran. She tore back the paper.

"I hope you like it."

Lizzie took her time exiting the room.

"Oh my. Ohhhh my." Fran pulled out yards and yards of blue fabric, the same fabric as Yancy's green.

"This is why I wore this dress. I wanted you to see how beautiful it looked all put together."

"I love it, Yancy. I just love it." Fran disappeared with the fabric trailing behind her. "This must have cost you a fortune," she called from in front of the hall mirror.

"If you need me to, I can get my seamstress to make the dress for you," Yancy said. "You don't want slaves fooling with this fabric."

"A slave? With my fabric down in that old nasty workyard? I wouldn't dream of having a slave touch this!" Fran came back into the room, her hand on her cheek as if the very thought made her flushed. "And I don't need your seamstress. What would I need your seamstress for? I have my own."

Dessie brought in cold drinks on a wooden tray and placed them on the table beside the women. Fran watched Dessie closely as she took the blue fabric and folded it into a neat square before placing it on the settee.

"Y'all be needing something else 'fore dinner, Missus?"

"No, Dessie. That'll be all."

Lizzie and Dessie nodded at the women before they went back to the kitchen.

Lizzie's children sat at the table slurping milk, white mustaches above their lips. Nate was big for his age—only five and already taller than other boys his age. His legs bumped against the chair beneath him. Although Rabbit was just a year younger, she was smaller. She held the cup in her pale hands and smiled at her mother.

"Who gave y'all milk?"

"Master Drayle," Nate said. He had learned recently that

Drayle was his father, but was still unsure what this meant. He called Drayle by the name everyone else did—Master—and he had not connected that Drayle was his "pa" as some of the other slave children called their fathers or called men who were like fathers to them.

Lizzie patted at the milk stains above their lips with the tail of her apron. "Well stay out of the way, y'all hear? We've got to serve this dinner. If y'all want to play, go on back in the storeroom. Go on now."

Dessie stirred a big pot of onion soup, bringing up slivers of the red and white bulbs to the surface. That would be followed by fried frog legs, Fran's favorite. The rest of the meal had been planned by Drayle who insisted the only thing Fran cared about were the frog legs. So he'd ordered up his favorites: pork roast, mashed potatoes, collard greens. Dessie had made soda biscuits from scratch, the same kind she made for breakfast. Mrs. Butterfield's husband still remembered Dessie's soda biscuits from his previous visit, years before.

During dinner, Lizzie tried not to concentrate on the conversation. Serving dinner when there were guests present, whether a special occasion or no, was always a serious affair in the Drayle household. Nothing could be spilled on Fran's hand-tatted tablecloth. Plates had to be taken at exactly the right time. Lizzie and Dessie had to distinguish between when a guest was actually finished and when they were merely taking a break. On days when there was no company Fran played games with them by pretending she was done—nudging her empty plate away from her and then picking up her spoon as soon as one of them approached. Whenever they made a mistake, she shouted at them so loudly that whenever they did have guests, the memory of her criticism was strong enough to make them nervous.

The dinner went off without any major slip-ups, and Lizzie offered dessert—a blackberry pie. Everyone declined except Mr.

Butterfield who looked pleased with everything that had been served so far.

The others asked for coffee and Dessie instructed Lizzie to pour the coffee while she spooned up some dessert for Mr. Butterfield. Lizzie hated pouring coffee because the slightest mistake could cause it to spill into the saucer. She was convinced Dessie had assigned the task to her on purpose. But the head cook was older, and among slaves that meant something.

Lizzie managed to pour all of the coffee without any mistakes, but as she moved to go back through the kitchen door, the door swung back toward her. The coffee pot hit her chest and the hot brown liquid soaked the front of her dress.

"I didn't mean to do it!" Nate's voice was shrill and scared.

Dessie grabbed Nate's shoulder and pushed him into the kitchen. Lizzie rushed through the kitchen to the well outside to pour cold water over her dress.

When she returned to the dining room, she found Rabbit on Yancy's lap. Nate stood behind the woman's chair watching his sister. His thick eyebrows came together between his eyes. Lizzie tried to think of something to say. The room was dead silent. Surely everyone at the table knew these were Drayle's children, especially the boy who looked just like him.

Yancy kissed and hugged May. "She's like a little white doll!" she murmured. Rabbit fingered the woman's bracelets and stared at her earrings.

"You didn't tell me you had such lovely new slave children, Fran."

"Well, they're not that lovely."

Drayle cleared his throat. "If you're done with that dessert, we could have another drink in the library."

"Sure thing," said Mr. Butterfield, following Drayle's lead.

The two men left their cooled coffee on the table.

Yancy reached for Nate to pull him onto her lap, but he stepped back. He didn't appear to be as enthralled with her as his sister was.

"Boy, go to Mrs. Butterfield. She asked for you. Now go on," Fran said.

Nate shook his head. Lizzie looked helplessly from one to the other. She wanted to entice her children back to the kitchen with the promise of more milk, but Fran was giving a different order.

Yancy reached out to touch Nate's hair. This time, he didn't retreat.

"Such lovely children," Yancy said.

"I suppose," Fran said.

Yancy waved her hand. "Now you know I would give anything to have some little colored children in my house. Now that we live in town, Mr. Butterfield only allows us to keep that old couple we've had for so long. I tried to convince him to buy me a girl— especially after our own children grew up—but he wouldn't have it. Said he didn't want a nigger child living in our house. Do these live in the house with you?" She tilted her face down, as if smelling Nate's hair.

"No," Fran said, watching Yancy. Then she did something that surprised Lizzie. She reached out for Rabbit and brought her close. The child leaned back between Fran's legs. "It's too bad you don't have children in your house, Yancy. I'll have to speak to Mr. Butterfield and convince him to buy you a new slave."

"Lizzie, have these children eaten?" Fran said without looking up.

"Yes, ma'am."

"Well, bring them some dessert. Do you like blackberries, boy?"

Nate was unable to resist the offer. "Yes, missus."

Lizzie didn't move.

"That's a great idea!" Yancy said. "Let's take it in the parlor. Let's take the children with us and fill them with sweets."

Lizzie stood there for a moment after the women and children had left the room.

When she returned to the kitchen, Dessie hissed at her: "Your childrens don't do what they told. You told them to stay out the way. Even you won't be able to save them this time. And they gone deserve whatever they get."

"You leave me and my children alone," Lizzie said.

Lizzie stood outside the parlor door listening with the plates of pie in her hands. Yancy Butterfield was laughing.

Lizzie pushed open the door with her foot and found the two women sitting with a child perched in each lap. Nate was telling them about Brother Rabbit and Brother Partridge. He was telling them how both Rabbit and Partridge liked the same girl. Partridge pretended his head was cut off by tucking it in his feathers, and convinced Rabbit that he should do the same because it was a noble thing. So Brother Rabbit went around trying to find someone to cut off his head. When no one agreed to do it, Partridge obliged him. After Partridge cut off Rabbit's head, he untucked his own and went down to the dance where he could have the girl all to himself.

Lizzie had not known Nate knew the story well enough to tell someone else. His speech came in short, excited bursts. The women laughed hard, as if they had never heard such a story.

Lizzie backed into the kitchen.

"What's wrong now?" Dessie asked when she saw Lizzie.

That night Drayle slept beside Lizzie while Rabbit and Nate slept beside Fran in her bed.

And Lizzie didn't sleep at all.

TWENTY

After Yancy Butterfield's visit, things changed. Lizzie had not thought Fran's momentary change of heart would last. She had been fully convinced Fran was only acting that way to impress her wealthier friend. But after Yancy's visit, Fran continued to spoil the children.

Never mind that Nate's skin was unmistakably brown and that he continued to wrestle with the decision of whether or not to trust her. Never mind that Rabbit was unnaturally pale with kinky blond hair. Fran was smitten and it showed.

Since Fran's love was expressed in short gusts of affection, the children still spent part of the day with Big Mama. But they stayed in the quarters under the strict instructions they were not to work. Fran ignored the fact that all of the slave children on the plantation had chores. The general belief among a southern slaveholder was that slaves must be introduced to work early so they would know no other way of being.

The children were now sleeping in Fran's bed regularly. It

worried Lizzie at first, but Drayle assured her it was good for both Fran and the children. Lizzie suspected he liked it because Fran no longer expressed an interest in his nighttime activities. If she had been uninterested before, she was now almost impatient for him to clear the room so the two freshly scrubbed children could climb into her bed and bury themselves beneath the covers.

Lizzie had never been allowed to sleep with her children. They had always slept in the quarters with Big Mama while Lizzie stayed in the house with Drayle at night. So it was with bittersweet tenderness that she prepared them for Fran's bed each evening. She bathed them in the quarters, in the big tub that sat behind a hanging quilt in the workyard. First, she heated the cast-iron kettle on the open fire. As she waited for the water to cool, she watched as they ran around naked and wrestled in the dirt. When everything was ready, she picked each of them up and set them down into the tub together. There wasn't much time for them to soak, so she started right in wiping and scrubbing the dirt from them. She took care to wipe behind their ears and scrub the creases of their necks. Each leaned forward as she scrubbed their backs. Then they stood while she washed between their legs.

Afterwards, she delivered them to Fran's room with a playful shove through the door that masked her real feelings. She stood outside in the hallway, her hands shaking, listening to Fran read a bedtime story.

When she returned to the room she shared with Drayle, he said she should be grateful that at least the children would learn to read. Lizzie tried to focus on this thought.

"One more time. And then I promise to leave you alone," he said.

She had determined she was not going to allow him to force her to do that again. Since the children had been born, he only asked her to do it every so often, usually when she was bleeding. As much as she hated it, her children were receiving special treatment, and she knew Drayle could stop it if he wanted to. She was living in a bedroom in the big house, wearing finer clothes than any of the other slaves. Her children drank milk and ate the best cuts of meat. She knew she had to weigh her answer carefully.

When he saw her indecision, he said: "I'll write you a pass to see your sister. You'd like that, wouldn't you?"

Lizzie frowned. She hadn't seen her sister in almost a year of Sundays. She had asked Drayle for a pass, but he had put her off. Polly's master never wrote passes for his slaves. He would beat a slave for even asking for one, according to Polly. She had sneaked off to see Lizzie a couple of times, but Lizzie discouraged her from doing it, afraid of what would happen if she were caught. It hurt to have blood kin so close but be unable to see her. If allowed a pass, she could find out for herself if the terrible rumor that her sister had been sold were true or not.

Drayle pulled his penis out and rubbed the shaft of it.

She turned her face away. She felt a sour taste rise in her throat. She blew out the stench between her lips.

"Lizzie, there are some things you don't understand."

"What do you want me to understand, Drayle? I understand you want me to do that nasty thing."

"What are you talking about? It's not some nasty thing. Women do it all the time for their men. Why there's a woman in town who—"

"I ain't like them women in town," she stated.

"I'm not like those women in town. How many times do I have to tell you not to use the word *ain't*?"

"You use it sometimes."

He picked up her hand. "If you loved me like you say you do, this wouldn't be a problem. Shoot, I bet it's a dozen gals down in the quarters who would take your place no sooner than you could shake a stick."

"Yeah well, they ain't got your children neither." As soon as she said it, Lizzie regretted it. That was the last thing she wanted. If Drayle wanted children by another slave, it would be easy, especially now that he knew he could make them. This was the only power she held over him. And now it was the only power she held over Fran. She had to be careful she didn't push him out there.

Her head moved and she felt Drayle tense. He placed his hand on the back of her neck and pushed.

Fran had decided Rabbit and Nate's clothes would no longer do. When she went to pick up her dress made in the silky blue fabric given to her by Yancy, she took the children with her.

Lizzie swept near the door so she could look through the front window. She knew Fran would protect the children as if they were her own, but Lizzie worried all the same. What would happen once Fran lost interest? What if her children mistook this for real love?

She looked up and caught Dessie staring at her.

"They be all right. Just one of them thangs slave children got to go through. Different ways to learn they lessons. Your childrens got to learn theirs thisaway, that's all."

Lizzie nodded. The floor creaked beneath her. The night before had been especially cold, and one of the cows had gone into labor and given birth to babies that had frozen during the night. The mother had abandoned her calves instead of keeping them close to her and warm. The story had shaken Lizzie when she heard it.

Lizzie polished the tall grandfather clock in the hallway, and took a rag to the floorboards. She walked and wiped until she got to the room she now thought of as Fran's instead of Fran's and Drayle's. A miniature wooden statue of Jesus on the crucifix. A snuffbox. There was no sign of Drayle in the room other than his clothes in the closet. Lizzie searched the closet for a box or some other container holding memories of Drayle's family and life before marriage to Fran. She found nothing. When she had asked Drayle about his family, he had only mentioned that both of his parents were dead and he had no siblings. It was as if he was as alone in the world as she was.

Lizzie opened the closet and fingered the dresses inside. She took one out and held it up in front of her. She was bigger than Fran now that she'd had children. But the dress had enough fabric to be let out and fit her just right. She put it back in the closet.

She found a book on the closet shelf and took it down and opened it. It was a child's catechism, and Lizzie could imagine the excitement of her children as they examined the pictures and Fran pointed out the large letters printed on the page. Lizzie lay across Fran's bed with the book open before her. She read softly as if her children were there listening. She had not read in the quarters lately. It struck her that her children did not know she could read. She would have to tell them. She would sneak a book out of Drayle's library and take it down to Big Mama's house. And the first chance she got, she would read to them just as Fran did. She didn't want them to think white people were the only ones to hold the magic key to these letters.

She put the book back on the shelf and smoothed out the bedcovers. She refilled the lamp with oil and polished the posts of the bed until they shone. She went over the windowsills with her rag until not a speck of dust remained.

She brushed her hair. Her thick naps didn't require much. She pinned them in her usual style. Fran had prohibited her having a mirror in the bedroom. She'd also limited Lizzie's clothes. She was not allowed to have more than three dresses.

Lizzie heard the clop of Drayle's boots on the stairs and hurried out of the room. She was bent down wiping the floor when he walked right into her.

"How are the cows doing?"

"We put them in the barn. There's four pregnant cows. Would you believe it? I put all four of them in the barn even though only two are due any day now. I figure they could keep each other company in case one starts whelping in the middle of the night."

Lizzie nodded.

"Where's Fran?" he asked.

"She took Nate and Rabbit to town."

Drayle scratched the back of his neck. He moved past her.

"I'll have my supper upstairs." When he got to the doorway of the bedroom they shared most nights, he turned around and looked at her.

"Hurry with your chores and come to bed," he said.

As she slowly made her way to the kitchen, she heard the excited voices of her children entering the house.

TWENTY-ONE

ran got out of the house more. She dressed the children in the finery she had bought them and took them on walks through the woods. When Rabbit scuffed her new shoes, Fran laughed. When Nate fell and got grass stains on his knees, she brushed him off and rubbed at his dirty face with a spit-moistened thumb. She walked the children through the slave quarters, pointing out various work tools and explaining the names of things. The slaves did not allow Fran to catch them observing the spectacle.

Eventually, Nate and Rabbit took note of their new status among the other slave children, refusing to play with them. The children made fun of the way they spoke. Nate kicked dirt at them and dared them to kick it back. The children did not dare, for they knew his threat was real. He would tell Miss Fran. Or Bossman Roberts. Or his *pa*. Nate had finally realized that Drayle was something more than his Master. Rabbit simply refused to speak to other girls her age.

The children still craved Lizzie's attention, but they preferred the time they spent with Fran because she gave them things. When Fran tired of them, Lizzie came and got them. They willingly went with their mother, but after a while with Lizzie they would begin to ask about Miss Fran again.

Lizzie saw how her children were changing, and tried to steer them back to their reality by secretly forcing them to continue with their chores. In the afternoons she made them change into their regular clothes. Both Rabbit and Nate knew better than to allow the other children to see them back in their old clothes. When they saw the other children coming, they ran and hid. After a few weeks of this, they told Fran what Lizzie was making them do and Fran put a stop to it.

Drayle delighted in Fran's new attachment to the children, but Lizzie was determined to change his mind.

"It ain't good, Drayle."

He fastened his belt and pulled her close to him even though the door to the bedroom was wide open. He was taking more and more liberties in the house, especially now that Fran was distracted by the children. "Not this again."

He turned toward the door and stepped into a wide beam of sunlight. Lizzie caught her breath. For a moment, she imagined Nate standing there in his shoes, filling out his clothes. The boy was the spitting image of his father for sure.

"I just don't want the children to be hurt is all. They've really taken to her."

"They'll be fine, Lizzie."

She pursed her lips after he was gone.

Nate ran out of Fran's room with Rabbit in pursuit.

"Give it to me I said!" Rabbit's face was pink.

"Hey!" Lizzie yelled.

They turned to her, ready to protest. She silenced them with a hand held up in the air.

"What are y'all doing running through the house? Nate, what do you have that belongs to your sister?"

"I ain't got nothing."

"He's a liar, Mama."

"I *haven't* got nothing," Lizzie corrected. She grabbed his balled fist and pried it open. A blue ribbon lay crumpled in his palm.

Lizzie took the ribbon from him and popped him on the back of the head with her hand. "I have told you about lying. And you know better than to run through this house like wild animals."

"Lizzie!"

Fran stood on the stairs, her face surrounded by a mass of curls. "What on earth are you doing?"

Lizzie pulled the children close. "Nothing, ma'am."

Fran rushed at her and slapped Lizzie on the face hard. "Don't you ever touch my children again, do you hear me?"

Lizzie nodded into the back of her hand. The children shrank back as if they were more afraid of their mother than the woman who had just struck her.

Nate began to cry. Fran grabbed May's hand and ordered Nate to follow. They disappeared into Fran's room and closed the door behind them.

Less than two weeks before Christmas, they received a telegram that Fran's sister and nephew were coming to spend the holiday with them. The house was thrown into a frenzy with Fran at the head of it all.

"I want all of the silverware polished once more," Fran said amidst a neck of family jewels, as if she had brought out everything she owned and donned it at once. "This is Christmas, after all."

Fran lifted doilies and opened drawers, moved vases and scooted chairs, sniffed meat and tasted milk, beat pillows and pointed out cobwebs. She moved about the house like a high priestess as she had not done all year, her velvet gown smelling faintly of mold and the bowels of the attic.

While Fran moved things around, Drayle tended to the moths. A sack of flour had been infested with worms and in the months since, slender moths had been fluttering out of closets and cupboards, lingering around candles, resting on walls. They nested in wools and silks, spun their sticky substance and left a trail of holes. Drayle brushed cocoon shells from the edges of floorboards and the creases of ceilings with a broom. They fell like gun casings, and Lizzie followed behind Drayle, sweeping.

Dessie made everyone wash up before entering through the back. She put a small tub of water by the door for any field slave entering the main house to wash their bare feet.

In the slave quarters, preparations were no less intense. The slaves worked in the fields an extra hour each day in preparation for the Christmas break Drayle would allow them. The overseer Roberts and his wife would also be leaving to see their family, so they worked the slaves extra hard to finish the list of tasks Drayle had set out for them.

Drayle directed the men, led by Philip, to groom and shoe the horses. When the horses grazed in the pasture, their heads down in relaxed concentration, they looked like statues except for the occasional swish of a tail. There were two Tennessee walking horses, three American Saddlebreds, and a Peruvian Paso bought for Fran's birthday by her father when she was a girl. Mr. Goodfellow also remained.

Fran rarely entertained her family. In fact, Lizzie could not remember the last time any of Fran's family had visited. The Drayles always traveled to Mississippi to see her folks.

After the house had been cleaned better than it had been in

months. After the vegetables had been washed and stacked in piles on the scratched wooden table in the center of the kitchen. After the salted ham had been brought in from the meat house and several chickens had been slaughtered and plucked. After the riding horses were shoed and the slave quarters had been tidied. After all this, they learned that Fran's sister would not be coming after all.

Two nights before Christmas, a carriage pulled up in front of the house. As the driver approached, the two women in the kitchen peeped out of the window to see who it was. Lizzie put down the jar of preserved berries and walked to the window to stand behind Dessie. They saw a man in a hat driving a carriage. He dropped the reins and proceeded to get down. Although they had not gotten snow that year, it was blustery cold outside. The slim figure pulled his coat about him and walked to the side of the carriage to open the door. A small child emerged.

"Who is that?" Lizzie whispered.

"I'll get the tea going. You get the door," Dessie instructed.

Lizzie did as she was told. She opened the door before the man had a chance to knock.

The child stood right in front of her and peeked around Lizzie into the hall of the house. Somewhere upstairs, the sound of Nate and May's chatter drifted down to them. It was after dinner and Fran was preparing them for bed.

The boy turned an ear toward the stairs.

"Is the mistress of the house here?" asked the citified coach driver.

"Yessir," Lizzie said. She watched as Philip unloaded a small trunk out of the back of the carriage. She let the man in out of the cold and went upstairs to tell Fran they had a visitor.

Fran came down the stairs and stared at the man who was now standing in her foyer with the boy, untying the scarf around the child's neck. Dessie stood by, ready to usher him into the parlor where a tray of hot tea waited.

"What can I do for you?" Fran asked.

"Mrs. Drayle, this here is little Master Billy. He has been sent by your sister to spend the holidays with you."

The child stuck his hand out, as if he had been properly rehearsed. "It's nice to meet you, Aunt Francesca."

Fran sputtered. "What? My sister? Where is she? I received a telegram that said she wasn't coming. She's *sick*." Fran emphasized the word *sick* as if she did not believe it.

He cleared his throat. "Yes, it appears that your sister has . . . ah . . . some health difficulties. She is hoping that you will do her the favor of looking after her boy for a while."

"For how long?"

"A few weeks, ma'am."

Fran looked down at the child in confusion. He looked past her at Nate, who was now standing behind her.

"Of course, of course." She reached into the front of her dress and drew out a piece of candy. The child walked forward and took it.

"That's mine!" Nate screamed.

Lizzie instantly knew things had taken a turn for the worse for her children.

TWENTY-TWO

His clothes were genteel but worn. He wore a set of blue knickers that were white at the knees. The ruffles on his shirt were no longer crisp, crumpled from napping in the back of the carriage. His reddish hair was straight with curly ends, as if it were just beginning to lose the last of its baby curls. He took the candy from Fran, but kept his eyes on Nate who stared at him unabashedly.

Fran opened her mouth to speak, but her voice sounded choked. "You're taller than I expected. You're welcome here, of course." She looked at the driver.

"He's six, ma'am. He explained to me during the trip that he just had a birthday." He paused. "I hope you won't mind if I go on my way. I have a schedule to keep, and I'm afraid I'm already behind. I have accommodations in the next town over, and I'd like to arrive before my host retires for the night. Tomorrow morning, I'm headed north—"

"Would you like to see your room, Billy?" Fran interrupted.

The child nodded in response.

"Lizzie, prepare the room across from mine. Dessie, have Philip take that trunk upstairs." Fran walked to the door with the driver. "I do hope you'll give my sister regards for me. Are you a friend of hers?"

"No, ma'am. I'm just a driver. She hired me to bring him. She regrets that she is not able to come herself."

"Yes, that's too bad." Fran looked back at the child.

As Lizzie took the child's hand and ascended the stairs, Nate followed.

When she got to the top of the stairs, Nate stood there looking curiously at Billy. It struck Lizzie that her son was dressed better than the white boy. Nate offered the wooden train car in his hand. The boy walked forward and accepted it.

"What's your name?" Nate asked softly.

"Billy."

"Do you like trains?"

Billy nodded. "I rode on one before. Have you?"

"No," Nate said, his eyes wide for a moment. "But I've got a whole train set. You want to see it?"

Billy shrugged as if he had seen a million train sets.

"Come on." Nate took his hand and guided him to Fran's bedroom, Rabbit following at a close distance behind them.

Lizzie heard Drayle stamping his boots as he entered the front door.

"We have visitors?" he asked.

"Yessir," Dessie answered.

"I'm not properly dressed to receive anyone. Tell them I'll wash up and be there in a few moments."

"It's just the child, sir," Dessie said.

And that was all Lizzie heard. She helped to carry the train set into the bedroom where Billy would be staying. She took her two dresses out of the closet, folded them, and made a stack on the floor outside the door. She guessed she would be sent back to the storeroom, but she wasn't sure. She turned back the bedcovers. The sheets had just been changed that day. It was late for a child. He would want to go to bed soon.

"You're probably tired from your trip," she said to Billy.

"Yes, ma'am."

The child had manners, she thought. And he hadn't been around slaves much. Philip entered the room with the trunk.

"Heavy?" she asked.

"Not so much," Philip answered.

Both of them knew what this question meant. Slaves always had an interest in knowing how long a guest would be staying. Each extra body meant more work.

"Where you want me to put it?" he asked.

"Just put it over yonder." After he had set the trunk down, Lizzie opened it and unpacked the boy's clothing, counting each piece as she went. As Philip left, she saw him look briefly down at her pile of belongings outside the bedroom door.

When she had finished putting away Billy's things, she turned and saw Drayle's figure in the doorway.

"Hello, youngster," he said. Both Nate and Billy looked up. Drayle looked confused for a moment.

Lizzie left them to get a washbasin. She went to the kitchen where Dessie filled it with hot water from a kettle on the fire. When she returned, Drayle was no longer in the room. Nate and Billy were sitting on the floor playing with the train set. Rabbit perched on a chair watching them. Lizzie placed the washbasin on the bureau.

"You've got to wash up," she said.

Nate smiled at Billy. "They always make you wash up in this house before you go to bed."

Drayle returned as she was cleaning behind Billy's ears. He watched Lizzie lay out sleepwear for the child. Nate and Rabbit had been sent down to the kitchen. After Billy was tucked into the bed, the two of them stepped out into the hallway.

"Lizzie, I'm afraid that you and the children will have to move out to the quarters. For now."

"The children? Why?" She understood that she would have to move. But the children?

"Because my nephew will use this bedroom."

He had not answered her question. She understood that Drayle would move back into the bedroom with Fran. But Lizzie had hoped the children could all play together, even sleep together in the extra bedroom.

She nodded and said "Yessir."

When she got to the kitchen, the children were sitting at the table. The kitchen was clean, and everything was put away. Dessie had already retired for the night.

"Miss Fran says we've got to move out to the quarters," Lizzie announced. She wanted them to believe their beloved Fran had decided upon this loss of status, not their father. It was better, she figured, for them to know sooner rather than later that the white people they loved would disappoint them.

TWENTY-THREE

Two days after she'd moved back in with Big Mama, the old woman died in her sleep. Although Lizzie believed in religion, she wasn't big on signs. Big Mama had been, though. And Lizzie figured Big Mama would have said God sent her and the children down there to be with her so she wouldn't die alone.

Lizzie expected Drayle and Fran to do something special to honor Big Mama since she was the oldest slave on the plantation, but they simply told the slaves to bury the woman however they saw fit. On the day of the funeral, Lizzie kept looking up toward the big house to see if either of them would come down, but they didn't.

Someone quoted a scripture and Lizzie read a poem from a book in Drayle's library by someone named William Wordsworth. The children cried the hardest. Lizzie returned to Big Mama's cabin alone and lit a fire. She had never talked much to Big Mama about her relationship with Drayle, and now she wished she had.

Philip had recently been over to the plantation where Polly

lived and confirmed to Lizzie that her sister had been sold. When the fire finally died down after a couple of hours, she wrapped herself in Big Mama's shawl. She cried for a little while. Rocked herself. Wondered if she would ever see Polly again. Polly had not had children. She had been alone before Lizzie. Now she was alone again, on another plantation somewhere. Lizzie had asked Drayle about finding her, but he reported that her former owner had been uncooperative. Without Big Mama and Polly, all Lizzie had were her children.

The longer she stayed there, the more she realized that sleeping in the slave quarters was difficult for a house slave. Each morning, while the slaves tied cloths around their heads and layered whatever clothing they could find to protect themselves from the cold before hustling out to the fields, she put on a dress and walked toward the house.

Her children still refused to play with the other slave children. Fran had filled their bellies and heads with false dreams, and they had a difficult time letting go of this. Rabbit became sullen and withdrawn, and Nate kicked when he was angry.

At first, the slave women barely spoke to Lizzie. But as the months passed, they included her in their conversations. Lizzie's speech fell back into the rhythm of her youth.

One unusually warm spring night, Lizzie went to bed in just a shirt. When she rolled over, she felt a hand between her thighs. She pushed it away, thinking one of the children was using her as a pillow. Then she felt the sticky hand wedge itself again between her legs.

She opened her eyes and a fat face loomed over her. He put a hand over her mouth. It was Baby. She hadn't spoken to Baby in a long time, and she could instantly sense that he was different. Not the Baby she'd known. She felt him try to pry her legs apart. She yelled and he punched her in the face. Her jaw burned. She kicked and arched her back. Even though she couldn't see around her, she guessed there was no one in Big Mama's cabin with her. The children were gone. She could hear singing. They were all outside and they wouldn't hear her even if she did manage to move his hand from her mouth. But he covered her mouth so tightly she could barely breathe. The look in his eyes scared her. He would do this to her. He would do this to her and the next day he wouldn't even glance in her direction. For once, she was glad her children had sneaked off.

He pinned one of her legs beneath his knee. She kicked with the other leg. And she understood what he wanted from her: just one push. He wouldn't even wait to satisfy himself. He just wanted to violate the master's woman. He'd do it with a finger if he could, but she kept his hands busy holding her down.

I'll tell. If she could speak, she would threaten him. But she wasn't sure if it would mean anything. Sleeping in the slave quarters meant she was subject to its rules. She could appeal to the elders. She could try to get somebody to beat him. But she had no family. Some women had brothers who provided this protection. Others had lovers who let it be known their women were not to be messed with. Lizzie had no one.

Except Drayle.

I'll tell. The words died in her throat as his fat finger made its way inside of her. He groaned. His grip on her mouth loosened and she bit him. Then she heard a loud thud.

He fell back and Lizzie rolled from beneath him and covered herself. She heard the skillet drop to the floor and then the sound of her son crying. She lifted herself up.

"Nate, come here."

Philip kicked the pan away and knelt beside her. "You alright?"

She nodded.

"Nate came here and found him on top of you. He came and got me. Why you in here sleeping when everybody else outside having a good time?"

"Nate, come here," Lizzie said. She didn't want to talk. She just wanted her son next to her.

A field hand stood in the doorway. "He dead?" he asked.

"Naw," said Philip. "He all right. Just help me get him out of here."

Lizzie scooted back into the corner, still holding on to Nate. "Where's Rabbit?"

"Outside," he said. They dragged Baby's big bulk out of the door.

Lizzie touched her hand to her sore cheek and knew it would be swollen by morning.

Lizzie and her children moved into Philip's cabin, the only one on the plantation built with hewed logs. He kept a neat and tidy room despite being a single man. Lizzie found Drayle in the kitchen one day and told him she was now living with Philip.

"Philip? That's fine, I suppose. He'll take good care of you and the children."

Drayle was right. Philip treated her and the children respectfully. He always left when she needed to undress.

Each morning, he left to give little Billy riding lessons. This kept Philip busy, and Lizzie and the children were often asleep by the time he returned. Lizzie was grateful for Philip's protection, so she kept the cabin as a wife would. She tended his laundry, brought back leftovers from the big house. He didn't say much, just clucked his appreciation and went back on his way. He grew closer to Nate, sharing more animal stories with the boy once he learned he liked them.

Lizzie wished Billy would leave. She did not feel any ill will toward him, but he was the sole reason she and her children were back in the slave quarters.

Fran never once inquired about Nate and May. It was as if they had never existed. Sometimes Lizzie's children came to the kitchen door to fetch something or run an errand. If they caught sight of Fran, she turned the other way. The children now looked as ragged as the other slave children. Despite their protests, Lizzie had finally taken away their fine clothes for good. There was no use for them in the quarters. The next time a slave with a pass visited the plantation, Lizzie gave them the clothes to sell in town.

Eventually the hurt looks on Nate and May's faces lessened as they realized Fran would not be their special mistress anymore. Lizzie dampened the hurt by bringing them treats from the house. She also took to hitting her children more, especially Nate. She didn't want a white man to be the first to beat her son. When he received his first beating, he would take it with the knowledge that a beating couldn't hurt him. He would have to learn how to be a slave now.

One day while Lizzie was shelling peas in the kitchen, she heard Fran scream from somewhere inside the house. She had never heard Fran scream like that, so she wiped her hands and hurried out to the front. Fran was kneeling over a small body and when she lifted her hands, Lizzie saw they were covered in blood.

Lizzie rushed forward, then stopped. It wasn't Nate. It was Billy. His head was bleeding and his eyes were closed.

"Lord!" Lizzie said.

Philip was talking fast. "He was riding. He was all right. And Mr. Goodfellow just bucked."

"Why did you put him on that one-eyed bastard? He's too big for a child!"

Drayle slammed the front door behind him. "What happened?"

"Your slave. He did this." Fran pointed at Philip. "He did this to my boy."

"No, no, no," moaned Philip. "I swear, Marsuh Drayle. I was right there. That one-eyed horse just bucked."

Dessie came out of the kitchen. "I sent for the doctor."

"Help me get him on the table," Drayle said to Philip.

"Don't touch him!" Fran screamed.

"We've got to get him off the floor, Fran."

Lizzie took Fran by the arms and pulled her up.

Dessie cleared the table, and the men lifted the child onto it.

Dessie brought out a wet cloth and wiped at the blood on the boy's head. Lizzie sat Fran down and rubbed her arms.

"He'll be fine," Lizzie said.

Drayle stood in the corner, watching Dessie clean the child up. He was trembling and it took everything Lizzie had not to walk over to him.

Because first, she had to tend to Fran.

TWENTY-FOUR

~

Sunday morning. Two male slaves jumped. The preacher hummed a tune and the elder women moaned. A young woman shook her hands in the air. Drums had been outlawed in the entire county so two young male slaves tapped out a blunt rat-a-tat on a tree stump. Others clapped a rhythm.

Then the singing began. A woman with a strong, clear voice stepped forward and sang. When she stopped and sat down, a man stepped forward and picked up where she left off, lyrics choppy and improvised. When he paused, another one took it up. The preacher shook his leg in obvious delight.

Lizzie sat back, slightly outside of the circle, each child perched on a leg. They stared curiously. Although several of the slave women danced with babies tied to their backs, Lizzie's children had never been to a Sunday meeting. During the last decade of Big Mama's life, she claimed she was too old to make it down the hill, and had made her own Sunday morning right there in her cabin where she quoted Bible verses from memory, holding the Bible right up to her nose as if she were actually reading it. Once Lizzie learned to read, she read the Bible to Big Mama on Sunday mornings while the children restlessly fidgeted before they were allowed to go outside and roam the empty quarters.

Sunday morning meeting was held a slight ways off from the plantation in a hollow. Most of the slaves eagerly made their way down the hill to the grassy clearing where their own homegrown preacher took up his most respectable aspect and preached to them. He couldn't read, but his memory was such that he could recite all of the books of the Bible in order, backwards and forwards. He had been raised by a Bible-loving woman who had a smattering of reading knowledge but had been too intimidated by her master to pass along that precious knowledge to her son. Instead, she taught him to memorize the passages. Pretty soon, the slaves learned the litany he recited at the beginning of each meeting: *MatthewMarkLukeJohnActsRomans. . . .* Naming the books of the Bible was a prayer in itself.

Lizzie knew her children were frightened by the dancing and shouting, but she also wanted them to know something about religion, especially now that Big Mama was dead. She put her arms around them. She closed her eyes and let the music seep into her.

She began to pray. She could not remember the last time she'd prayed so hard. She prayed for Billy who was back with his mother and recovering from the gash in his scalp. She even prayed for Fran who was heartbroken now that her nephew was gone. She prayed the Lord would straighten out Dessie's back. She prayed for Big Mama who was sleeping with the angels. She prayed that she would see her sister Polly again. But most of all, she prayed Drayle would free her children.

And then one of the women took her children from her and another lifted her to her feet. They pulled her into the dance, and Lizzie tried to imitate their movements. They swished their skirts around and Lizzie did the same. They shook and trembled and some even spoke in tongues. Lizzie did the same, the language coming from somewhere inside of her she had not found before. They surrounded her. The elders moaned while the men and women welcomed her into their circle.

"Hallelujah!" the women shouted.

Despite the clumsiness of her steps, they forgave her mistakes. She danced and the women embraced her.

The drumbeats slowed and the women knelt to the ground. They clasped their hands together in supplication, and the preacher spoke above them all. He spoke of trials and tribulations, rivers and mountains, and paradises. Oh, if they could only make it to the other side. They just had to hold on.

As she walked back from the meeting, her children skipping happily behind her, she felt lifted. A light filled her chest.

The three of them entered Philip's cabin, a noisy bunch. Lizzie swung the door open wide.

Standing in the center of the one-room cabin was Drayle. He held his arms out.

He had come for her, and she willingly went to him.

PART III

1853

TWENTY-FIVE

Once again, Drayle and his two slaves took the steamship up the Mississippi to the mouth of the Ohio River. All slaves traveling on the *Madison* slept on deck, chained to iron posts, surrounded by cargo that included bales of cotton, bundles of sugar, hemp, and tobacco. Although they had always worked in the sun, the slaves' skin turned even darker on the river and they eagerly awaited the cool of sunset when the shadows would stretch long again. Most slaves were headed downriver, so by the time Lizzie and Philip reached Cairo, Illinois, and veered northeast on the Ohio, most of the other people sleeping on deck were roustabouts and deckhands. By her third summer of travel, Lizzie had become accustomed to the strange accents, mostly German and Irish, of the poor whites. Yet she was still confused by the sight of these whites working alongside the free blacks on the ship.

The first time she saw a steamboat she could not believe her eyes. She stared at the wide hurricane deck, small pilothouse, two chimneys shooting black smoke. How on earth did the ship move against the powerful downstream river current, which any slave knew could sweep you to your death in seconds? She feared the floating house would sink. Or explode. On the first day, there was a storm and the boat swayed dangerously. She became so sick she thought she might be pregnant. But she learned quickly that this feeling in her stomach was not uncommon on the water. One of the chambermaids gave her a brew to drink and it helped. Lizzie wanted to ask the woman about life aboard the ship, but the woman's hardened face did not invite idle chatter.

The ship made stops along the way. Even before it reached the riverbank, the passengers could hear a cacophony of noises—bells ringing, people shouting, horses clattering. Lizzie watched as men loaded even more cargo onto the decks, sometimes piling it so high the passengers could not see out of their stateroom windows. It took several men to roll a single bale of cotton up the gangway. Then they tied a rope around it and pulled it up using a capstan until they had secured its place among the stacks.

Lizzie tried hard to forget the voyage that first summer. Instead, she concentrated on Drayle's desire to protect her. She tried not to remember the man's body on top of hers, pinning her down on the rough sack of cotton seed she'd made her bed. When the memory threatened to surface, she focused on the image of the black sky she'd watched as the man moved on top of her. She'd flexed her arms so tightly that the chains had gouged her wrists and left her bleeding, but she tried not to remember that as well. In her rearrangement of this memory, the ordeal had not lasted long.

Philip had been nearby, seen the entire incident, helpless in the chains that prevented him from moving close enough to help. Her shouts had been lost in the sound of the river current and steam engine. In the end, she'd had no choice but to acquiesce to the violence and pray it would end quickly.

Philip told Drayle what happened the next day, and he immediately moved Lizzie to his stateroom. The room was small, about six feet square, with a bed, small table, and chair. Despite its size, it was as fine a room as Lizzie had ever seen, but she chose to sleep on a narrow slip of floor. When he saw that he could not convince her to share the bed with him, he made a sleeping pallet for her out of his own clothes and Lizzie lay there at night. In the daytime, she was taken back to the upper deck and chained near Philip where he kept a close eye on her. The head deckman ordered his hands to leave this particular favored slave alone. Then, at night, Lizzie retreated again to the protection of Drayle's room where he let her sleep undisturbed.

This third summer, in the year 1853, Lizzie stepped down the gangway behind Philip, her ankles chained to his. Drayle had already disappeared in the coach of a carriage headed up the hill to the train depot. Lizzie and Philip were assigned to a man, a handler of sorts, who saw to it that they made it without incident from the levee to the depot. Two trains left daily headed north on morning and afternoon runs. The three arrived at the station around noon and had to wait for the train's next departure. The sun was hot and there was not a roof under which the two slaves could stand. The handler placed iron clasps around their necks that were so tight, they left marks. They were seated backs to one another in the middle of the platform, joined together tightly enough that they could only move to scratch an itch, one body against the other. Sweat ran down them and soaked the wooden platform around them.

When the train arrived, the handler took his time loading them, waiting until all the whites boarded first. Once the slaves were settled into the hindmost train car, the man released the iron clamps from their necks and chained them by the ankles to iron bars bolted to the floor.

Lizzie preferred the train to the ship by far even if the train did reek with the odor of livestock. The loud din of it, the clucking of the chickens in the cages above her, the roar of the engine, the steady lurch as they tumbled along the iron T-rails did not bother her as much as the ship.

She slept most of the way to Xenia. Sometimes, she stayed awake long enough to hear Philip tell stories of rabbits and foxes and men with conjuring powers. Each summer, Philip had murmured these stories to her during the voyage. She would listen while she looked out the window at the Little Miami River, a tributary of the Ohio that surged along beside the rail. Other times, she retreated into her head, thinking of the women she was soon to see again. During those moments when she was jolted awake, she held on to his hand and listened for his clucking sound beneath the roar of the engine.

The rail stretched sixty-eight miles from Cincinnati to Springfield, but they would disembark at Xenia, hours before the train reached the end of its line. She wondered what Drayle was doing in the forward car. She'd caught a glimpse of its interior—green fabric stretched taut and tufted over spaciously placed seats. She closed her eyes and tried to raise the voices of her children in her head over the train's loud chuffing.

At Loveland, the train slowed to a stop and an elderly colored man boarded. He tipped his hat when he saw Lizzie and struck up a conversation with Philip. His hair was sketched with gray, and in the places where the hair had thinned, the skin shone through. He was a narrow-skulled man and reminded Lizzie vaguely of a rat. When he looked her way, Lizzie recognized the glow of his eyes as the beginnings of blindness.

"Where y'all headed?"

Philip finished sizing the man up before he spoke. "Tawawa House, suh."

"Tawawa who? I is headed to Columbus myself. I been down to Kentucky looking for my family, but the old house is run over

with weeds. She ain't there no more. Ain't nobody there no more."
He looked down at his hands.

"You got folks in Columbus?" Philip asked after a few moments.

The man shook his head. "I reckon I gots to start over." He smiled. His teeth were crooked and brown. "But I is a young man yet. I reckon I can find me a new family. A job."

His voice sounded unconvinced. He took a paper out of his coat pocket and waved it at them. "These here is my papers. Reeeeeal United States government papers. The man say can't nobody take 'em away from me."

Lizzie leaned forward to catch a glimpse of the writing on the paper. She could barely make out the curves of someone's handwriting.

The train slowed and Lizzie braced against the seat in front of her. A chicken squawked overhead and stirred the others. Soon the car was filled with the racket of chicken clatter. As the birds struggled against one another, the car filled with a dust laced by the occasional feather.

The door to the train rattled open and a white man in a gray uniform pointed at the senior.

"You there! Off my train."

He reached for his cane. "Why, sir? I paid my fare. I is going to Columbus."

"I don't care what you did. I don't want you on my train." He pointed at Lizzie and Philip. "These two are traveling with someone. You aren't."

The elderly man pulled himself up and looked back at the two. Lizzie moved a foot and her chain rattled against the floor. The man looked down with a start, as if he had not realized they were slaves. Then he turned from them without another word and used the handrail to step down from the train car.

Lizzie turned her thoughts again to Drayle and the white cottage. She thought of the parlor and the stove that burned coal. She thought of her friends—the warmth of Reenie's laughter, the squeak of Sweet's voice, the determination of Mawu's shoulders—and took comfort in the world that awaited her.

TWENTY-SIX

~

Lizzie wasn't sure if Mawu forgave her for what she'd done the summer before. Everything seemed to be fine, but she knew that memory was a funny thing. It reared its head at the least expected of times. She felt as if she were holding her breath, waiting for the punishment Mawu would enact to avenge herself. They had never even said goodbye, and here they found themselves back in each other's company at the resort again.

For Mawu's part, she acted as if nothing had ever happened between the two women. Her tongue was its usual sharp self, but it wasn't particularly aimed at Lizzie. Not so far.

When she saw Lizzie for the first time, Mawu offered her an even-toned "how you been" and Lizzie replied with a low-voiced "mighty fine." The other times the two women had seen each other had been in the presence of Sweet and Reenie, so things had seemed like they were back to normal. This day was no different.

The four women were visiting the Bath of Gold, named by the Shawnee because of the shining metallic rocks that lay beneath its surface. They had seen it from the top of the ravine a few times but had never descended into it to check it out. Usually, the white guests chose this spring over the four smaller ones, both for the refreshing cool of its clear, soft water and its two spring houses divided by sex. Swimming in the pool had been Mawu's idea, and Reenie had checked on how long the families would be gone. They weren't expected until well after dark, so the slaves had an unusual stretch of free time.

Sweet's belly rolled in deep waves, the skin still stretched from her last pregnancy, and the fat on her legs jiggled as she walked. She walked into the water, squealing as she went.

"Ohhhh!" she yelled out.

Mawu and Lizzie were already in the water. Mawu's head bobbed once and then dipped beneath the surface. Lizzie could still see her. The water was so clear she could see all the way to the bottom.

"Reenie, come on and dip your feet in!" Lizzie shouted.

Reenie pulled her knees to her chest and scooted farther back from the water's edge. "Don't you worry none about me." Even several feet back from the edge of the water, she looked nervous.

The evening sky was a warm color. It made the stones glow more red than gold. Mawu swam over to a rock and climbed up. She stretched out like a nymph and leaned back on her hands. Water rolled down her thighs.

"Ooh, girl don't you have no shame? What if somebody see you?" Sweet said.

"Let 'em see." Mawu shook her hair out.

Lizzie swam over, inspired by Mawu's brazenness. She climbed up on the rock and blew water from her nose. She looked down at her own body and then studied Mawu's. She couldn't help but notice Mawu's taut skin showed none of the sag of her own. Mawu looked unreal in the deepening shadows, like a ghost that would disappear at any moment.

"It sure is nice out here," Lizzie said. "This water makes me feel real good."

"Why you think the white folks come here?" Mawu swirled a finger in the rivulets of water on her stomach.

Sweet swam over and watched the two women quietly for a moment. "You think this summer gone be any different?"

"What you mean?" Mawu said.

"You know. You think the menfolks will be more decent? I just want to have some peace and quiet," Sweet said.

Lizzie understood what Sweet was trying to say. As much as she could, Sweet wanted to enjoy the summer the same as the white visitors. She wanted to have her own kind of vacation, free from the pressures of the plantation.

"Peace and quiet. What that is?" Mawu said.

Lizzie wondered if the memory of Tip's humiliation had risen in Mawu's mind. She tried to change the subject. "Don't y'all think Reenie looks different this summer?" Lizzie couldn't figure out what it was that looked different about the eldest of the group.

Sweet held on to the side of the rock. "Seem more sad, don't she?"

Mawu whispered: "A lifetime can pass between these summers. No telling what done happened since us been gone."

"You sure the mens ain't gone be back for a while?" Sweet glanced back in the direction of the resort.

"Reenie told the woman at the hotel to ring a bell if she sees them coming," Lizzie said. "How are your children doing?" she asked Sweet.

"They doing just fine," Sweet said, her face lighting up. "I been teaching my youngest how to read. I swear that boy a natural born storyteller. I think he gone be a preacher."

Lizzie thought of her Nate, too angry at the world to ever preach. It seemed like the older he got, the more sullen he became. He had his bright moments, but for the most part he wore a frown these days. Drayle said children had natural born tempers that couldn't be messed with. Lizzie wasn't sure that was true.

"How is that boy of yours?" Lizzie asked Mawu, still trying to gauge the woman's feelings toward her.

Mawu gave her an empty look and said, "What boy."

"Reenie?" Sweet said. They looked over at the other side again. Reenie had lifted her skirt and was standing in the shallow part of the water.

"I thought she wouldn't set foot near the water," Lizzie said. Reenie had told them that she was so afraid of water she wouldn't even allow the preacher to baptize her in a knee-deep pond.

"Guess she done changed her mind," Mawu said.

Lizzie waved at Reenie. The woman closed her eyes and turned up to the sun. Lizzie caught a glimpse of Reenie's younger self. It reminded her of the first time she had met her. They had been almost certain they might be kin. They'd later learned they weren't related by blood at all. But they were still close and each seemed to know exactly what the other was thinking. Sometimes. Right then, Lizzie thought she knew what Reenie was feeling. The water felt like relief. Being in it made it easy to forget the words, licks, disappointments that had sliced at every little part of them over the years.

Reenie stepped deeper into the water. The pool rose to her thighs, hips, stomach. The three women watched, perhaps believing Reenie would paddle over to the other side and join them. So when Reenie took one more step and disappeared beneath the surface, none of them reacted right off.

The drops of water on Lizzie's skin turned cold. "Reenie!" She sprang into the water, followed closely by Mawu. The mineral pool dropped off swiftly from the wide shallow ridge to the deeper center, and when Lizzie saw Reenie bob up out of the water, coughing, then down again, her arms flailing, she knew the woman had already taken in a mouthful of water. It seemed Lizzie could not reach her fast enough. She wiggled her body, moving through the water like a fish.

She could see Reenie's dark mass in the clear water ahead of her. When she reached her, Lizzie locked an arm around Reenie's neck and tried to pull. The older woman punched the water with her fists. Lizzie could see her opening her eyes and mouth. Bubbles raced to the surface. She caught Lizzie in the face with an elbow and Lizzie sank, momentarily stunned. Lizzie had a piece of dress in her hand, but she wasn't sure which part.

Mawu clutched Reenie from the other side, and pulled at one of Reenie's arms. Mawu hadn't sucked in enough air, and was clearly struggling to get to the surface herself. Reenie kicked Mawu in the stomach, and Mawu choked. The three of them burst through the surface of the water, sputtering and Lizzie finally felt the ground beneath her toes.

"What was you doing?" Mawu demanded when she had caught her breath and was standing on the shallow ridge, the rocks beneath her bare feet. Sweet was sitting on the grassy bank, her stroke not good enough for her to help the other women. She was crying softly, hugging her knees.

"Leave me be, leave me be," Reenie said.

"What do you mean, *leave you be*," Lizzie said as she and Mawu pulled Reenie up onto the bank.

The three women sprawled out on the grass. Lizzie tried not to think about what all of them were trying not to think about. Reenie coughed up water, loud hoarse coughs from deep within her chest. Lizzie looked down at Reenie's hand and saw it before the others. The tip of Reenie's finger was missing. It looked as if it had been sliced cleanly off. The skin had grown over the wound and it looked blunt and hard.

"Get up." Mawu motioned to Reenie.

When Reenie didn't respond, Mawu said it again with more force. "I said get up."

Reenie sat up, her bottom lip quaking. She muttered something the rest of them did not understand. Lizzie helped Reenie to her feet and pulled the wet dress over her head. She wrung it out over the grass. Reenie's naked body stood wrinkled and thin in the afternoon light.

"Shut up with all that mumbling," Mawu said, still talking in her mean voice. Again, Reenie listened. The talking stopped.

They waited for Lizzie to get as much water out of the dress as she could. Lizzie put her own dry dress on Reenie and put the wet one on herself. The coarse cloth would dry quickly in the sun.

After they had all dressed, they walked toward the cottages, quietly, as if to fend off the admission that Reenie had almost crossed a line they dare not mention. Mawu had been the only one of them with enough courage to stand up and say Reenie was not going to take them to that dark place.

Sweet walked beside Reenie and held on to the woman's elbow. Behind them, Mawu and Lizzie watched Reenie's back, poised to catch her should she fall. The cold of the wet dress numbed Lizzie's skin. Mawu moved toward her and put an arm around her waist. Lizzie leaned into her, hoping it meant she was forgiven but suspecting the gesture had nothing to do with her.

They walked back to the resort, four shadowed figures holding in yet another secret on only their third day back in Ohio that summer.

TWENTY-SEVEN

For the next three days, Drayle traveled with the men to hunt and fish. Lizzie kept herself busy by going to the hotel each morning. The colored servants readily doled out chores, and Lizzie was glad for the work. She tried dutifully to get everything done, all the while observing the white women as they preened over their hair, chatted about the latest fashion, fussed over their children. They were mostly Cincinnati women, up for a short vacation with their husbands, wives of elected officials, lawyers, businessmen. The hotel offered suites of rooms for families choosing not to rent cottages.

While working in the main hotel, Lizzie learned that while the men went off together, the women stayed behind and relinquished secrets to one another.

One woman whispered of a lover half her age who liked to kiss the soles of her feet.

Another spoke of her ill mother and how she would be relieved when the elder woman finally "met her Maker."

A petite woman who looked very young to be married, even to Lizzie, spoke of how she sometimes spanked her servant on the bottom, giggling as she described how she forced the woman to pull down her underpants and bend over.

Between snatches of gossip, Lizzie admired their dresses—floating affairs that were fuller than any dresses she had ever seen. She was so curious about these that she sneaked into one of the rooms so she could rummage through the armoire. She found a hoop with wires of metal. Did they put this over their petticoats? Lizzie knew she would never recover from the thrill of these skirts. Even Miss Fran didn't own one. Before the white women headed into town, they put on the finishing touches: bonnet, gloves, a small cape, and sometimes a parasol. And the shoes! Delicate little things held tight by ribbons.

When they wanted to bathe in the outdoor spring, the women changed into dark, woolen dresses with weighted hems. They met in the hotel lobby, tugging at their puffy hair bonnets as they chatted excitedly.

But Lizzie was especially impressed by the marvelous expense of the children's outfits. She had never seen children so adorned. From the cover of her broomstick or dusting rag, she observed the young ones—the smart hats, expertly gathered knickers, ruffles, lace, ribbons, and bows. She had never known a child to wear silk before. It was too expensive. But some of the older girls wore dresses in the style of their mothers—in cotton and silk.

On the day before Drayle was to return, Lizzie took Mawu with her to the house. They chose to clean the front parlor where a group of white women sat around a table with bowls in front of them. A woman dressed in white spoke as she circled the table. The women stirred their concoctions. Lizzie and Mawu tried to get close enough to peer inside the bowls. The substance was yellowish brown and smelled like lemon. After much stirring, they spread the thick substance onto their faces. Then the leader of the group told them to wait for a few moments while it hardened. One woman claimed that her face burned. But the others said they felt they could feel their complexions clearing up.

"Quick!" the leader called to Lizzie, clapping her hands. "Refill these buckets with fresh water," she said.

"Yes, ma'am," Lizzie answered under her breath.

"She's a *slave*," Lizzie heard someone say behind her as she and Mawu left the room, a bucket in each hand.

They returned with the water and watched as the women splashed their faces over the bowls.

Later, Lizzie and Mawu tried to reproduce something of the same. They sat on the steps of Lizzie's cottage and mixed aloe with lemon juice and egg. Mawu was certain that she had heard mention of tree sap. Lizzie disagreed, arguing that the tree sap would be too hard to rinse off.

Reenie and Sweet arrived just as the two arguing women had agreed to let Lizzie win.

"What in Sam Hill are y'all doing?" Reenie asked. Sweet put down a rag stuffed with dirty clothes.

Lizze paused. "We're . . ." she thought of a word she'd read once, ". . . beautifying."

"Well, I'll be. Do it to me, too," Sweet said. She sat beside them on the steps, and Lizzie spread it on her face. Surprisingly, Reenie sat too and turned her face up to be lathered with the thick mixture. When Lizzie was finished with everyone else's faces, Mawu did the same for her.

They sat patiently waiting for it to dry.

"Y'all seen them white women doing this?" Reenie asked.

"Mmm hmmm," Mawu said. "Some citified woman was showing them how."

Lizzie tracked a ground beetle as it made its way toward her foot. The sun in the sky was almost reaching dusk, and even though they had passed the hottest part of the day, she still felt the moisture dampening the back of her dress. The four women were quiet for a few moments, not wanting to mess up their faces.

Lizzie finally spoke, "Y'all think this gone make our faces white?"

"Maybe," Sweet murmured.

The women left their things and walked down to the pond. They crouched close to one another beside the bank and splashed water onto their faces. Afterward, they studied their reflections in the pool. Lizzie picked at the mole on her nose. She wished she could pull it off.

Reenie dried her face on her dress. "I reckon this ain't gone change the years on this old face."

"Can y'all imagine," Mawu began, "what the slaves back home would say? They would think us done gone plum crazy!"

"Is I white yet?" Lizzie asked.

Reenie put a finger on Lizzie's chin, lifting her face to the light. "No'm. You is still the color of maple."

They made their way back up the bank to the steps of Lizzie's cottage. Even after Sweet had tied her laundry to her back and Reenie had tucked the reading primer back into her skirt and Mawu had pinned her hair, the women did not leave.

"Y'all wait here," Lizzie said. She disappeared into her cottage and returned with a small bundle. She untied the knot. Inside were four small candies wrapped in red paper and two pamphlets.

"Miss Lizzie, you didn't!" Sweet exclaimed.

Lizzie folded the top of the cloth back over her prizes. "If you don't want it, just say the word. I'll eat this candy myself."

Mawu reached out to grab the bundle, and Lizzie jerked it back. "I'll beat you first!"

"Hush, now!" Lizzie shouted above their laughter. She pressed a candy into each woman's palm. They carefully unwrapped their treasures and placed them into their mouths.

Lizzie closed her eyes. She sucked it, scared that if she chewed, it would not last as long. When Lizzie had swallowed the last bit of it, she relished the lingering taste of caramel on her tongue. She put the wrapper to her nose and smelled it. It made a soft crinkling sound.

Only Reenie ate hers quickly. "You got to enjoy thangs before they is taken away," she murmured when she was done.

Lizzie opened the cloth again. The two pamphlets remained.

"What them is?" Sweet whispered.

Mawu snatched one up.

"Abolition," Lizzie whispered.

Sweet took a step back. "Marse will kill me for sho if he catch me with that."

"I can't read yet nohow," Reenie said. "You keep it."

Lizzie sighed. "Y'all meet me here tomorrow night. I'll read it to you."

"I can read it my own self," Mawu snapped even though they all knew she was not literate.

"We can read it together," Lizzie said, fingering the wrinkled pages of the stolen pamphlet.

Lizzie's hands were black with coal dust. Even though the coal chips were in bags, its edges were covered with soot. She took two bags from Philip and put them behind the stove in her cabin. She did not use coal often during the summer. The cottage was hot enough as it was. She tried to do most of her cooking outside, only using the stove every now and again to reheat. So she knew instantly that his gift of coal was only a pretense.

He offered to carry the bags for her, but she refused. When she turned around, he was standing in the middle of the parlor, his bulk dwarfing the room. He looked different somehow, as if he had combed his hair and greased his face. Lizzie hesitated before offering him a seat.

Not surprisingly, he refused. He was not supposed to spend any time inside the cottages except to enter and exit on the occasional chore. Both of them knew how dangerous it was for him to accept a seat inside.

"You look like you've got something to say," Lizzie said.

He wiped his hands on his pants, streaking black marks down each leg. That gave Lizzie something to do. She brought over a washbasin and dipped a rag into it before passing the rag to him. He used it to wipe his pants, unintentionally spreading the smudges. Then he mopped his hands for longer than it took to clean them. The cloth grew dark. Before he gave the dirty rag back to her, he folded it neatly. He dried his hands on his shirt while he waited for her to clean her own hands in the water.

"It's that woman, huh?" she said when she was done.

Philip looked surprised. "How you know?"

"Cause you're making a mess. It's got to be that woman." They had only been in Ohio a little over a week.

"She's probably forgot all about you by now, Philip."

He shook his head and shifted to the other foot. "Naw she ain't. I seen her last night."

"Last night?" Lizzie had not seen the girl around the hotel this summer. And she did not think the barber had visited since their arrival. But Philip did look as if he had been grooming himself. She did not doubt his words.

He nodded.

"Where?"

He hesitated and Lizzie knew why. The memory of her betrayal of Mawu was still fresh. He was wondering if she would do the same to him.

"Philip, you're like my brother. Ain't no woman on earth closer to you than me."

"Not no more."

She felt her throat burn.

He started toward the door. She followed him and grabbed his forearm as he descended the back steps.

"Don't you do that. Don't you make me feel like I'm a stranger," she said.

When he turned back to look at her, his eyes were red. She wanted to tell him that she had learned her lesson. She would not tell again. Even if it meant trouble for somebody she cared about.

She looked around to see if anyone saw them. They sat down on the step beside one another.

"Her name Virginia. She born free, but her daddy used to be a slave. He crossed the river with her mama when she was still in her stomach. He got his own barbering shop in Dayton."

Lizzie gave Philip her most thoughtful expression. She tried not to let him see that she felt his love was even more impossible than hers. "He doesn't mind his daughter loving a slave?"

She felt Philip tense beside her and she knew she had touched a sore spot. Surely he had thought about that. Surely he'd considered that the woman's father might feel Philip was beneath his daughter.

"That woman love me!"

Lizzie nodded, determined to remain quiet this time.

"He want to free me. But if something don't happen soon, I reckon he'll tell his daughter to move on. He got three daughters, and the other two is already married. I don't know nothing about no barbering business, but she say if I get freed, her daddy gone help me learn a trade. Only thing I know is horses. I reckon I got to learn about city living."

He looked off toward the main hotel. Not far from them, a tall, slender colored servant fed a group of oversized ducks that had been preening their feathers on the edges of the pond. They squawked in anticipation of the bread and flapped their wings, sending bristly feathers into the air.

"If she don't love me, I don't know what I'm gone do." He cupped his forehead in his palm.

Lizzie really wanted to know how and when he was sneaking off. At night? Through the woods? But she knew better than to ask. Philip was only asking for her ear, nothing more.

He turned and took Lizzie's hands in his. "I got to ask something of you."

So he wanted more than an ear. "What?"

"You close to Marsuh. I reckon you can talk to him about selling me. If anybody can change his mind, you can."

Lizzie shook her head. "He already said no when the barber asked him outright. And Philip, if I can't get him to free my children, what makes you think I can get him to free you?"

Philip dropped her hands and slapped his thigh. "Hell, Lizzie, those ain't just your childrens. Those his childrens, too. He won't free them cause he don't want to lose them. They his blood. But I ain't. He can always buy another slave with the money he get for me."

Lizzie felt dizzy. Philip had spoken of Drayle freeing her children as if he had given it some thought. She had never heard Philip talk that way. He had an opinion. *Drayle would never free the children.*

"Lizzie. Lizzie."

"You're like blood to him, too, Philip. When he bought you, you were just a boy. He doesn't say he thinks of you as a son, but when he talks about you it sounds like he's talking about Nate."

"You and me different, Lizzie."

"He won't sell you neither," she said. He stood, and she saw the wound she had carved into his shoulders. "He'll beat you before he sells you," she added, unable to stop herself.

Philip didn't turn around to see the slash of malice on her face. He just walked away without saying another word.

TWENTY-EIGHT

They were on their way to see the white woman. Lizzie couldn't remember whose idea it had been in the first place, but Mawu was leading. And she was rushing. Lizzie wanted to walk slowly and enjoy the cool shade of the trees. Their steps competed with one another. Lizzie also wanted to forget her conversation with Philip earlier that day. But she couldn't. "Hey girl, slow down!"

Mawu stopped and looked back at her.

"I've got something to ask you."

"All right." Mawu slowed until they were walking side-by-side.

"Philip wants me to ask Drayle about freeing him."

Mawu tilted her chin and turned to look at her. "That woman?"

Lizzie nodded.

"So what you asking?"

"Should I?"

"Why not?" Mawu stopped walking.

Lizzie grabbed the long, arching stem of a butterfly bush. She pulled it to her nose and inhaled the flower. "Because it might be him or my children that get freed and not both."

Mawu waved a hand. "Oh, Lizzie. Is that why you feeling that way? Pssh."

"What is that supposed to mean?"

Mawu didn't say anything.

Lizzie frowned. It was as if Mawu agreed with Philip that Drayle would never free the children.

Mawu stopped and placed the side of her hand against her forehead. "That way, right?" She pointed. They had not seen the woman yet that summer, and they were expecting her to still live on the same plot of land.

"I hope she ain't dead."

"Why do you care?" Lizzie asked.

Mawu shrugged. "I don't suppose I care much about no white woman."

"This one is different, huh?"

"Maybe."

Lizzie stopped and scooped a grasshopper off a nearby leaf. She closed her hand around it and it scrambled in her palm, trapped.

"I'm glad you ain't still mad at me. I never meant for you to get hurt."

Mawu stopped and turned to look at her. "Your man. He God to you?"

"Yeah, he's good to me," Lizzie replied.

"No. I say is he God to you?"

"What do you mean?"

Mawu paused for a moment. "Tip done got another slave-woman pregnant. He ain't bring her cause she pregnant. He don't like to mess with no pregnant womens. So he brung me. Say he got a thing for me even if I does hate him."

Lizzie let the grasshopper go and it jumped out of her palm onto the ground beside them. For a moment she thought it had hurt itself. The jump from her palm to the ground had been a long one. But then she saw the blur of it as it leaped into the bushes beside the path.

A majestic cedar rose before them like a spirit. Lizzie couldn't tell if it was welcoming or warning them. Two of the arms looked as if they had been sawed off. Or perhaps fallen off during an ice storm. She had heard about the harsh Ohio winters. She knew all about ice storms, but she couldn't imagine the amount of snow they said Ohio got. She had only ever known Tennessee winters. Sometimes a bit of snow and sometimes not.

They approached the cabin from the back and threw pebbles at the back door from their cover in the woods. The weeds had grown up tall around the yard, but it did not look as if the cabin was abandoned. Lizzie thought she recognized the husband's hat hanging beside the door, but she couldn't be sure.

Just as Mawu gave a look to signal they should turn back, they heard someone moving. Then they saw her. She looked the same from a distance. Hair covered. Long plain dress. Wide hips and shoulders ambling along and then as she neared them, slowing down. She squatted down before a patch of yellow flowers and rifled through them. She searched carefully, as if for the perfect one, finally selecting four. She stretched and stood, rubbed the back of her hand across her forehead.

"Hey!" Mawu called out.

Glory turned around. Even though Mawu had called out to her, neither she nor Lizzie revealed themselves. Glory pulled the bonnet back a bit so she could see around her. The sun peeked from behind a cloud.

"Who's that?"

Lizzie stepped out from behind the tree. "Us."

Glory shocked them with the speed with which she dropped her bag of flowers and rushed toward them. Lizzie thought the woman would hug them both. But just as she got close to the two slave women, she stopped, as if she had checked herself.

"You're back. I knew you'd be back," Glory said, breathless.

"How come us ain't seen you around the place?" Mawu asked.

"Some other farmer is providing for the hotel this summer."

"Why?" Lizzie asked.

Glory rubbed at her cheek. "My husband took sick this winter. He really never got better. A bad cough. He still works as much as he can, but he can't do too much. It's just enough to keep us fed and to sell some in town."

Glory was still stout and healthy looking, but her eyes had taken on more of a sunken quality. "Everybody come back?"

Lizzie nodded.

"What brings y'all out here?"

There was no hiding the fact they were too close to Glory's cabin to just happen to be nearby. There was nothing else nearby but the cabin. So the question was really, *what do y'all want with me?*

Lizzie looked at Mawu and waited to see what her friend would say.

"Where your husband at?" Mawu asked.

"Gone," Glory replied, falling easily into the clipped cues the women knew they had to speak in order for their friendship to remain secret. What she meant was that *he is gone for a spell and yes we have time.*

"I got something to ask," Mawu said.

Lizzie scratched a bug bite. She had no idea what Mawu was about to say.

"Shoot," Glory said.

"I need you to help fix me." Mawu looked down at her waist. Then she put her hand over her private area. "I need you to help fix me permanent."

Glory shook her head.

"I don't aim to give him no more childrens," Mawu said, eyeing Glory steadily.

Lizzie coughed and then coughed again, as if there were a hair in her throat that she couldn't get to.

Mawu hit her on the back. "You all right, girl?"

Lizzie nodded.

"What you got to cook in that cabin?" Mawu asked.

"Some potatoes. A fresh rabbit," Glory answered.

"Well, that's all us need. My mammy taught me how to make the best rabbit stew you ever sank your teeth into."

Mawu showed a mouth of crooked teeth as if to prove it. Glory removed her capelet. In a few moments, the three women were walking toward the cabin, Mawu stopping here and there to pick an herb.

Lizzie couldn't help but wonder what the sight of them must have looked like: a brown woman, a red woman, and a white woman. Thin, short, and fat. Tennessee, Louisiana, and Ohio.

The three women were just as different on the inside, too. One of them was hoping to give up what the other cherished and the third longed for.

TWENTY-NINE

The hastily dispatched telegraph from Georgia said it might
be cholera. Diarrhea that spread as rapidly as a brushfire in
the woods. The women never got a copy of the telegraphed
note themselves. But they knew from the cook who heard it from
the maid who heard it from the horse groom that the place back
where Sweet lived was in trouble.

For days, Sweet waited to hear word of her children. That week
was a difficult time, not only for Sweet but for all of the women.
Each of them remembered Sweet's dead baby from the summer
before. And they knew she could not handle any more dead babies. There were four children left: three girls, one boy. Each one
with the light skin born of the nightly couplings with her master.
And as she walked around the place, stiff as stone, it was hard for
those who watched her petite frame to believe she had birthed so
many.

The women knew better than to ask. They could tell from

the look on her face she knew no more than they did. So they all prayed silently at night, into sheets, pillows, blankets. Lizzie asked Drayle after the third night of no news if Sweet's master would send her back to check on her young ones. Surely her master needed to go back to check on his plantation himself. Surely he was worried about his own family, if not the coloreds then the whites. Even though his wife was long dead, he had five white children of his own. But according to Drayle, he had made no such plans, perhaps afraid if he did go back, he would fall victim to the illness as well.

Then they learned that his white children had been evacuated from the place. And those who were sick had been separated from those who were well. And the sick ones had been taken off the land and put away somewhere safe. Temporarily, those still there believed that this had stopped the rage of the infection.

Sweet didn't know if her children were with the healthy ones or the sick ones. So the women waited, wondering what kinds of midnight supplications Sweet made to her master to find out about her children. Wondering if he cared that these were his children, too. Not just his property, but his own flesh and blood.

But they also knew that for white men there was no such thing as separating the two. They were his children, yes. But they were also his property. And like most property they could be replaced.

This was the women's deepest fear. That a white man would feel his slave children could easily be replaced with new ones, as if it were an exchange at a dry goods store.

Mawu, Lizzie, and Reenie sat on the low bank of the pond, each keeping her hands occupied with different tasks while their minds focused on one thing. They spoke of things light, like what they would cook for dinner and how quickly dust seemed to gather in the corners of their cottages. They watched as white hotel guests walked by. Mawu spun a story about a man back on her place who could catch flies in his mouth, snapping them up like a frog.

Chew them and eat them? Reenie asked.

Well, if he ain't eating them, he holding them in there mighty long, Mawu answered.

Tomfoolery, Lizzie said.

The three women allowed themselves a welcome chuckle. Until they saw Sweet approaching them, carrying something spread across her arms. It looked like a garment of some kind. The three women waited. Lizzie scooted over to make a space for Sweet in the middle, so that she would be flanked by the rest of them.

When Sweet made it over to them, they could see she was carrying a dress. She passed through Lizzie and Mawu and stretched the dress out on the ground between them. She arranged the folds of it. The dress was black, but varying shades of black. Sweet must have run out of fabric; it was clear that she had stitched together all the black fabric she could find. Only the neckline and the sleeves were edged in white lace. Lizzie recognized the lace as the same fabric the hotel used for the cottage tablecloths. This made Lizzie study the rest of the dress and wonder where Sweet had gotten the other pieces of mismatched cloth.

"This for my baby. My Sarah."

"Dead?" Reenie put down the potato she was peeling. "Your child dead?"

Only Sweet's mouth moved. "My oldest. The one that took care of the others. She had a face from the heavens."

"I'm so sorry, Sweet," Lizzie whispered. "I'm so sorry."

Sweet shook her head. "No. This a good thing, in a way. I was worried about her. She was too pretty. Some old man was bound to start trying to mess with her. I didn't want her to end up like me. So now she gone to the Lord where she can be a true angel."

Lizzie reached out and touched the dress. "You made this for her?"

"Ain't it pretty?"

"When you leaving?" Mawu asked.

Sweet smiled. "We ain't going."

"What you mean, you ain't going?" Mawu's eyes flashed.

"It's all right, Mawu. I just need y'all to do this."

"Just say it," Lizzie said.

"Go and bury this here dress in the woods. Next to my other baby. The one without a name. I can't stand to be there myself. But I know y'all will do right by her."

"I is gone say a prayer," Reenie said.

Sweet closed her eyes and then opened them. She nodded her gratitude and headed back to her cottage.

All three women stood, and Reenie looked off at the sun to see how much time they had.

"Supposing we ask one of the men to come help us?" Lizzie asked.

"No," Reenie said. "Us can do this our ownselves."

Lizzie and Mawu picked up the dress and carried it between them as if there were really a body in it. Lizzie carried the top portion and Mawu carried the bottom. Reenie led. On the way, they stopped and got a shovel.

They found the spot where Sweet's infant girl was buried, near the intersection of two forest paths that crossed one another. It was marked by a small tree. Lizzie took the shovel and dug while Mawu and Reenie folded the dress into a bulky square. The hole wasn't man-sized. It was just large enough for the folded dress. Reenie placed the dress in the hole while Mawu hunted for rocks. They covered the hole with a hill of smooth rocks.

The three of them held hands and formed a circle around the two graves. Mawu said a prayer in a language neither Lizzie nor Reenie understood, but they all felt the spirit of it. When Mawu got quiet, Reenie withdrew a wooden cross from beneath her dress and kissed it.

Three nights later, there was a knock at Lizzie's back door. Drayle was sleeping on the sofa, so she opened the door quietly. Sweet stood there with a shirt and pants, already folded.

"This here for my boy. My only boy."

And then she disappeared into the darkness.

The next day, the women repeated their ritual.

Two days later, Lizzie woke and found a dress folded so tightly on her back porch step that she did not know what it was at first. She looked around, but no one seemed to notice the bundle. She took it to Reenie who immediately put down her washing and nodded. Mawu couldn't join them that morning because her master was home. Reenie said a few words so powerful and angry they made Lizzie cry a bit.

It had been two weeks since the first word of the sickness. And Sweet had one child left. They were afraid to ask, dreading more news of the dead. And knowing that if three of her children were gone, and they all lived in the same cabin, then it was likely the other was sick as well. They didn't want to believe that God would be so cruel to take her last child.

But they imagined feverish nights, nights of stomachaches and loose bowels and cold rags on foreheads, one sick caring for another.

Sweet stayed in her cottage, and when the women knocked on the door after witnessing her master leaving with the other men, there was no answer. They peeked through the window and saw her sleeping on the bed. They watched for the rise and fall of her chest. They knew grief like this could kill you. They left her alone after they saw signs of life.

Three days later, Lizzie could no longer wait and decided to enter Sweet's cottage. She had heard of other plantations being in trouble like this, but she had never known any slaves on them well enough to feel the effects of it.

As she walked, she was conscious of the burden of her steps and tried to think of what she would say. She stood outside the back door of Sweet's cottage for several minutes. And when the proper healing words did not enter her mind, she decided her presence would have to do.

She found Sweet in the middle of the room, sitting amidst a mountain of shredded fabric. Her hair was disheveled, lips covered with the white crust of dehydration.

"What are you making, Sweet?"

"Making."

"We ain't seen you around in a few days."

"I told you. Making."

Lizzie took up some of the fabric in her hands. Some of it was coarse cloth. But some of it was good—muslin, cotton, wool. Parts of it looked like undergarments, lace, sackcloth.

Lizzie recognized the top portion of a girl's dress. The lower half of it was a neverending patchwork of textures. Lizzie went into the bedroom and saw that the bed was barren of sheets, the closets empty of clothes. Everything had been used. Maybe Sweet's man was grieving, too. Surely he knew Sweet had sewn up everything in the cottage.

The stitches weren't even either. Some were loose, others bunched the fabric into uneven folds.

"You got some more?" Sweet licked her lips.

Lizzie quietly observed the odd look in Sweet's eyes. Then she left and went back to her own cottage and got a pair of pants she had discovered behind the stove, left by some previous guest. She went to the kitchen at the back of the hotel and asked the women if they had any fabric to spare. They wouldn't give it to her until she told them Sweet was making a dress for one of her children.

The cook who ran the kitchen must have understood because she commanded the younger women to gather every scrap of cloth they could find in the house that wouldn't be missed. They came back with heaps in their arms.

Lizzie took it all back to Sweet's cottage and dumped it in a pile on the floor in front of her. The grin on Sweet's face motivated Lizzie to go and search again. This time, she visited Reenie and Mawu to ask for fabric. Both of them gave her what they could spare.

"She all right?" Reenie asked as she handed over a pair of worn bloomers.

"She all right," Lizzie repeated in a low voice.

"She making it?" Mawu called through her cottage window.

"She making it," Lizzie said.

When Lizzie returned to Sweet's cottage, she saw the woman had hungrily grabbed up the nearest piece of cloth to her and ripped it apart. She was sewing it onto the neverending dress and as she worked, drool made its way down her chin. Lizzie decided to leave her alone.

Two days later, they were sorting eggs when Sweet came to them. Mawu had just accidentally broken an egg and found a tiny leg inside. She had thrown the egg into the grass, frightened by the omen. Sweet lay the dress out in front of them on the ground.

"They all dead now. They all gone to meet the Lord. They in a better place. They crossed over." She spoke in a loud, clear voice as if she had rehearsed the lines. She touched the dress lovingly. Then she stretched out on it, rolled over on it.

She stood and faced the women. "Now bury her. Bury my last baby girl."

She walked off. The women wrapped the delicate eggs and tied their bundles around their waists. They folded the dress to lessen the weight of it, and Mawu took it and balanced it on her head, holding it with one hand as she walked.

They dug the hole beside the other four mounds. Mawu wanted to stick flowers between the rocks. Reenie said the flowers would die, just like everything else. Lizzie thought it was a good idea. Mawu found yellow daisies and stuck them among the rocks. She promised to come back later and freshen the flowers. They looked down at the rock-covered mounds. They didn't quite look like human graves because of their small size. But they did look like something human hands had touched.

The three women knew there was no telling what had actually happened to the bodies of Sweet's children. They knew that when sicknesses like this happened bodies were burned. Even if they hadn't been, it was likely Sweet would never see her children's graves. They would not be marked. Her children would now be among the missing. But it wasn't as bad as if they were sold off. Nothing was worse than that.

The three women held hands again. But this time, none of them said a prayer out loud. Instead, they prayed in their hearts and sent their pleadings through palm kissing palm. And although they didn't admit it to one another, both Lizzie and Mawu thanked God that their own children were safe and sound back on their plantations.

THIRTY

When the women did not see Sweet the next day, they decided to go to her cottage. The door was open and the
women passed through the front room. They found
Sweet lying naked on the bed, no sign of her master ever having been there in the night. The cottage was bare, as if someone
had swept up the bits of thread and fabric that had been strewn
throughout the rooms, erasing the evidence of her grief.

Sweet had developed a rash. It covered her face and neck and
part of her shoulders. Mawu went out and filled a tin cup with
water. Reenie pulled Sweet up and put the cup to her lip. Later the
women would have to cut Sweet's hair, it was so tangled and mat-
ted with dirt.

Reenie said, "Drink this. Drink up."

Sweet drank without protest. There was nothing to wipe the
wetness from Sweet's chin, so Lizzie used her dress.

"You still got a life, don't you?" Mawu said. "You still got a life?"

Lizzie didn't know what to say. Four children gone. Five in the last year. She just didn't know what one mother could say to another when her own children were safe and sound, bellies full, cheeks fat, backs smooth, soft hands, soft feet, minds that could read, lips that could pronounce words grown slaves had never heard of. She was trying not to feel her own fortune. Trying not to feel that this could have been her laying in this puddle of stink, sewing big chunks of cloth into a dress for a child she would never see again.

"You ate anything yet?" Lizzie asked.

Sweet looked up, her eyes glassy.

"You hungry?"

Sweet's eyes rolled back in her head before she looked in Lizzie's direction. Lizzie gently lay Sweet's head back. She went out to the hotel.

At the back of the hotel, all she had to do was mention Sweet's name and they pressed a loaf of bread under her arm and a bowl of creamed corn into her hands. The cook said, "God bless her. God bless her."

Mawu fed Sweet as if she were a baby. She broke off a piece of the bread, dipped it in the water, and put it into Sweet's mouth. Sweet chewed slowly. Between bites, Reenie put the cup of water to Sweet's lips to make sure she didn't choke.

When they were reasonably certain Sweet had had enough, Lizzie took the bowl and washed it at the well and set it outside the cottage door.

When she went back in, she heard Reenie talking, "You cry, now. You hear me? You let it out. You got to get it out your body. This thing you making, it ain't gone do you no good."

When Lizzie looked down, Sweet's hands were moving. At first, she didn't know what Sweet was doing. Then she understood. As if the fabric were still in her hands, Sweet was sewing away, her thumb pressed against an invisible thread, as if holding her place.

Lizzie found a small square of slate framed by wood. The cook managed to get her a piece of chalk. It was a precious find and Lizzie planned to take it back to her children. In the meantime, however, she would use it to teach Reenie a few of her letters. Reenie had been practicing with her primer since the summer before, but this was their first formal lesson.

Lizzie had thought to begin with A since that was the first letter of the alphabet. But then she changed her mind and began with teaching Reenie how to read and write her own name.

"How you keep track of them big letters and little letters? How you know which is which?"

Lizzie smiled. Reenie smelled of lavender. The older woman gripped the sides of the slate until the bones flexed over her knuckles.

"R-E-E-"

"How many E's in my name?"

"Three," Lizzie answered. "Can you count, Miss Reenie?"

"Not much." The chalk slipped out of her hand.

"Like this." Lizzie showed her how to hold it.

"I can add little numbers like two plus two and four plus four. But something climb over ten and I gets myself in trouble."

Lizzie wiped the slate. "Let's try again."

Reenie concentrated and the chalk slipped out of her hand again. She threw the slate into the dust.

"I is too old, Miss Lizzie!"

Lizzie picked it up. "No you ain't. Let's try it again."

"Miss Lizzie, I want to tell you something. About my finger. How I lost part of my finger."

Lizzie put the slate down.

Mawu was running toward them from the main hotel. Reenie straightened her back and her face hardened. News was coming their way and whatever she'd had to confide in Lizzie would have to wait.

THIRTY-ONE

They wore the same dresses they'd worn the summer before during the dinner in the hotel, dresses carefully tucked away in trunks stored in the hotel attic over the last year. Dresses they'd instinctively protected when Sweet was sewing up everything in sight. Dresses they'd often thought about over the winter months when they were back home on their plantations, trying to make it through each day.

They'd tried to forget what happened to Reenie the night of the dinner when they'd first worn them, only speaking of it once. Reenie had described the night in a hushed tone early one morning. She'd told of how she'd carefully taken the dress off before she let the manager touch her. So that it, unlike her body, would remain inviolate. Every time he came for her, she made certain she never looked as enticing as that first night, so that each coming was a bigger disappointment than the last.

They should have been surprised the white men allowed them to go to Dayton. But they had come to learn that in this place with the magical water, things were different. Later, they would learn the trip was a gift for Sweet. It was her master's way of giving her a piece of joy. Henry had not returned that summer, but his more vocal brother George had. George had been ordered to stay behind at the hotel. His owner had work for him to do.

One of the colored hotel porters was entrusted with money to buy Sweet something nice, but he would steal half of it and spend the rest on their meals and a cheap trinket for her. The slaves did not trust the porter because it was rumored he had turned in more than one runaway slave for the reward money. The word on him was that he believed slaves needed to earn their freedom by saving up for it. His own grandfather had done this very thing, buying his own freedom and his wife's before settling in Ohio. Born into freedom, the porter believed in the legal rights of white men.

The slaves could not help but envy him. They observed the neat coat he wore with the shiny buttons, the polished black-soled shoes, and how he, every now and then, extracted a watch from his inner pocket and flicked open its lid at just an angle where they could not see its face.

Without the whites, the five slaves and one free colored weren't allowed to ride the omnibus that shuttled Tawawa House visitors between the railroad depot and the resort. So they took a wagon. When they got to the depot, they piled into the back car of the train.

"I heard something," Mawu whispered to Lizzie after the two had squeezed into the narrow seat.

"What's that?" Lizzie asked.

"Ain't you noticed it's not that many folks here this year?"

"I guess."

"They closing it. They selling it."

"What?" Lizzie asked.

"Hush. Don't want that porter to hear us talking."

Lizzie lowered her voice. "What's this you're saying?"

"You ain't gone see none of us again. They closing the hotel," Mawu said.

Lizzie had heard nothing about this, and she intended to ask Drayle about it. She did not believe it was true.

She leaned back over and spoke closer to Mawu's ear. "What about fixing yourself? You know. So you won't have children again. Are you still going to do it?"

Mawu looked at her lap. "I reckon not, Miss Lizzie. I can't do it round Sweet. It ain't right."

Philip opened a window to let some air into the stuffy car, and Mawu's hair, having grown even longer over the winter, flew out around her face, the hair so thick as if a scalp did not exist. She held it back with one hand and placed the other in her lap.

The six brown-faced men and women were mostly silent the rest of the trip. The train rocked them into intermittent naps. It was as dark as nighttime when they left the resort, and by the time they arrived in Dayton, the sun had risen high over the buildings on the outskirts of the city.

The four women were unable to control their excitement as the city came into view. Even Sweet, who had been so quiet in the days following the death of her last child, spoke up. A servant from the hotel had given Sweet a steel needle as a gift, and she used it to make sure their dresses still fit, mending holes, tightening bodices, and letting out seams. And she had done it all in what appeared to be a healed spirit.

The women did their best to dry their faces and air out the spaces beneath their arms. They did not want to look like slaves. Lizzie patted Sweet's wet forehead with a small square of cloth.

The hotel porter whistled and a tall, thin boy ran to the back of the station and came back driving a wagon. The wheels on the wagon were slightly bent and looked as if they would wobble right off.

"I want some sweets," Mawu said.

"I want to go into a store and buy something," Lizzie said.

"Your man give you money?" Sweet asked.

"A little," Lizzie said, feeling selfish. She didn't want to share.

"You think they gone let us go into a store and buy something without no note from our master?" Mawu asked.

"This ain't the South," said the porter. "Colored folks go in stores all the time here."

When they got to the center of downtown, the women eased themselves off the wagon, taking care to hide their ragged shoes beneath their dresses.

The streets of the city were just starting to fill with people, mostly looking as if they were going to work. One group of leisurely white women passed by, the women turning and raking their eyes over the colored women's dresses. The four slave women sped up. Only Lizzie glanced back. She noted that none of the women wore the wide hoops of the white women vacationers back at the hotel.

The porter suggested they get breakfast. He led them to an alley where they found an open door to a colored diner. Some of the diners turned to look; others ignored them and continued slurping down their breakfasts. The tables turned over quickly as men pushed back wooden chairs, scraping the floor, then put on their hats and headed off to their daily lives.

The six of them found a large enough table in the back, and a woman approached them. None of the slaves had ever been waited on before in a public establishment. Lizzie sat high and straight, and when her breakfast came, she tried not to eat too quickly. Reenie studied the other diners to see how they did it. Mawu stared at the menu written on the wall above the counter. The diner was quiet except for the noise of forks against plates. There was only one other woman in the entire place.

After breakfast, they walked through the streets. The porter explained that they were in the colored section of town known as Little Africa. Lizzie delighted at this. She waved at a woman who mistook her for someone else. She was surprised that so many of the buildings were made of brick. Large windows covered the fronts of businesses. Lizzie and Sweet read the names of signs for Reenie and Mawu. *Blacksmith. Shoemaker. Dry goods.* The porter explained that they were walking down Franklin Street.

Lizzie knew clearly in her mind that the men had not known how dangerous it was to allow their slaves to go into Dayton. Then again, perhaps whites did not understand how it felt not to be able to go where one wanted to go, dress how one wanted to dress. They took simple things like movement for granted.

She turned around and saw Philip hanging back, talking to a large woman wearing a dress even nicer than hers. Philip touched the woman inside of her elbow and Lizzie recognized her. The barber's daughter. They were standing in front of a shop with a red, white, and blue pole with gold finials hanging outside. Inside, three colored men wearing white coats stood behind chairs raised high off the floor. Lizzie recognized the tall, straight profile of the girl's father.

Philip and the woman walked over to Lizzie.

"This here be Lizzie," Philip said. "She from back home."

Even though Lizzie had seen the woman working in the hotel during the previous two summers, they had never had an opportunity to speak. She took Lizzie's hand in a proper way, the way Lizzie had seen white women take other white women's hands. She brought the slave's hand to her mouth and kissed it, smiling at Lizzie from a wide, pleasant face. "Pleased to meet you."

And Lizzie knew then that she would not let another night pass without talking to Drayle. She made up her mind while standing on the street in Dayton. Even before she confirmed the truth of the rumor that they were, indeed, selling the place, she knew that she would use her favored status to pay Philip back for his kindnesses. If her children could not be free and filled with new possibilities, then maybe Philip could.

That evening, Drayle heated a kettle of water on the stove. Lizzie took off her dress. It was something they weren't able to do back at their place, one of the rules Fran had established with her husband and his mistress. In minutes, Lizzie was soaking in the tub. He ladled the water over each of her shoulders.

After the water had grown chilly and Drayle had emptied a fresh kettle of hot water into the tub for the final time, she stood and he dried her, reaching beneath her armpits, ordering her to squat so he could dry between her legs.

"Drayle. I've got to ask something."

He shook his head and tensed, as if he expected the usual question. It angered her that he always became so upset at the prospect of her asking to free their children. She closed her eyes and tried to press down on the sick feeling in her stomach.

"I want to talk to you about Philip."

Drayle turned and faced her. Lizzie read the relief clearly written across his features. "What is it?"

"Drayle," she began. "You know that Philip is a man, don't you?"

"A man?"

"He's always done everything you asked of him. He's been faithful to you. In fact, he's one of the best slaves you own."

"True," Drayle said.

"And now it's time," she said, "to give back to him. To thank him for all those years he gave you. To thank him for being faithful."

"What are you talking about, Lizzie?"

"Drayle, you've got to free him. You know it. You've got to free that man!"

"Free him? What on God's earth—?" He paused and looked at her suspiciously as if trying to ascertain whether another escape plot was being hatched.

"The time has come. You can't keep a man like him in chains forever."

"But he's one of the most valuable slaves I own. You're telling me to just give up my valuable property. Free him. Just like that. That's what you're saying."

"No, Drayle, let the old man buy him. The man offered to buy him. Sell him and get your money. If you got your money, would that make you happy?"

She felt chilled. She was still naked and Drayle held her gown in his hands, suspended. Then he pulled the gown over her body. She picked her fingers through a knot of tangles in the back of her head that had clenched up in the steam of the water.

"Drayle, you'll do it, won't you? You'll do what's right?"

"Come on, woman." He grabbed her arm and pulled her into the bedroom.

She yanked back. "No, not this time. This time you give me an answer. You won't give me an answer about my children. You won't give me an answer about anything. But . . ." She lowered her voice. "Give me an answer about Philip."

She understood the risk she was taking. White folks had a way of having a limited number of acts of generosity. If he listened to her about Philip, the chances of freeing her children would decrease. She tried not to dwell on this.

"Why are you pleading his case all of a sudden?" He looked around the cottage, as if searching for clues of betrayal.

"You know that man is like a brother to me. He ain't never been more than that, and he never will be. Now what are you going to do? Are you going to be a man and free him?"

"Shut up, woman. Don't you call me out of my name."

"I didn't call you out of your name. Tell me something, Drayle. Are you the kind of master everybody back home makes you out to be? Or are you something else?"

He looked down at the brown nipples peeking through the thin fabric of her shirt. "I'll think about it. Is that good enough for you? I won't say no and I won't say yes. I'll say—"

"What?"

"Let me think about it. How about that?" He reached for her hand.

But for the first time since she could remember, she refused him. And that was the way it was that night. And that was the way it would be for a few nights more.

The last words out of his mouth before he fell off to sleep were: "We never should've allowed y'all to go off to Dayton."

THIRTY-TWO

Early the next morning Lizzie rose and lit the outside fire in preparation for breakfast. On her way back from the hotel, laden with the day's provisions, she spotted Mawu running toward her. "Lizzie, Lizzie, Lizzie," Mawu was saying over and over. Not loudly, but enough where Lizzie could hear the z's carrying through the air.

When Mawu reached her, she circled her arms around Lizzie.

"What is it?" Lizzie asked. She peeked over Mawu's shoulder at the sun and could see it was perched at breakfast time.

"What is it, Maw?"

Mawu pulled back and put both hands on Lizzie's shoulders. "Sweet."

Even before the words that followed, the words that would deliver Mawu's message, Lizzie knew something was wrong.

She clenched her teeth and dropped her bundle, leaving it on the ground where it fell. Mawu led her away from the cottages into the woods. Lizzie knew where they were headed. The five little graves. For a moment, hope flickered inside of her. Maybe it wasn't bad. But as Lizzie and Mawu approached the bodiless mounds of dirt covering the dresses and pants and shirt, she saw her friend laid out on her back, on the ground, hands folded across her chest, as if she had already been carefully laid to rest. Her eyes were closed, one side of her face covered with a cloth, the other side smooth as if recently wiped clean. She was still wearing the dress she had worn to Dayton the day before.

Reenie was already there, standing off to one side. Mawu pulled Lizzie right up to Sweet, and they both dropped to their knees.

Lizzie's eyes roamed over Sweet's body. "What happened?"

Reenie shook her head and told the women that Sweet had been discovered in the ravine by early morning hunters.

Lizzie shook her head. "I don't understand. She fell?"

"Must be," Reenie said. "I guess she lost her way in the dark."

Lizzie started to cry.

"But she do look happy, don't she?" Reenie said.

"How could she be happy?" Lizzie spoke to Reenie in a tone she had never used with the elder one before.

"Because there's a afterworld," Reenie said. "And in that afterworld, all our sadness go away. The Bible say that the Lord will wipe your tears away."

Mawu spat on the ground. "The Bible! The Bible! That's all you niggers talk about!"

"She freer than you is. That's for sho!" Reenie's spittle flew in Mawu's face.

They were silent.

Finally, Lizzie whispered, "Sweet."

~

They held the ceremony for Sweet at night, after the day's chores were done. All of the slaves were in attendance and a few of the house servants. None of the white men came, although Sweet's man had been there earlier, knelt over the body for some time. At least that's what Philip told Lizzie. While Philip and George dug the grave, the white man sat beside her. And although they did not see tears, the men witnessed the hump of his back, the shake of his shoulders.

It was late when it all began. The men brought tall candles set into stakes. They planted them into the ground around Sweet's body. It was a dark night, the crescent moon barely lighting the clearing. There was no box to put her in. The men had not had time to build one because the white men had insisted her body be buried quickly. There was also no cooling board on which to lay the body. So they just dug the hole as deeply as they could, nearly six feet under, so that the smell of her decaying body would not reach the surface.

There was no preacher to stand over her and make sure her soul made it to the right place. They all stood silently, waiting for someone to step forward and give Sweet's body the honor it deserved.

It began with a song.

> *Mary had a baby.*
> *Yes Lord.*
> *Mary had a baby.*
> *Yes my Lord.*
> *Mary had a baby.*
> *Yes Lord.*
> *People keep a coming*
> *But the train done gone.*

They listened to the song as if they had never heard it sung before. And it did not matter that they usually sang it at Christmas. Reenie's voice lifted over the other night sounds and floated into the darkness. She had a rich, deep voice. And although she rarely sang and wouldn't ever call herself a singer, she barely missed a note that night. She sang the song slowly, befitting a funeral, not rapidly like they sang it when they were working.

Only Mawu stood a bit apart from the group, her face a mask, a chicken dangling from her hand. After Reenie had finished her song, Mawu opened her mouth: "They say he fed the hungry with a few loaves of bread. They say he turned water into wine. They say he walked on water. They say he calmed storms. They say he healed the blind and the deaf. That's what they say."

The chicken clucked, a string connecting its tiny neck to her wrist. She stopped speaking and picked the chicken up, spun it around until its neck broke. The wings started to flap. She turned it upside down and stuck a small knife in its mouth, making a slicing motion. Blood spilled onto the front of her dress. She lifted the chicken in the air and closed her eyes, mumbling something inaudible over the wind and rustling trees.

"Enough!" Philip shouted. He looked upset.

The two men rolled Sweet's body into the grave. George shoved dirt into the hole, mumbling "God bless you" as he worked.

Reenie took Lizzie's hand and walked away. Behind them, Mawu walked, holding the chicken out in front of her. Philip and George moved pile after pile of dirt into the hole, the blood of the dead fowl splattered on the ground around them.

THIRTY-THREE

I t was only after Sweet's death that they decided to read the pamphlet, as if the loss of her had stirred in them a more urgent reason to know about these freedom-loving whites. On the first morning that she read, only Mawu and Reenie sat beside her. Later, Philip and George would join them. But that first time, it was just the three women sitting in the parlor of Lizzie's cottage. Lizzie pulled the couch over to sit just in front of the two women. Reenie put out a plate of bread, and Mawu sipped from a cup of tea.

"The Philosophy of the Abolition Movement" by Wendell Phillips. This is a speech delivered in Boston on January 27, 1853.

Lizzie cleared her throat, and decided to start at the beginning. She had looked the pamphlet over several times and there were words she could not accurately pronounce because she had never heard them said aloud before. But she was pretty certain of the general meaning of what she was about to read. Even so, her hands shook. She wondered what the women would think if they knew that it had been Glory who had stolen the pamphlet and given it to her. Glory, the faithful Quaker, had stolen it out of the bag of a man at the post office.

> *Mr. Chairman,—I have to present, from the Business Committee, the following resolution:—*
>
> *Resolved, That the object of this Society is now, as it has always been, to convince our countrymen, by arguments addressed to their hearts and consciences, that slaveholding is a heinous crime, and that the duty, safety and interest of all concerned, demand its immediate abolition, without expatriation.*

Lizzie wanted to stop and read those words again. She had never heard a white man talk in such a way. For a moment, she faltered, wondering if she'd mispronounced the word "heinous." But she continued:

> *I wish, Mr. Chairman, to notice some objections that have been made to our course, ever since Mr. Garrison began his career, and which have been lately urged again, with considerable force and emphasis, in the columns of the London Leader, the able organ of a very respectable and influential class in England. I hope, Sir, you will not think it a waste of time to bring such a subject before you. I know these objections have been made a thousand times; that they have been often answered; though we have generally submitted to them in silence, willing to let results speak for us. But there are times when justice to the slave will not allow us to be silent. There are many in this country, many in England, who have had their attention turned, recently, to the AntiSlavery cause. They are asking, "Which is the best and most efficient method*

of helping it?" Engaged ourselves in an effort for the slave, which
time has tested and success hitherto approved, we are, very prop-
erly, desirous that they should join us in our labors, and pour into
this channel the full tide of their new zeal and great resources.
Thoroughly convinced ourselves that our course is wise, we can
honestly urge others to adopt it. Long experience gives us a right
to advise. The fact that our course, more than all other efforts, has
caused that agitation which has awakened these new converts,
gives us a right to counsel them. They are our spiritual children:
for their sakes, we would free the cause we love and trust from
every seeming defect and plausible objection. For the slave's sake,
we reiterate our explanations, that he may lose no little of help by
the mistakes or misconceptions of his friends.

Lizzie read slowly, and when she noticed Reenie picking at the
hem of her dress, she decided to skip ahead a bit.

The charges to which I refer are these: That in dealing with slave-
holders and their apologists, we indulge in fierce denunciations,
instead of appealing to their reason and common sense by plain
statements and fair argument;—that we might have won the
sympathies and support of the nation, if we would have submit-
ted to argue this question with a manly patience; but instead of
this, we have outraged the feelings of the community by attacks,
unjust and unnecessarily severe, on its most valued institutions,
and gratified our spleen by indiscriminate abuse of leading men,
who were often honest in their intentions, however mistaken in
their views;—that we have utterly neglected the ample means that
lay around us to convert the nation, submitted to no discipline,
formed no plan, been guided by no foresight, but hurried on in a
childish, reckless, blind and hot-headed zeal—bigots in the nar-
rowness of our views, and fanatics in our blind fury of invective
and malignant judgment of other men's motives.

Mawu whistled. "Ooh, I didn't know you could read so nice, Miss Lizzie. I can't hardly understand for listening to the sound of them words. What that man saying there?"

"He's saying that the abolitionists have been accused of being too . . . too vicious, too mean, and he doesn't believe this to be true. He believes these folks that accuse them of this don't know what they're talking about. He believes that the cause of freedom is just and right and they must do all they can to get rid of slavery."

Reenie's eyes were wide. "Oh my sweet Jesus. Go on," she urged. "Go on."

Two days after Sweet was laid to rest, the white men discovered Philip sneaking off the resort to meet his woman. No one knew how they found out. But the word got back to the slaves that Philip had been meeting her halfway between the colored resort and the white one. Lizzie thought of how often slaves did this back in Tennessee, meeting halfway between plantations and making their love felt on the forest floor. In contrast, she thought of how direct Drayle was back on their place, exercising his rights wherever and whenever the mood hit him.

They all waited around wondering what would happen next. No one had seen Philip, and Lizzie searched frantically for Drayle, but he, too, was nowhere to be seen. From her porch, Lizzie could make out Reenie hanging laundry behind her cottage and Mawu walking on the other side of the lake carrying something on her head.

Lizzie swept the dust out the front door of her cottage. Back at the plantation, Drayle might have gotten away with giving Philip a light scolding and perhaps having the slave trader visit the place to scare the slaves into thinking that Philip might be sold off. But here, in this Northern climate, where he was under the scrutiny of the other Southern slaveholders, Drayle would probably decide to take a sterner approach.

Lizzie had to get to Drayle first, remind him that Philip was still his favorite slave. It was no longer a rumor but a well-known fact that this would be their last summer at the resort. Most likely, Drayle figured that if he could get Philip back to Tennessee without this woman, he would be able to get his slave's mind off her.

Once, Drayle had bought a beautiful woman for one of his slaves after the man's wife died in childbirth. The young woman had been intended to salve the older man's grief. They had taken up residence together in one of the slave cabins, and it was not long before the young girl had genuinely fallen for the kind old man. It had been an unexpected but welcome outcome to the forced coupling. Lizzie thought this was probably what Drayle was hoping for now, that he could purchase a woman for Philip that would solve everything.

Lizzie tried to block out any image in her mind of Drayle having Philip beat. Besides, who would beat him? There was no overseer here to perform Drayle's dirty work, and Drayle had never been one to perform such an unpleasant task himself. There was that one hotel porter who would do anything the white men told him for a price, the one with the watch who had accompanied them to Dayton. George would do it if so ordered, but she doubted that he would complete the task with any zest. And the slaveholders knew this.

As the different scenarios passed through her mind, she saw a figure that looked to be about Philip's size approaching from the distance. He was flanked by two men holding him by the arms. Lizzie shaded her eyes with her hand. From where she stood, it looked as if Philip's legs were chained. As the three men got closer, she heard the telltale clink of metal against metal. She clutched the arm of her broom.

The men led Philip to a tree just off the edge of the pond. It

was a scrawny young pawpaw tree that even in the height of summer had never bore any fruit. Nor was it full enough to offer very
much shade. They chained him to the tree and walked away.
Philip scooted along the ground until he was beside the tree and
rested his back against its narrow trunk.

Lizzie leaned the broom against the wall of the cottage. She
wiped her palms across the front of her dress. Even though she
could not make out Philip's face, she knew he had already been
beaten. He did not have the walk of a beaten man, but she knew
how such things worked. He had been beaten and left out in the
hot sun.

She heard someone moving inside the cottage, and it startled
her. She pulled open the door and saw Drayle moving about the
room, packing a bag. "Drayle? What did you do to Philip?"

He ignored her and continued to move around the room. She
watched as he put the tin cup and plate he used for camping into
the bag.

"Where are those socks you mended for me?"

She went into the bedroom and took a thin pair of socks out
of the drawer with a patch across the toe. She returned and gave
them to him.

"Talk to me, Drayle. What's happening?"

"Hand me my fishing rod."

She took the rod out of the closet. Considering the time of day,
she knew he would probably camp overnight. But surely he didn't
plan to just leave Philip there.

He hoisted the pack of supplies over his shoulder and finally turned to her. "Don't you even think about going near him,
Lizzie."

"What?" She tried to shame him with a certain look she used
now and again. "You're going to just leave him there?"

"You hear me? This is between me and him. Don't you even think
about going near him. You or nobody else, but especially you."

Surely he didn't plan on leaving Philip out there all day and night. There wasn't much shade out there, and the Ohio sun was as hot as the one in Tennessee.

She remembered when she was a child and still lived on the plantation in Weakley County where she was born there had been a dog that hung around the slave cabins. It hadn't belonged to anyone in particular and no one had ever given it a name. They just called it "Dog." The dog lived on scraps thrown to it here and there when the slaves had finished eating. As it got old, its back legs started to give out. So it took to sitting around more and more until finally it stopped walking altogether. No one had the heart to kill it. One morning, as the slaves went off to the fields, some-one placed the dog in a shady spot near a tree.

When the children gathered around the tree that evening to hunt for the sticks they used for toys, they discovered the dog lying in the same spot where it had been left. One of the children called his father who came and picked up the dog's lifeless body. He told the children to run along, and he went off somewhere to bury it. Lizzie could remember the dog's skin: it had been raw and peeling beneath the dog's thin brown and white pelt. She had dreamed that night of what it must have felt like to be that dog, becoming so hot until her vision blurred and she could barely suck in enough air to cool herself. She had heard of adults com-plaining of such symptoms while working the field all day, but even they wore hats to cool themselves. The dog had been unable to do anything to lessen the punishment of the sun once it moved its position in the sky.

"Who's going to feed him and give him water?" she de-manded.

"You stay away from him, now. You hear me?"

Lizzie must have looked as if she intended to follow no such order because his voice turned cold.

His words were slow. "I'm going to leave instructions for the hotel servants to keep an eye on that tree." He spoke of the tree as if it existed and Philip didn't. "If I so much as hear that you or anyone else has gone near it, I will have Nate whipped until he's black and blue."

Lizzie froze. He had never threatened to do such a thing. Nate had never been whipped in his life.

"Nate? Whipped? Have you lost your mind?"

She felt it and saw his hand swing back at what seemed like the same time. It happened so quickly she didn't have time to dodge out of the way.

"I have told you time and time again to watch your mouth when you are talking to me. You are just a woman and, on top of that, nothing but a slave woman."

The blood on Lizzie's lip didn't taste like anything. It wasn't salty like sweat or sweet like mucus. She lapped it up with her tongue and squeezed her lips together.

His eyes were red, the look of a parent who has just slapped his child. She had seen that look in Big Mama's face before.

"I'll be back in a day or two," he said. He turned away from her and left her standing there wearing a new feeling.

THIRTY-FOUR

~

At first, no one dared go near Philip because they did not know who had been set up to watch him. The slaves watched the hotel servants and the hotel servants watched the slaves. Lizzie, Reenie, and Mawu tried to devise ways they could sneak out in the middle of the night and get him water. Philip was tied to a tree right at the edge of the water, a tree easily visible from any of the nine cottages surrounding the pond and also from the hotel's main lounge. The white women set up a picnic nearby on the first day and watched him while they ate. Two children threw rocks at him, narrowly missing for the most part.

George spent the first couple of days watering the flowers along the water's edge. When he got close enough for the water to reach him, he doused Philip down. Philip tried sticking his tongue out and drinking water that way. On the second day the two men got smarter, Philip digging a hole in the ground and George managing to fill the hole with water. Philip used his tongue to lap up the water before it soaked into the surrounding dirt.

Another day went by and Lizzie walked by the tree, close enough to Philip to see that his lips were white and cracked. He tried to say something to her, but his words got muffled by his swollen tongue. Lizzie went to Reenie's cottage and sat in a chair while Reenie folded clothes.

"We can't just leave him out there," Lizzie said. "It's too hot."

"He can survive," Reenie said. "Philip a strong man. Strong as an ox."

"That's what everybody thinks about him." Lizzie shook her head. "But he ain't strong as people think. He's got a soft spot. I've seen it. And it's probably worse now that he's got that woman on his mind."

Reenie picked up Sir's overalls and folded them down the front of her dress.

"And Drayle ain't never been too hard on none of his slaves, let alone Philip."

Reenie stopped folding and eyed her. "Every slave got the survivor in him. You don't got to get beat every now and then to remember how to make it through something."

Lizzie tried to believe what Reenie was saying.

The next morning was the fourth day since Drayle had left and no one had been allowed to feed or water Philip. It was only because he moved a bit here and there that they knew he was still alive.

The three women sat on the steps of Mawu's porch. George came and sat down on the grass in front of Mawu's cottage.

"Somebody done fed and watered him," George said.

"Who?" Lizzie asked.

"I don't know. One of the coloreds at the hotel, I reckon."

Mawu sucked her teeth. "Them people ain't never helped nobody but theyselves. I doubt it."

"Why do you think somebody fed him?" Lizzie asked.

"Cause look at him. He look a little better today than he did yesterday," George said.

"I haven't gotten close enough to see," Lizzie responded.

"I did. And as far as I know, he ain't had water in two days. Can't nobody survive that long in this sun without at least a dip or two of some cool water."

"Maybe it was that Quaker woman," Mawu said.

"I ain't seen her in a spell," Reenie said.

"She could be sneaking on the property at night," Mawu said. "Maybe."

"Maybe it was one of those abolitionists," Lizzie offered, thinking of the pamphlet.

"Look," George said. They all looked east and saw the group of white men returning, long fishing poles hanging from their shoulders.

The women stood, their respite over. Lizzie hastened back to her cabin, eager to convince Drayle to end his punishment of Philip. Over the past couple of days, she had decided to try the tactics she'd used on him in the service of her children. She would not refuse him this time.

When she heard Drayle's footsteps swishing through the grass, she met him out on the porch and pushed him into the wooden rocker.

"Let me help you with your boots," she said.

She pulled each boot off and lined them up beside the door. Then she pulled off his socks and massaged his feet. They stank like the outdoors, but she rubbed them anyway, paying particular attention to the large bunion on his right foot.

He enjoyed her attention for a few minutes before smiling down at her.

"Lizzie?"

"Hmm?"

"If I tell you that I've already decided to sell Philip, will you still take care of me?"

She dropped his foot and it fell with a thud onto the wooden porch.

"For real?"

He nodded.

She studied him for a moment, then leaned down and kissed the stinking, sweating toe.

This time, Philip and George joined them. The four slaves sat mute before Lizzie as she read.

> What is the denunciation with which we are charged? It is endeavoring, in our faltering human speech, to declare the enormity of the sin of making merchandise of men,—of separating husband and wife,—taking the infant from its mother, and selling the daughter to prostitution,—of a professedly Christian nation denying, by statute, the Bible to every sixth man and woman of its population, and making it illegal for 'two or three' to meet together, except a white man be present! What is this harsh criticism of motives with which we are charged?

"Slow down, Miss Lizzie. I don't want to miss a thang," George interrupted.

Lizzie's next words were slow and deliberate:

> The South is one great brothel, where half a million of women are flogged to prostitution, or, worse still, are degraded to believe it honorable. The public squares of half our great cities echo to the wail of families torn asunder at the auction-block; no one of our fair rivers that has not closed over the negro seeking in death

a refuge from a life too wretched to bear; thousands of fugitives skulk along our highways, afraid to tell their names, and trembling at the sight of a human being; free men are kidnapped in our streets, to be plunged into that hell of slavery; and now and then one, as if by miracle, after long years, returns to make men aghast with his tale.

Lizzie stopped reading. She paused for a minute although no one asked her to explain.

Drayle told Lizzie that while camping he had decided to let Philip go. But first, the barber would have to agree to a price Drayle would set himself. A price that would allow him to buy another slave with a reputation as good as Philip's. He had come to this decision because Reenie's man had convinced him the slave would be no good anymore. He would either try to flee or spend the rest of his days resenting Drayle for it. Philip had a permanent pass that allowed him to run Drayle's errands or exercise the horses throughout the woods. Sir insisted that those days were over. And even though Drayle objected, Sir ominously reminded him that some slaves had even killed their masters over such disappointments.

Drayle convinced Lizzie he was doing this for her as well. Because she'd asked and he respected her wishes. She'd known it all along, she said to herself. This would be the good deed to answer all other favors. A man, he would most likely argue later, could only give up so much of his property.

When the barber arrived to bring the money, the small group of slaves watched from afar, Philip among them. The daughter was not present to help, so the assistant laid out the tools and rinsed the brass bowl. It appeared to Lizzie that the barber's arms moved with especially exaggerated flourishes as he whisked the cloth off Drayle's face and brushed the white man's shoulders clear of fallen clips of hair.

The assistant removed the rocks from the back legs of the rocking chairs so the men could sit upright. The other three white men paid the barbers and took their leave. The assistant cleaned up the tools and left Drayle and the head barber on the porch alone. The slaves could see the gray-haired man resting against the rail, his white coat blending with the white of the wood.

"You reckon you gone be able to leave with him today?" George asked.

It sank in for Lizzie that Philip would not be returning to Tennessee this time. And if this were really their last summer at the resort, she would never see him again. She tried to etch his features into her memory as she had done to her friends when she was nine years old and being sent to the auction block. She hoped this time the memory would stick.

"I don't know," Philip said, unable to hide his joy.

"Well, it ain't like you got nothing to pack," Mawu said. "You probably just gone climb in that there wagon and be on your way."

"Maybe you'll get a whole new suit of clothes," George said. "You gone enter the barbering trade?"

"I don't know. I gots to pay the man back his money. But the onliest thing I know is horses. I ain't like these cityfied folks." Philip brushed at a fly crawling on his forehead.

"You gone learn quick," Reenie said. "Tell me, Philip. How do freedom taste?"

Philip looked at her and smiled. "Miss Reenie, I got to say I honestly don't know just yet. I reckon I won't know till I get my free papers."

Lizzie studied Drayle and the barber and saw that neither had changed position. She knew that Drayle had Philip's papers in his pocket. She had looked at them just that morning and run her fingers over them. The papers looked real, sure enough. Written up by someone in a flowing and official-looking script, even better than those of the old man on the train up from Cincinnati.

"You be sure to send me a letter, Philip. Even if you've got to get somebody to write it for you." Philip could not read and write, and Lizzie wondered if he would learn now that he was free.

Philip reached out for her, and she hugged him for a long time. His chest felt warm against hers. She remembered the nights she had spent in his cabin, how he had kept a respectful distance. She'd always appreciated that. But now she wished she would have let him take her just one time. To remember him by. It wouldn't have been much for her to give herself to him. At the time, though, she'd felt differently. She'd seen being with Philip as a way of disrespecting her children's father. But now she knew she could have done it. She could have shared something with him a little more than friendship and a little less than love.

The good news was that now he would get real happiness. She felt protective of him. Tender. And jealous all at the same time.

"He got them!" George exclaimed. "He got the papers!"

Philip released her and they both strained their eyes to see if it was, indeed, a paper in the barber's hand.

"Hallelujah!" Reenie shouted.

Mawu turned to Lizzie and spoke quietly. "That was a good thing you done."

Just as they'd thought, Philip left with the barber that very afternoon. Each of the slaves gave him a token to take with him. Reenie gave him a wooden cross her brother had carved for her years before. George gave him a nectarine he had stolen from a nearby orchard. Mawu gave him a sack containing some herbs she said would protect him from evil spirits. Lizzie gave him a note she had carefully written the night before containing the address of the plantation in Tennessee.

That night, Reenie told Lizzie as they drew water at the well she would no longer have sex with the hotel manager. Lizzie replied she had not known that it was still going on. Reenie looked at her with a half-surprised expression and continued to pump water. Lizzie remembered the summer before when Reenie's own brother and master had promised her to the hotel manager. All of them had seen Reenie making the evening walk to the hotel for the remaining days of the summer. But since none of them had seen Reenie making that walk this summer, they'd figured that the relationship had ended.

But it obviously hadn't. If he was bold enough to continue the relationship across summers, then he would not take no for an answer. Reenie's master had made a trade of some kind, and most likely he would have to give up whatever the manager was giving him in order to free Reenie of her obligation.

In the days that followed, Lizzie saw less and less of Reenie. A week after their conversation, she went to Reenie's cabin to see if the woman had really been able to end it. The men were gone for the night on an overnight camping trip, and since she figured Reenie would be obligated to the hotel manager on a night they were gone, she wanted to see if her friend was in the cottage.

She saw a light in the window and went around to the back door. She tapped.

"Miss Reenie?"

She saw the lace curtain in the kitchen window inch back. A moment later, she heard the floorboards creak. The door cracked open.

"What you want?" Reenie answered. Her eyes moved past Lizzie.

"I just came to talk."

"You by yourself?"

"Course I'm by myself." Lizzie looked behind her just in case. Reenie was making her nervous.

Reenie opened the door just enough for Lizzie to slide through.

Lizzie looked around once she had entered. "Are *you* alone?"

Reenie grabbed her arm. "What you mean?"

"What's wrong with you? I'm just asking. And I thought I heard something besides."

Reenie scooted a chair into the middle of the floor. "Sit," she commanded.

Lizzie obeyed.

Reenie went to the closet and stood before it. "If you tell anybody, she dead. If you tell anybody, you gone have blood on your hands."

"Tell what?"

Reenie opened the closet door. A girl peeked out.

Lizzie's hand flew to her mouth. "Who is this?"

"Shh!"

The girl began to cry.

"Hush, baby," Reenie said. "Miss Reenie gone take care of you." She took a piece of bread out of the basket and handed it to the girl. The child broke through its hard crust with her teeth. Then she scooped out its soft whiteness with her finger and stuck it in her mouth.

Lizzie looked the girl up and down. She was dressed like a slave. Or, at least, she was dressed like a slave trying not to dress like a slave, wearing pants like a boy and a large shirt tucked into them. The shirt wore a patch across the arm as if the sleeve had been ripped off and then put back on. Her hair was cut short like a boy, too, but there was no mistaking the soft feminine features.

Reenie wiped the girl's runny nose with her own sleeve. Then she tucked her sleeve in to hide the wet spot.

"Whose child is this?" Lizzie wondered if the older woman was going crazy. They had all been grieving since Sweet's death. And Reenie had been through a lot over the past year.

Reenie pulled the girl in close. "She mine and she yourn, too. She belong to all of us."

"What are you saying?"

The child relaxed and leaned against Reenie. "She come up from Kentucky. Them free women in the hotel done asked me to look after her for one night. She be on her way tomorrow."

Lizzie finally understood. She rose to her feet and glanced nervously toward the open window. The air in the cottage had cooled noticeably since she'd arrived.

Reenie was watching her closely. "What you thinking?"

Lizzie felt it. A test. Even after all this time, a grain of mistrust remained. "But how?"

"I can't . . ." Reenie stopped as if trying to think of the word. "I can't explain. A lot of people help this here child. I ain't the only one."

"Oh." That was all Lizzie could think to say.

The child took another nibble of bread. Lizzie looked around the cottage, trying to determine if this was the first runaway slave Reenie had helped. Nothing looked out of place. Only the child.

"When?" Lizzie asked.

"After Sweet died. Didn't something change for you after that?"

Lizzie searched inside herself. Something had, but she couldn't really give expression to it. And she certainly hadn't gone as far as Reenie to act upon it.

"Why you come over here tonight anyway?"

Lizzie looked at her friend. She couldn't say she had come over to see if Reenie was still seeing the hotel manager. She couldn't say she had come over to ask how Reenie had gotten away from him and taken back her body. And ask how she could take hers back from Drayle and still maintain favor. The child watched as if awaiting her answer as well.

"Well," Lizzie began. "I really just came over cause I'm lonely, what with Sweet gone and all." There. That was enough of the truth to be counted as honest.

"You want a piece of bread?" Reenie asked.

Lizzie nodded.

THIRTY-FIVE

ater, Lizzie would try to put the pieces together and would
wonder if the first fire provided the idea for the second. She
would recount every little moment of the summer in her
mind—from Sweet's death to Philip's freedom—and wonder how
she'd missed the little signs that had, no doubt, been there all
along. She would experience a store of emotions, and it would be
months before she would boil it all down to grief.

The crowd at the picnic was the lightest it had been all summer. There were more Southerners in the crowd than Northerners, the thick drawls and parasols a telltale sign that the Southern
visitors outnumbered the others. Reenie reported that she'd
overheard the hotel manager speaking about the situation. Ap-
parently, the Northerners no longer wanted to come to the resort
as it was being overrun by Southerners. Most of them had short-
ened their visits. Some were said to be offended by the presence
of negro wenches.

Lizzie and Reenie were standing together when a colored

child unwrapped a muslin cloth, exposing a small fish inside. She pulled a few sprigs of some kind of herb from her pocket and tucked them one by one into the folds of the fish. Then she wrapped the fish again and placed it on the outer edges of the fire.

Neither of the women knew where the child had come from. They assumed that she belonged to one of the hotel servants and had been assigned to perform some chores for the day. Lizzie and Reenie each held the end of a long stick skewering partridges. They had spent the entire morning plucking the feathers from the birds and cleaning out the organs. Now they held the stick just high enough where it would not catch fire, and rotated it slowly so the birds would cook on the inside before they charred on the outside. Once the birds were done, they slid them off and piled them onto a long board. Then Reenie carried the board over to another table where Mawu and two other colored women from the hotel ladled sauce onto them.

Each time she was given a pail of fresh raw partridges, Lizzie slid the birds onto the sticks, careful to pierce each at its thickest point. As she held the birds over the fire, she searched for Drayle's face in the crowd. She had not often seen him in the company of the other resort guests, and she wondered what he would be like.

He was standing about thirty feet away from her in a group of men who were smoking. He only smoked when they came to Tawawa because Fran didn't allow it at home. The men laughed, the scent of their cigars mingling in the air with the scent of the meat.

Lizzie looked with wonder at the colored child kneeling beside her. She was fascinated by free colored children. She wanted to reach out and touch the girl's head, but she could not take either hand off the heavy stick of partridges. She was so busy looking between the birds and the girl that she didn't see the white woman approach her.

"What's your name?"

Lizzie looked around for someone else. But when she glanced into the white woman's eyes, they were fixed on her. She looked down. She could tell from the accent that the woman was a Northerner.

"Lizzie, ma'am."

"Lizzie. Is that short for something? Elizabeth?"

"Eliza, ma'am."

"Who do you belong to, Eliza?"

Lizzie tried to figure out where the question was coming from and where it was going. "I belong to Master Drayle, ma'am."

Lizzie peeked over at the woman and saw her eyes searching the crowd of men.

"Which one is he?"

Lizzie tilted her head. "The one in the tall boots, ma'am."

Despite the heat, Drayle had not taken off his riding boots and still held his crop in one hand.

"Is he good to you, Eliza?"

Lizzie nodded and said what she knew was expected of her. She remembered Mawu's question, *He God to you?*

"Yes, ma'am," she said.

Lizzie took a chance and looked up into the woman's eyes. The woman looked visibly relieved. "Good. 'Cause I can't stand men who are brutes. A lot of slave owners are brutes, aren't they? At least, that's what I hear. That's why I detest slavery."

She wanted to ask the woman about the pamphlet, about this Wendell Phillips. Did she know him?

The woman moved on. When she joined the next group of women, she must have said something about Lizzie because they all looked over at her and gave her little half smiles. Lizzie looked at them for a moment and then turned her attention back to the partridges. Her arm was tired. She needed to relieve herself, but her partridges were still too raw to eat.

The child's fish had cooked more quickly. She unwrapped the cloth to check on it, and Lizzie guessed from its aroma that it was probably just about done.

A white child approached the colored girl and sank to her knees. "Is that fish ready yet?"

The colored child nodded reluctantly. Lizzie could feel the child's disappointment as she realized that her treasure was about to be taken from her. The servant child put the wrapped fish on the ground. She knew she had to give the fish to the other girl, but her anger would not allow her to hand it over just yet. If the girl wanted it, she would have to pick it up and take it herself.

The white girl smiled triumphantly, and as she leaned over to take the fish, the end of her dress grazed the hot ember. Lizzie saw it when it happened, but she did not know it had caught fire until the child had already felt the heat of the burn on her leg. The white girl screamed and the fish flew out of her hands. She jumped up and ran. Reenie put down the partridges and ran to the well. The colored girl picked up the fish and stuffed its slippery flesh into her mouth with her fingers, sliding the bones out between her teeth.

A white woman threw the quilt she had been sitting on over the child. It, too, caught fire. There were shouts all around as people realized what was happening. One of the men ran after the child and caught up with her before throwing himself on her. They rolled on the ground. The child was still screaming loudly, and the smell of burnt flesh filled the air as the doctor yelled, "Let me through! Let me through!"

Lizzie looked around for Drayle and saw him standing alone, a bit off from the crowd. The ground around him was littered with forgotten cigar ends, still glowing. Only he remained, his fingers grasping the butt of his cigar and his mouth frozen in the round shape of a deep exhale.

She turned back to the birds on the ground beside her, and felt her eyes sting from the heat of the fire. Then she looked again at Drayle, and as the burning child's screams simmered, she saw him take another puff of his cigar and wipe his forehead.

Lizzie was so busy watching Drayle that she had no memory of Mawu at that moment. She wished she had looked her way. Later, she wondered if she would have seen the reflection of the fire in her eyes.

THIRTY-SIX

⌒

The second fire happened that very night. The men poured out of the cottages in their dressing gowns, faces lined with the tension of sleep. The fire rose like a vengeful ancestor over the lot of them.

Mawu and Tip. It was their cottage. Lizzie searched the faces for her friend and found her, standing on the fringe, indecent in her gown, arms hanging slack at her sides, crying and choking through something that resembled tears.

Lizzie saw Reenie hurrying along with a pail of water in each hand. Out of the darkness, Drayle pushed two pails stuck inside of each other into Lizzie's fist and commanded her to the pond. She joined the long line of frantic men and women, sooty-faced colored and white, slave and free, who moved back and forth between the pond and the cottage. One of the men yelled something unintelligible, and Mawu reached out into the darkness as if trying to clutch someone. Swollen white sores ran the length of her arm.

"She hurt. Mawu hurt," Lizzie said to the closest passing negro.

In a moment, Reenie was there. Both of Mawu's arms had been burned from the shoulder down to the hand. The skin had started to pucker, a fret of scales and blisters. Mawu looked down at her arms as if they belonged to someone else. Her face appeared untouched, smooth as a speckled stone, brown and iridescent in the light of the moon and the fire.

"I tried, I tried."

"Hush. We gone take care of you." Reenie had to yell over the shouts of the men.

Lizzie wanted to ask. What had she tried to do? Had she tried to save Tip and failed? Lizzie looked off toward the cottage. It was a lick of flames, dark smoke blasting into the air and sending down a sprinkle of ashes.

"But you don't understand, Miss Reenie. You don't understand. I tried, I tried."

"Sweet Jesus," Lizzie heard Reenie say. "Anybody ask, you tell them she burnt and I is taking her back to my cottage, you hear?"

Lizzie nodded, the empty pails swaying in her hands.

"Is she all right?"

Reenie shook her head. It surprised Lizzie. Like asking the doctor if someone was going to be all right and hearing the truth for a change.

"She got more than burns to deal with."

"Lizzie! Fill them buckets, girl!" Drayle shouted at her as Reenie and Mawu hurried off.

Lizzie ran back to the pond. One of the slaves standing knee deep in the water helped her get them full. When she turned around, she saw Tip waiting behind her, an outstretched pail in his hand and a pasty look on his white face that made him appear ghostlike.

But he was not a ghost. He was just as real as the fire still panting hungrily behind him. She glanced off in the direction that Reenie and Mawu had gone. Now she understood. She understood what Mawu had tried to do.

And while she had a strange feeling in her belly she might never see Mawu again, it never crossed her mind she might never see Reenie again, either.

THIRTY-SEVEN

When she heard that both Reenie and Mawu were missing, Lizzie felt as if her insides had been broken into a thousand pieces. She wanted to crawl inside herself like a turtle. Later, she would describe it to Glory as time moving at an indescribable speed, carrying buckets of water one minute and carrying her heart in her hands the next.

After the news spread through the resort, Drayle changed toward her. Everything became a barked order and she was locked in a room at night.

Lizzie ran the day over and over through her mind. From the girl with the burned legs—the way the skin merely looked sunburned—to the oozing sores on Mawu's arms. From the dark smoke rising from the cottage to the empty feeling in her stomach that came with the knowledge that she was the only one of the four left. She could not understand what she had missed, why they had not included her in their plans. She wasn't sure how she would have responded if they had, but she mourned the lack of invitation.

The only thing she could come up with was that they had not forgiven her for the summer she told on Mawu. They still thought of her as a traitor.

After the cottage fire was put out, Drayle had told her to make her way back. She had considered sneaking off to Reenie's cottage, but she had thought better of it. Drayle's eyes had made two holes in her back, and she'd figured it wasn't smart to anger him at that point.

She couldn't keep her face out of the window that night. Drayle followed her home soon after and made her come to bed. But after he was asleep, she got up and sat in the window again. The smell of ash was still in the air and the moon was bright enough for her to just make out Tip's cottage where two men were still dousing the smallest flames. It wasn't really a cottage anymore, just a black shell standing.

How long had they known they were making a run for it?

Two days later, Drayle shouted orders to George to get their trunks up to the hotel where the omnibus would pick them up. There was still no news of Reenie and Mawu's whereabouts, but every day she could hear the dogs. The same dogs they'd used to hunt wild birds and pheasants and possum were now being used to hunt her friends. She had heard that the reward money was so big, every slave catcher in the county was out looking for the women.

She hoped Mawu had covered her hair. In her mind, she warned the woman like a mother would a child. She advised the two to split up. She wrapped hot biscuits in a cloth and tucked it into their aprons.

Tip walked around the resort with a righteous anger on his face, as if someone had kidnapped his mother. She wondered if he was angrier that Mawu had escaped or that she had tried to kill him first.

You ain't the only one wondering about a betrayal, she wanted to say to him. But she didn't say anything because whatever rights she'd had before Reenie and Mawu had escaped had ended. Now it seemed everyone was watching her. Reenie's Sir even tore a piece of her dress one day and gave it to one of the dogs. The dog smelled and licked it while she watched. Then Sir grinned at her, as if to let her know that he could find her, that he would find her if she had a mind to take off after the others.

Each hour that passed by that she didn't hear they had been caught was like a jubilation. She hoped they made it all the way to Canada. She had heard that in Canada coloreds and whites could marry. She wondered if there was a country north of Canada, and what possibilities existed there.

She also wished for two more things: that she could be with them and that she could return to her children. It felt like her right arm was being pulled one way and her left arm being pulled the other. She knew it wasn't a right way to feel.

While she was packing her trunk, she tried to pack her fancy dress, but Drayle told her to leave it behind. Leaving the dress, saying goodbye to it, was like leaving a part of her new self. She wished she had given the dress to Sweet to tear up and sew. Maybe it would be of better use in the ground where they'd buried the clothes in honor of her children.

On the day they woke up to leave, it was still dark outside. As she walked to the hotel, she found no joy in the early morning bird chirps.

She moved slowly because she wanted to remember every moment of the free soil. She remembered Reenie asking Philip to tell her what freedom tasted like, and she felt a thrill at the knowledge that Reenie would be getting her own taste now.

Drayle watched her. He appeared to be half asleep, his eyes drooping low, but when she glanced his way, she sensed the alertness. What did he think she was going to do? Try to make a run for it? There were dogs and slavecatchers throughout the woods. She supposed that Drayle was already regretting his decision to sell Philip. His eyes were saying he had no intention of letting her go.

The walk from the cottage to the hotel seemed longer than it had ever been. Even though the air still carried an early morning chill, she felt sticky beneath her breasts. Drayle walked behind her, and it felt like he would walk behind her for the rest of her days.

Once the omnibus was loaded, she climbed onto it. Drayle sat beside her the way he always did, as if she were his real woman. She pulled the cloth tight around her hair and the sides of her face.

As the omnibus rolled forward, she thought to herself that this would be the final time she would feel *this* human. She thought about her children and how overjoyed they would be to see her again. Both of them. The slate board was wrapped carefully in a cloth and tucked into her things. Drayle had taken the dress, but he hadn't known about the slate. She had also managed to bring along two pieces of chalk. She thought of the free child at the picnic and wondered if she could read. The girl had been about Rabbit's age.

And there was one more thing she had managed to escape with: the pamphlet. She needed to find a safe place for it, somewhere it could sit for a few years. She planned to give it to Nate once he was a man, so that he too could feel the heat of the words and channel his young anger into the righteous fury of this Wendell Phillips.

She tried not to look back at the cottages or the hotel because she did not want to feel any worse. She just wanted to think of her children and not think about Reenie or Mawu or anybody else. She took solace in knowing that there would be no more good-byes.

But just as they rounded the bend in the road, she couldn't stop herself. She looked back anyway. It was too late. The hotel and cottages were too far back behind the trees.

But there was a figure. Lizzie closed her eyes and opened them again. The woman was still there.

In the middle of the road, smaller after she opened her eyes the second time, was Glory. She didn't have on her bonnet, so Lizzie could just make out her face, the square of her chin. Glory lifted her arm up and did something like a wave.

Lizzie waved back. There had been someone to say goodbye to after all.

PART IV

1854

THIRTY-EIGHT

⁓

They returned to the resort that summer for the fourth time, after all. And this time, Fran came with them.

On the ship, Lizzie slept in the servants' quarters adjacent to Fran and Drayle's stateroom. She wondered where she would sleep once they got to the resort. She pictured Fran in her cottage, tucked into her sheets, soaking in her bathtub, drinking from her cups.

Leaving her children had been more difficult than ever. Nate was almost eight years old—big enough to work in the fields and to look after his sister. Rabbit was a year younger, but she had an old soul. Lizzie sometimes felt the girl could see right through her mother's put-on strength. As if the girl could sense the most cowardly part of her. As if the girl already knew the secret that Lizzie had not told anyone, had not even half admitted to herself.

Fran had been pestering Drayle about putting the children to work, and even though Drayle had held her off, Lizzie could tell that the woman was wearing him down. Drayle had never gotten over losing Philip. Even though he had sold his favorite slave at a fair price, he acted as if Philip had escaped. He didn't even like for Lizzie to mention Philip's name. Recently, Drayle had started training Nate to care for the horses. It was exactly what Lizzie had expected.

Nate was eager to bid Drayle's wishes. Lizzie could see how much her son wanted his father's attention and how he would jump the sun and the moon to get it. If he wasn't busy showing off how strong he was by lifting something too heavy for him, he was reciting something from a book. Lizzie was proud of the fact that he talked like a white boy with nary a touch of slave in his speech. She only wished that the other slave women were there so she could brag about him in a way that she could not brag about him to other slaves.

She leaned her forehead against the train car window. She passed the time by counting the houses built along the banks of the Little Miami River. Her stomach pitched with each tumble of the train. The glass was hot against her skin. She missed Philip's stories.

Drayle had warned her this wasn't a vacation this summer, mysteriously saying that he had unfinished business. She hoped that it had nothing to do with trying to buy Philip back. She wanted Philip to enjoy his freedom with his new wife. At the same time, she didn't want to offer up her son as a replacement. As usual, she found herself having to choose between her interests and another's.

She wondered why Drayle had brought her along at all. Since Reenie and Mawu's disappearance the summer before, they had not spoken about the two women. She had been afraid to ask lest he think she had a mind to follow.

As soon as they got to the hotel, she planned to make her way to the kitchen so she could find out the latest news.

When they finally arrived at the resort after eight days of

travel, the grand white hotel did not look the same to Lizzie. The paint was not fresh, and a yellowed curtain blew through a broken window pane. The grass was not trimmed very low, and some of the flowerbeds were empty. A gaggle of geese sauntered by, following a servant carrying bread.

Fran looked about her, as if disappointed that the resort did not appear the way she had expected. Lizzie wished the woman could have seen the place at its height. When Drayle entered the hotel to sign the register, Fran instructed Lizzie to fan her while they waited. Lizzie stretched over the trunks in the back of the omnibus so she could reach her. The leather was hot. Her lip twitched. Lizzie wished there was someone there to fan her. *I suppose I am the spoiled nigger she says I am.*

When he came back, he pointed to Lizzie and said, "They fixed up your bed" as if she was supposed to know what he was talking about. She hopped off the back of the omnibus and grabbed the square of cloth pinned around her belongings.

In the kitchen, the head cook Clarissa smiled at her and while Lizzie had waited for such a warm welcome for the past three summers, she found that it did little to ease her mood.

"You looking good," the older woman said to Lizzie. "You done gained some."

"I reckon so," Lizzie responded. The cook put up her arms to stretch, and Lizzie pretended to take it for a hug. She pulled Clarissa close, and when the woman squeezed her back, Lizzie felt a flower open up inside of her.

She asked if Lizzie had eaten, and when Lizzie told her no she fixed a plate. She motioned for Lizzie to go outside and wash up. Lizzie stepped into the sideyard. The spigot on the water pump was rusted and a bee circled its mouth as if it held the attraction of something other than water. She put her hands beneath the cool liquid, and closed her eyes.

Clarissa served mashed potatoes, gravy, and chicken. Lizzie

was hungry. A chambermaid on the ship had brought her a plate of leftover food every evening, but once she'd boarded the train, there had been no more meals. After she finished the chicken, she felt sick. She tried to hide it from the ex-slave, thinking it wouldn't take much for the woman to guess her condition.

Lizzie indicated she was ready to go upstairs. Clarissa called out for a servant who showed Lizzie up the back stairway. As she led the way, the girl asked if she had ever seen where the hotel servants slept. Lizzie answered no. When they opened the door, the girl pointed out that the men and women slept on opposite sides of the attic. The wall between the two spaces had been erected after Clarissa explained to the hotel manager that no self-respecting free colored woman would share a bedroom with a man. The servant pointed to a narrow bed that was sinking in the middle.

"I guess a bed, even a sinking one, is better than a dirty old pallet any day," the girl said softly, watching Lizzie.

Lizzie slid her bundle under the bed and thought of her bedroom at home. This free girl was assuming that because she was a slave, she slept on a pallet. She wondered what the girl would think if she saw the spacious room Lizzie called her own in Drayle's house. The drawer of underwear. The wooden horse on the dresser.

Lizzie wasn't used to being idle, but the new sleeping situation had her off balance. She was used to tidying the cottage and washing Drayle's clothes and warming his dinner. Why had they brought her here?

She considered asking the girl her name, but thought better of it. The last thing she needed was another friend who would desert her.

She wanted to kill Drayle. While she was sleeping that night, she made up in her mind that she didn't want to kill it. She wanted to kill him instead. He was the one who had gotten her into this mess. He was the one who had been lying to her for all these years, who wouldn't let her children go free.

She had to kill him. And unlike Mawu, she had to succeed.

She caught herself mumbling when she woke up. The room was so hot, she felt as if she were boiling. There wasn't a window that opened in the attic and even though the door was ajar, the air wasn't moving.

She pushed her way out of the bed, pulled off the sheet, and walked down the back stairs. She was used to finding cool spots in the kitchen, so she had no problems locating one here. She balled up the sheet and made a bed of it.

But still she couldn't sleep. Because in her dreams, she had done it already. She had killed him. Would doing something like this weigh on her children's spirits? Would they pay for her decisions? Big Mama always used to say that the sins of the mother and the father rained down on the heads of the children.

She finally gave up on trying to sleep and stepped out the back door. Everything was quiet except for the occasional sound of a dog barking. She walked, stopping when she saw a piece of paper nailed to a tree.

$100 REWARD for NIGGER WENCH.
Ranaway from Tawawa House resort, near Xenia Springs, OH on the seventh day of August, 1853. Answers to the name
REENIE
5 feet 6 inches high with a straight nose for a negro; no teeth remaining but does wear a set of false ones; deep voice like a man. She was raised in the house and will likely look for work as a cook.

The paper made Lizzie go cold.

She had only meant to walk to the pond and back, but her feet had their own mind. Before she knew it, she had arrived at the cottage and was peering in the window. She wasn't sure if Drayle would be staying in the same cottage as the one he had shared with Lizzie. A part of her had hoped they wouldn't, that Drayle would be sensitive enough to know the cottage had been special to them. But there lay the couple, sleeping as sound as babies. Drayle's arm lay across his wife's chest. They didn't look any more comfortable than she had felt in the attic above the kitchen.

As she tried to make her way back, she tripped over something in the dark that sounded like metal. It clanged loudly. She looked down and saw Drayle's metal camping dishes, lined up against the outside of the house, still dirty from the last visitor. Surely Fran would wash them for him, she thought, as she put the cup back in its proper place.

"Who's there?"

Jesus! It was Drayle and there was no place to hide. She stepped closer to the side of the house and pressed up against it. She figured if he went left, she would go right. If he went right, she would go left.

He came out the back door and walked to the water pump, as if he figured he would get himself something to drink while he was up.

She couldn't help herself. She needed to claim him, needed to know there was still that connection between the two of them, even if she was angry at him. She crept up behind him and put her arms around his waist.

He jumped and turned around. "Girl! Don't you sneak up on me like that. Are you crazy? What are you doing out here this time of night?"

His eyes moved past her shoulder.

"You spying on me?" he said.

Then he pushed her back into the shadows and kissed her. It had been a while since he had kissed her on the mouth. Lately, their lovemaking consisted of a few grunts and then he was through. Most of the time it was from the back with her dress still on. She had noticed that sometimes he couldn't seem to get it going good enough. Then he would tell her it was her fault.

She let him kiss her for a few minutes until she started to feel sick again. She pushed him back and lay an arm across her stomach.

"What's wrong with you woman? You ain't—"

"No!" she said. "Something I ate."

He grabbed her shoulders. In the dark, his face looked boyish. He seemed to be enjoying the secrecy of the meeting. He told her to turn around and bend over. She didn't say what she wanted to say, that she didn't feel like it.

It lasted a little longer than it had lately. While she was bent over, she spied a sharp piece of metal on the ground. While he was carrying on behind her, she stared at it. It was just close enough where she could reach it. *Swing it around. Hit him with it.*

But she couldn't do it. *I'm not Mawu.*

And then he was quiet. And she knew he was through.

THIRTY-NINE

~

It was the Quaker woman who led her to Mawu. Lizzie had started to know the Tawawa Woods, the deep ravine in its center, the five mineral springs, Massie's Creek, but she still did not know them well enough to navigate directions. Once they arrived, she was surprised Mawu was so close. With that hair, she'd figured Mawu would be long gone by then. All of this time and she had been living right under the slavecatcher's nose. Only Mawu could do something like that.

The first thing Lizzie noticed as Glory approached with the two horses was that she was pregnant. The woman's rounded belly made her pause. Lizzie wanted to share in the news, touch it, give her a silent prayer. But she was in no place for such celebrations. She tried hard to feel warmth, especially since she'd known how much Glory wanted a child.

She forced words from her lips, "You've done it I see."

Glory smiled and put a hand on her middle. "Yes. My very own. I'm hoping it's a girl."

"A girl?" Lizzie wanted to chastise her for such talk.

"Yes. If it is, I'm going to name it Eliza. Like your given name."

Lizzie didn't bother to hide her surprise. Why would this woman want to name a baby after her? Why not Mawu or Reenie or Sweet?

"You don't have to do that."

"I know I don't," Glory said. "But I want to. I need this baby to have a strong love like yours."

Lizzie shrugged and climbed onto the horse. It was a gentle mare and not as large as the one Glory rode. As they started off, Lizzie noted she was a better rider than Glory. And she took pleasure in the fact. She had learned a lot about horses from Drayle over the years. The one-eyed horse had finally been sold, and Lizzie remembered him now. This mare felt much less solid beneath her. She coaxed it to follow Glory's horse off the trail.

Glory was delivering fresh goods to the hotel again. Her husband wasn't sick anymore, so he was back in the fields. As they rode at a leisurely pace, Glory described the turnips and tomatoes she grew in her garden. Lizzie asked what Glory and her husband would do once the resort closed this summer. Perhaps they would return to taking their goods into town and selling them, Glory answered. Some were hoping the hotel would be sold to new owners who would maintain it and keep some of the help. Glory hoped for the same thing.

They picked up the pace a bit, and rode until they got tired. Then they rode some more. Just when Lizzie was about to suggest they stop for a rest, they came upon a cabin. It looked run over. Deserted. A tree grew right out of its side edge, as if the cabin had been built on top of its roots. It cracked the wall and angled south toward the sun. Mold covered the gaping hole. Glory jumped off her horse and tied him up. Lizzie descended more slowly, suspicious all of a sudden. Although she trusted this white woman, they were still in slavecatcher territory and she didn't want to be mistaken for the wrong runaway slave. If she disappeared, Drayle would assume she'd run away. And Glory would be able to collect a reward.

A curtain moved in the window. When Glory was certain none of the sounds around them were human, she walked up to the door. It opened without her having to knock. She motioned for Lizzie to follow. They stepped into the dark cabin before they could see who opened it. Behind the door was Mawu, a cloth wrapped around her hair, earrings dangling from her ears. She looked exactly the same, only thinner.

"Mawu!" Lizzie whispered. Mawu reached out for her. The embrace did not end quickly. Lizzie wanted to kiss her face, wanted to cover her up with joy.

"Miss Lizzie," she said.

When they let go of one another, Lizzie looked around. The cabin was dark because the curtains were made out of a thick, opaque cloth. But even in the darkness, she could see its coziness. There was hardly any dust. The wood plank floors were swept clean. Lizzie wondered if Mawu had been expecting them. How did Mawu and Glory communicate? That had been a long ride.

"You looking good, Miss Lizzie," Mawu said.

Something about her diction sounded different. Lizzie looked in the corner of the room. Three books sat neatly stacked. Had she learned to read? Or did those books belong to somebody else? Lizzie searched for signs of somebody else living there.

"It's just me," Mawu said, watching Lizzie. "Reenie long gone."

Mawu brought out three jars of cold tea and the two slave women settled themselves into two ragged armchairs while Glory sat on something that looked like it was carved from a tree stump. A beetle came up through the floorboards. Mawu stomped it with her foot before sitting back down.

Lizzie crossed her arms over her stomach. "I think I might be having another one."

Mawu's eyes traveled down Lizzie's body and back up again. "How long have you knowed?"

Lizzie unfolded her arms. She hadn't talked to anybody about it yet, and it hurt to let her secret go.

"Not long. I don't even feel it moving yet," she said. "What am I going to do?"

"That's the same thing I was gone ask you."

Glory looked from Lizzie to Mawu.

"Kill it," Lizzie said, before she could think.

Mawu's face didn't change, but Glory choked on her tea.

"Don't," Glory said. "Give it to me. I'll take care of it and raise it right alongside this one. Don't kill a baby from God."

"Ain't from God," Mawu snapped. "From the devil, if anything."

"You don't know about God. You left your boy behind," Glory said.

"He'll be all right."

"What kind of mother." Glory left the statement unfinished.

Lizzie had never heard Glory speak so angrily before. She, too, wanted to know how Mawu could have left her son behind. Had she sent him word of her whereabouts? Did she plan to try to buy his freedom? Did she even care?

Glory was still staring at Lizzie as if to say *don't you do that*. Lizzie knew she ought to feel bad about it, pitiful as Glory's face was, but she didn't. She really couldn't say that she felt anything at all. It seemed like lately, her feelings had been drying up.

"Ain't no other choice now, Lizzie. You got to escape. You got to get out now," Mawu said.

Lizzie looked down into her glass. She'd heard somewhere that there were folks who could look at the bits of tea in their cup and tell the future. She counted the flakes of tea swimming in the bottom of her jar, but she didn't see a sign. The leaves didn't form into anything that resembled a hatchet or a rifle.

"Course if it was me, I'd kill it. If you sick, it's gone make it hard for you to escape."

Lizzie thought about her children like she always did when escape crossed her mind. How could she get word to them? Tennessee seemed so far away. Like a different world.

"I reckon that man fancy he love you. You don't still talk that nonsense about loving him, do you?" Mawu watched Lizzie.

That's what she'd told Mawu before. She'd told of Mawu's plan to escape because she loved her, but also because she loved Drayle. But something was shriveling up inside of her. The love she did have left felt old and useless.

"Where's Reenie?" Lizzie asked.

"I don't know. Us was together for only that first night. Us didn't have no plan. Us was just running for our lives. Then us split up cause all the slave catchers was looking for two women together. I do hope she made it. I had a vision the other night that us gone meet up again some day."

So Mawu still believed in her heathen religion. Most folks would have said they would meet up again in heaven. Mawu probably meant she would meet Reenie in Canada or Africa. Lizzie had begun to believe that slaves had a right to venture off course once in a while when it came to religion.

Lizzie looked down at Mawu's hands and saw the burn scars. They were raised and welt-like and lighter-colored than the skin around them, and she could tell that the scarring went up her sleeves. When Mawu caught Lizzie staring, she did nothing to hide her hands.

"This is what you got to do. Everybody expect you to leave at night. That be when there is the most men out looking for runaways so they can get that there reward money. But you got to fool them. You got to leave in the middle of the day. You got to walk just like you free. I got a man can make you up some free papers look just like the real thing. Course it's gone cost money. You got money?" Mawu asked.

Glory took Lizzie's empty glass and went to refill it. When she came back, she grabbed Lizzie's other hand. Glory's hand was cool and wet from where she had been holding the glass. She let go of Lizzie and sat back down on the stump.

"If you ain't got no money, us can get some." Mawu kept on without waiting for an answer. "You know Philip married that woman and now he a barber. Did you ever think he would go from being an outdoors man to cutting hair? They say he picked it up right quick. I bet he rich."

"Philip?" Lizzie said absently.

"Yeah, Philip," Mawu continued. "He'll help if us ask him." Mawu fixed Lizzie with a stare. "But my question is, is you ready? Cause I ain't gone help you if you is gone act the way you acted in the past."

Lizzie tried to focus in on Mawu's features. The woman's face had not changed. It was still steady and cold. "Why did y'all leave without telling me, Mawu?"

Mawu stole a look over at Glory. Glory understood and announced she was going to check on the horses. When the door closed behind her, Mawu said: "Wasn't no time."

"What do you mean? You knew what you were doing long before you did it."

"No. I mean, I knew what I tried to do. I tried to get rid of Tip once and for all."

"You burned down that cottage to kill him."

"He never said nothing bout it or they would have had the law after me. I would be a dead woman. But he knowed what happen. I believe the only reason he wants me back is so he can punish me hisself. Lord knows what would happen if he caught up with me now."

"Why are you still around here then? You ought to be in Canada by now."

Mawu put her glass down. She lifted out of her chair.

At that moment, Lizzie understood why her friend had remained. She had waited for her, the last of them.

"You got to leave, Lizzie. This your only chance. Promise me."

Lizzie couldn't say anything. She was too dizzy from Mawu's love.

Mawu held on to Lizzie's shoulders. "Promise me. Promise me, Lizzie."

Lizzie shook her head. She couldn't promise. She couldn't say anything. She couldn't even look Mawu in the eye.

FORTY

As Lizzie and Glory rode back to the resort from Mawu's cabin, the rain began. For the next three days, it rained without ceasing. The water came down in gusts, along with a tropical-force wind that sent wetness through open doorways and windows, created troughs of water between the hills, and swelled the streams. When the rain finally let up, mottled gray slugs emerged from the ground, leaving trails of mucus on steps and paths. Dozens of them appeared around the property, and the children who were visiting with their parents that summer collected a few and placed them in jars.

Drayle had gone on a camping trip with the men, and did not return as promised. While he was gone, Fran instructed Lizzie to tend to the cottage. Lizzie washed and ironed the clothes, scrubbed the floors, dusted the wood, beat the rugs. While she cleaned, Fran sat in the highback armchair with a cloudy look in her eyes.

In the afternoons, Lizzie spent time with the women in the

hotel kitchen, helping them to prepare the evening's supper. She liked sitting and talking with the free colored women while they peeled turnips, mashed squash, shelled nuts, sliced tomatoes, sifted flour. Lizzie had never spent so much time with them, and she was delighted by their tales. She begged them to tell her more about the men they courted or the monthly neighborhood dances.

The rain had a calming effect and lifted their moods. But it did not help to dissipate the overall gloom at the resort, the knowledge that the servants would have to find work elsewhere.

The first morning she woke and did not hear the pelt of raindrops, Lizzie dressed quickly and rushed outside to see the sky. She was hoping for sun, but was greeted with the same dark clouds scudding across the tops of the trees. She could smell another rain shower as she made her way to the Drayle cottage. As she walked, she saw the manager of the hotel and it looked as if he was walking toward her. She wondered what he thought about Reenie's disappearance, and if Reenie's master had blamed him at all for the unexpected disobedience of his favored slave.

Lizzie tried to walk in a different direction so she would not pass him. But he had already spotted her.

"Hey! You there!" he shouted.

She tucked her chin down as she neared him. Several pains sprang up at once: an ache in her knee, a shot in the elbow. She could feel herself becoming physically ill the nearer she came to him.

He pointed to a batch of firewood. "Gather up that wood and stack it outside the kitchen door."

He walked away.

She pulled out her skirt and placed the wooden blocks onto it. She moved all the firewood in five trips. Afterwards, she looked around and didn't see him. She hurried off to Fran, all the while picturing Reenie and the things he must have made her do.

⌐

Lizzie poured a cup of warm water over Fran's shoulders.

"Back home, it's unheard of to take a bath in the middle of the day. Up here in Ohio, I imagine the ladies do this sort of thing all the time. They probably don't have to work as hard as us Southern women. I'm so tired of working. I've told Drayle that we need to sell the farm and all the slaves and everything else and just move to the city."

"What city, ma'am?" Lizzie asked softly, scrubbing Fran's back with a brush.

Fran waved a hand. "Oh, any city will do. As long as there's no work involved. I want a husband who comes home at a decent hour. They say city men are always out in the streets, working and carrying on, but I wouldn't allow that. I want to live in a house that doesn't have a bunch of slaves walking around. Maybe one of those fancy houses like I saw in Washington, DC. I think I rather like it up North. I like the way they . . . carry themselves."

"Hmmm," Lizzie responded. She tilted Fran's head and cleaned her ears.

"Of course, my mother is a country woman, a Southern woman through and through. My daddy was always talking about his daddy's Scottish heritage. I've always wanted to go to Scotland. I guess I'll make it to Europe someday. The farthest I've traveled is . . . let's see . . . here or Washington, DC. I don't know which one is farther from Tennessee. Now that I think of it, those are the only two *important* places I've ever been."

Fran stood and Lizzie wiped her dry.

"In my next life, I'm not going to marry an ordinary horse-man. I'm going to follow my parents' wishes and marry some kind of aristocrat. Maybe I'll marry a real European aristocrat. A count or a . . . or an earl."

"That would be something else," Lizzie said. Lizzie followed

Fran into the bedroom. She powdered the woman from the neck down. The rain beat against the closed window as if asking to be let in.

"My sister sure does live an exciting life. Sometimes I wish I could trade places with her. Sure, her husband left her. But she's got that blessed child. And she travels all over the place. I wonder if Drayle would mind if I traveled with her sometime. I'd probably be gone at least a year, but oh what a year it would be! I could probably see the world in a year's time! I wonder what one of those big ocean steamships look like. They probably look entirely different than a Mississippi rowboat."

"Yes, I reckon they do," Lizzie said and reached for Fran's dress.

Lizzie could not believe it. A letter from Reenie? How could this be? Reenie could not read or write. Surely this was something that would endanger Reenie. Clarissa had gotten the letter from the butler who had gotten it from the porter who had picked it up in Xenia. It was addressed to "Lizzie Drayle." The letters on the envelope were smudged, but she could clearly read the postmark: "New York."

New York! Even Miss Fran had never been to New York. Lizzie tried to picture what this New York must look like. She had read about it in newspapers, but she found she could not come up with convincing images. So she just thought of Cincinnati—the biggest city she had ever seen—and imagined it was New York.

The letter brought to mind Reenie's story of how she lost the edge of her finger. On the night Lizzie had visited Reenie's cottage and discovered the runaway slave girl, the two women had sat up talking after the child went to sleep. Sir had issued a rule on their plantation that no slaves were to learn to read. Reenie had always wanted to read. Her mother had been taught by Sir's daddy when he was alive, but the woman had never passed it on to her daughter. Reenie kept the primer with her mother's letters in it, and it was this book that Sir found in her cabin. He burned it right in front of her, knowing that he was also burning her mother's memory. She'd hated him for it.

But what he hadn't destroyed, she said, was her desire. She'd gotten another book, stolen from the house that she believed no one would miss. It was more difficult than her last one and didn't have any pictures. She kept it in her skirt so that she could pull it out whenever she had a spare moment. When Sir felt the book's hardness while grabbing her from behind one day, he'd taken it from her. She'd fought him to get the book back, and when he slapped her, she picked up a flower vase and hit him in the head with it. It broke, and the man was astonished to find he was bleeding. Furious, he ordered her down to the stables where a slave was made to slice the tip of her finger right off.

Lizzie sat on the porch of Drayle's cottage, cupping the open letter in her palm, remembering Reenie's story. She read the name at the end first.

"With love I remain, Reenie."
"I remain, Reenie."

"Reenie."

The first thing Lizzie noticed was the penmanship. It was perfect, with looping *g*s and tall *h*s. She wondered if she would be able to write like that if she studied long enough.

She took a moment to thank God for her ability to read. She didn't want to have to share this bit of heaven with anybody:

May 8, 1854
My dearest Lizzie:

I hope this letter finds you. I have asked my friend - - to write and mail this letter in my stead because I am still learning to read and write properly! But I so desired to get a letter to you and let you know that I am doing fine. I am a free woman, Miss Lizzie, and I have a job as a maid in a rich family's residence. They treat me fine, and gave me my very own room. I cannot go into detail how I escaped, but just know that I met many kind people along the way. There were many times that I thought I would not make it, but someone always appeared ready to give me a helping hand. My faith in the Lord is stronger than ever. I do hope that you will lean on Him in your darkest hour. How are your children? Have you heard anything about Mawoo? I know that I will never receive an answer from you as I cannot give you my address, but I thought I'd ask so that you know that I am thinking of you, my dear friend. Whenever I think of you and Mawoo and Sweet, it makes me happy and is about the only thing that I can remember from my past days, other than my darling girl, that brings me Joy.

Miss Lizzie, you will always remain in my thoughts. I do hope to see you again one day, in this life or the next.

> With love
> I remain,
> Reenie

Lizzie wanted to hold on to the letter, wanted to take it back with her to the plantation, and tuck it into her things. But she knew she had to get rid of it. Keeping it could only bring harm to everyone involved. She would have to burn it.

Before she did, however, she wanted to read it again.

FORTY-ONE

Lizzie started drinking the tea the next morning. First, she prepared herself as much as she could. She said her good-byes and prayers. One moment she was thinking of it as a baby—a boy or a girl, a younger brother or sister to Nate and Rabbit. The next minute she was thinking of it like a seed—a large seed, perhaps—but a seed no different than what one found in the middle of a plum or peach. Whenever she felt doubt, she brought up the image of this seed in her mind.

There really had been no decision to be made. If she kept this baby, she would not be able to escape very far. Everyone knew the journey North could take weeks or even months. She would also have to figure out a way, once she was settled, to make enough money to buy Nate and Rabbit's freedom. If she kept the baby and returned to Tennessee, she would be adding another slave to Drayle's plantation. And she had no intention of doing that. No intention whatsoever.

So she followed the instructions given to her by Mawu, used

the herbs gathered by the red-headed woman before she left her cabin that day. Drink the tea every four hours for several days. The only thing she knew the tea contained were squaw root and pennyroyal. And it was bitter. She brewed it in the hotel kitchen, holding the bag of herbs close to her chest in case anyone noticed. At first, she felt the same. Would this really work? But on the second day, she began to feel nauseous and the bleeding started. It was a heavy bleeding that threatened to travel down her leg if she didn't wrap up tightly enough. It soaked her rags so thoroughly she could smell the dark, rich scent of the blood once it dried.

Each day, when Glory delivered the goods, she met Lizzie on the back steps of the hotel kitchen and asked how she was doing. Lizzie tried not to look at the white woman's pregnant belly when she answered.

"Fine," was her answer each day. Then she would take the food off Glory's cart and place it inside the kitchen.

On the third day, the cook sniffed the jar with the steeping herbs while Lizzie was tidying up the pots.

"Bless you child," was all Clarissa said.

On the fourth night, Lizzie cramped so badly that she had to take to the bed. The young girl on the bed next to hers placed a pile of rags beneath her so her blood would not soak through to the mattress. Lizzie felt hot and feverish, and her entire body tingled. Every few minutes, her stomach cramped up into a knot and she had difficulty breathing. Then it would pass.

Clarissa sent Glory up to check on her the next morning.

Glory knelt beside Lizzie.

"How are you feeling?"

Lizzie shook her head. "Not so good. I can't stand to drink this tea anymore."

Glory spread Lizzie's legs and pulled back the rags. The blood

was thick and clotted and lay curled in bulbous lumps like tiny
dead mice.

"How much have you bled?"

Lizzie started to cry. "I don't know, I don't know."

Glory dried Lizzie's forehead. "You'll be fine."

Lizzie reached for Glory's hand. Glory patted it. "Shhh. Hush
now. You'll be fine. Just don't drink any more of that tea. Let the
Lord take away your pain."

Lizzie nodded.

"I've got to go. I'll tell Clarissa in the kitchen to send you up
something to eat. You've got to keep your strength up."

Lizzie nodded and let go of Glory's hand. A few minutes later, Clarissa sent up a bowl of soup. Lizzie tried to sit up in bed and drink it.

The same girl who had shown her to the attic on that first day
now cleaned and changed Lizzie.

"I don't even know your name," Lizzie said to her.

The girl smiled, but did not respond. It was her turn to reject
the intimacy.

Lizzie stayed in bed all day, mostly sleeping and resting, sometimes staring at the wall. What if she wasn't pregnant after all?
What if she had panicked for nothing? Mawu had said it was better to drink the tea than worry, that she had to drink the tea before she started feeling the quickening movements in her belly.

When she felt low, she pulled Reenie's letter from beneath her
mattress and read it again. It gave her hope, if only for a second.
Reenie had been able to escape because she had no children to
mess with her mind. She made a clean break because the only
daughter she had ever known had been sold off from her. Lizzie
wondered if Reenie was trying to find that daughter now. Surely,

she was. Surely any free slave would work to find their family. But where would she start? How did you find someone who may not even have the name you gave them when they were born?

Lizzie could tell the time of day by the color of the light in the room. Even though she had just awakened, she knew it was an hour after supper when Drayle appeared in her doorway. He was freshly shaven and wore the trousers she had washed and pressed for him the week before. His blond hair lay neatly combed to the side, its thinness camouflaged.

He sat on the bed beside her and took her hand.

"I hear that my little Lizzie has been sick," he said.

She shook her head. "I'll be fine. Just a bellyache is all."

He stood up and closed the door. She wasn't ready. Not yet. What if one of the women returned? And how could she tell him she had just gotten rid of the child he never knew he had?

He unbuttoned his shirt.

The girl had just cleaned her bedclothes, so they were fresh. But Lizzie was still bleeding, and although the cramps had subsided for the moment, she was nauseous. She felt that she would vomit at any moment, as if the vomit sat right at the back of her throat.

He had to lift her to move her because she was nestled in the center groove of the bed. He lay beside her naked and stroked her chin as if she wore a light beard.

"I've missed you. I wish I hadn't brought Fran this summer. This is our place," he said.

She had wanted to hear those words from him, but now that she got them, she did not know what to do with them. She did not feel the satisfaction she had thought she would.

He lifted her gown and fumbled with the rags tied around her. He was naked and she was fully clothed.

"You're bleeding?" he asked.

She nodded.

"That's okay," he answered. "I don't mind."

She had always hated that Drayle was foul enough to occasionally take her when she was bleeding. Men were not supposed to do such things. And she did not know how to tell him she was not bleeding in the way he assumed. Her stomach rolled, and she fought at the bitter taste in her throat as he pushed his way into her.

She screamed out, and he put a hand over her mouth.

"Quiet!"

He did not move his hand from her mouth, and she felt she could not breathe. She wanted to stop breathing, so she would not have to deal with this anymore. She would lose Rabbit and Nate, but she would join her unborn baby. She squeezed her eyes shut and held her breath.

When he was finished, she could smell the stink of her own body.

He used the end of her gown to clean himself, leaving streaks of red.

"My Lizzie," he said, not looking at her. He left the door open.

The next day, Lizzie felt worse.

Clarissa was climbing the stairs to her room. Lizzie could tell by the way the steps creaked. Every other step, the woman stopped to get her breath. When Lizzie heard her coming, she knew it was important.

"Your mistress want us to move you. She want you to come to the cabin."

Lizzie shook her head, remembering Drayle's visit. "Tell her I can't work just yet."

"She know that, Miss Lizzie. She want you to come over there so she can get you better. At least that's what they tell me."

The only thing that was going to get her well, Lizzie thought, was the proper expulsion of this baby. Once the baby and all its remnants were gone, she would be better.

If Drayle would just leave her alone, it would be a matter of time before she got better. In that cottage, she was more vulnerable to his desires. Fran would make her a pallet on the floor and fuss over her for a while before using her as a giant ear. The real problem, Lizzie knew, would be the night. Drayle would have no problem taking her on the floor of the living room while Fran slept on the other side of the wall.

"I ain't going," Lizzie said.

Clarissa shook her head. "Oh no. You not gone get me in trouble. You going. That's why I came up here to tell you myself."

Lizzie tried to sit up, and Clarissa helped her. "Miss Lizzie, this just the life you got. Until you do something about it, you got to deal with what the Lord bring you."

Lizzie she was surprised to hear these words from the woman. *Until you do something about it.* Was that a message?

"Miss Clarissa, you can't help me down those stairs. You better send that young girl up here."

"You best believe I ain't gone help you nowhere. I just came up here to deliver the news and let you know I'm here for you if you need me. And I'm gone send over food for you each day now. You hear?"

Lizzie nodded weakly.

You know we were only supposed to stay here two weeks. We're lengthening our trip on account of you," Fran said.

Lizzie sat in the bundle of sheets on the floor and leaned back on the sofa. Fran had done a good job of securing the rags around her private area. But neither wanted to risk her getting blood on the couch, so she sat on the floor for the time being.

"I appreciate that, Miss Fran."

Fran sat at the table staring at Lizzie. She sipped from a glass of water. Every now and then, she looked as if she wanted to ask a question.

"Where's Mr. Drayle?" Lizzie asked. She was still nervous that he would return that night and try to have his way with her.

"He's with the men."

"Oh."

Lizzie looked down again. She wanted to be alone.

"You know, I was always jealous of you."

"Jealous?"

"Of course. You never knew?"

"No, ma'am. I'm just a slave, Miss Fran, and an ugly one at that."

Fran looked down into her water. "So many things. I was jealous because you gave him children when I couldn't. Jealous he brought you to this summer resort without me. It was downright disrespectful!"

Lizzie had thought about this, but she had never questioned the unwavering rule of white men. They did what they wanted. That was the way of the world.

"Lizzie, envy and hate are two different things. I envied you. But I did not, and I do not hate you."

Lizzie nodded. She understood the difference between the two words. What she did not understand was the difference in how Miss Fran would treat her based on the distinction. If Miss Fran did not hate her, why was she trying to make her children go work in the fields?

FORTY-TWO

⁓

That night, Fran slept on the sofa in the living room while Lizzie slept on the floor. In the other room, Drayle slept alone in the bed. Lizzie woke to the strange arrangement, startled. She could hear Drayle snoring. As soon as Lizzie moved to rearrange her gown, Fran woke up.

"Lizzie?"

"Yes, Miss Fran?"

Fran opened her eyes and pushed up onto her elbows. Her eyes were swollen, as if she had not slept well.

"Everything fine?"

Lizzie realized that Fran was keeping watch over her, making sure that Drayle did not try anything. Fran had never done such a thing before, so Lizzie was confused.

"Well, I am a bit thirsty. But I'll get it."

"No." Fran swung her legs off the sofa. "I'll get it."

Lizzie listened to the pump outside. It made a swishing noise.

When Fran returned, she had a glass for both of them. She sat on the sofa beside Lizzie and they drank quietly.

The water refreshed her. Lizzie remembered what Fran had told her earlier, and she felt an urge to reassure her in some way.

"Miss Fran?"

"Yes?"

It was dark, but the moon shone through the window and before long, the shadows in the room had brightened. Fran's curly hair had become unpinned, and there were a few tendrils framing her face. Lizzie looked at her and thought to herself that it was she who had envied Fran, not the other way around. It was she—Lizzie—who would have given anything at one point to be in Fran's place, to have Fran's lustrous hair and skin and position.

In this unfamiliar setting, Lizzie could clearly make out Fran's vulnerability. The white woman stared at Lizzie as if she needed to know what the younger slave woman wanted to say to her, as if she didn't have a closer friend in the world who understood the problems of her intimate domestic life better than Lizzie did.

"The reason I've been sick is because I drank a tea."

Fran nodded. But Lizzie could see that she did not understand. She had never been pregnant, and she did not make the connection.

"A tea that gets rid of a baby."

"Oh!" Fran's hand flew to her mouth and the sound that escaped was enough to stop Drayle's snoring. Lizzie heard him grunt, shift, and settle again.

Fran leaned forward and her breath blew across Lizzie's face. "I ought to slap you!" she said.

It was not the reaction Lizzie had expected. "But I didn't want it. I didn't want another baby." She wanted Fran to know she was not intentionally having any more children with the woman's husband, that something inside of her had changed. Couldn't Fran see it?

"How could you?"

Lizzie was silent. She didn't know what to say. She could see the shine of Fran's eyes.

"Did Nathan know?"

Lizzie shook her head. Would it make Fran feel better if Drayle had known? Lizzie tried hard to figure out the right thing to say.

Fran wiped an eye. She touched Lizzie on the shoulder. "I am sorry. I am sorry for you."

Fran lay back down on the couch and pulled the covers up to her neck although Lizzie could see that the woman's eyes remained open.

For the next two days, Fran acted as if their conversation had never happened. She continued to eat beside her at the table. Lizzie had never sat at the table with Fran, so this was uncomfortable for her. In the evenings, Fran made her bed on the sofa beside Lizzie. Lizzie slept on the floor, wrapped up tightly so that her blood would not stain the wood.

During the day, Drayle left the two women, unusually quiet as he observed them. As Lizzie's strength picked up, she became more relaxed as she felt that she could better handle any advances he might make.

Finally, Drayle announced to the women they were to begin packing up to leave. Lizzie had known they would be leaving soon. They had already been there almost three weeks. She had not seen Philip, so she assumed Drayle's business had not been to buy his former slave back. She knew if Drayle really wanted Philip back, he could just claim him—with or without free papers—and put him on the first ship downriver.

Over the past week, Lizzie had bled so much that she was pretty certain if there had been a baby there, it was dead now. She tried not to imagine the pretty hair, fat cheeks, and toothless grin. But everywhere she went, she smelled it. The wetness of its slick head on a hot night. The quiet scent of baby piss and sour soiling after feedings.

And everything soft reminded her of it as well. Even her own hairy softness. Would it have had blue eyes and white skin like Rabbit? Or dark intense ones like Nate? How tight would the curls have been? And would it have been her first child to inherit her moles?

On the other hand, she was working on convincing herself that she had not been pregnant after all. The increase in urination, dizziness, nausea had all been a part of her imagination, delusions created by a brain that feared another pregnancy. The tea had merely brought her monthly cycle back, forced her to expel the blood that had accumulated. She concentrated on the seed.

And yet, she could not edge the feeling that she had done something terribly wrong. She walked around with the weight of her secret. Fran's reaction had not helped, either. Neither of the women had told Drayle, and each time he spoke to Lizzie, she resented him for not seeing through the lie. She didn't smile, didn't talk, barely ate in the days following her admission to Fran. All she did was obey. Somebody told her to do something and she said "yes ma'am" or "yessir." That was all she could bring herself to say.

She made up in her mind that she wanted to see Mawu one more time. She asked Glory to take her. This time, she rode on the back of Glory's horse and they traveled slowly so the horse's movements would not jar her tender belly or Glory's hardened one.

Mawu did not seem to be expecting them. She cried out when she saw them dismounting the horse, and she waved them into the cabin quickly.

"What's wrong?" Lizzie asked.

Mawu looked from Lizzie to Glory. "I'm moving on. Got word that the slavecatchers is checking cabins in these part of the woods. I been here long enough."

"They searched my house," Glory said. Lizzie looked at her, and it occurred to her that Glory could get in a lot of trouble for what she was doing.

"Where will you go?" Lizzie asked Mawu.

"I don't know," Mawu answered, staring evenly at her.

Lizzie took Reenie's letter out of her dress. "I wanted to give you this. I burned the envelope, but it had New York on it."

"What is it?" Mawu asked.

"A letter from Reenie."

Mawu grabbed it from her. She pressed it to her lips.

"What does it say?" Glory asked.

Lizzie recounted the contents of the letter. She knew it nearly by heart.

Mawu looked up and smiled. "She fine. She fine."

Lizzie would remember that look on Mawu's face for many years to come. The letter had done exactly what she thought it would.

"And it came from New York," repeated Lizzie.

Mawu nodded. She went to the wall and removed a plank. Behind it was a cloth folded up into a small square.

"Take this." Mawu opened the cloth and revealed a thin metal necklace. Birds were carved around the length of its metal links.

"Where did you get this?" Lizzie asked.

"The man what taught me the magic. He say it bring me luck. Now I give it to you."

Lizzie put the necklace to her lips.

"And this for you, too," Mawu said, handing her a piece of folded paper.

Lizzie spread the paper out. There was a drawing—squares and triangles and octagons all linked together in a pattern. It wasn't the prettiest drawing Lizzie had ever seen, but it looked carefully done. It reminded her of a quilt, only irregular, as if the quilter had gotten confused along the way.

"You drew this for me?" Lizzie asked.

Mawu cursed. "Girl, is you always thinking about love? That there's a map. That's how you gone find me. I done already remembered it. Now you remember it. Then burn it with Reenie's letter."

Lizzie studied it. "What does it all mean?"

Mawu explained that the triangles were houses where she could hide. Stay away from the squares. Circles were transporters, people who would take her to the next station.

Lizzie studied the drawing.

"How do I tell what direction I'm going in? What if I get off track?"

Mawu paused. "Look here." She refolded the paper and then unfolded it again. She pointed to the crease. "That there's the ravine. That will point you in the right direction."

Lizzie looked doubtful.

"Or so they tell me. I ain't started the journey yet my own self. But I hear tell that the families will point you north. As long as you is going north, you is going up the page like this here."

"I don't know," Lizzie said.

"Is you coming or ain't you, Lizzie? I ain't got no more time for you. I is leaving tonight. I'll be a day ahead of you if you leave tomorrow. Us is safer if us ain't together. But I is gone leave a message for you with whatever family I meet. I is gone send you signs."

Lizzie still held the drawing. "I've got a sister."

"That sister done been sold," Mawu said.

"Lizzie, has God told you what to do?" Glory interjected in a soft voice.

"Shut up." Mawu grabbed Lizzie's hand. "I ain't gone make you. But I'll be looking over my shoulder for you. You hear?"

Lizzie nodded.

On the way back to the resort, Lizzie did not say a word to Glory.

FORTY-THREE

The indecision paralyzed her. They told her to mop the floor. She did it. They told her to sweep the steps. She did it. They told her to go help in the kitchen. She did it. They told her to go sit in the corner until somebody else told her what to do. She did that too.

After dinner, she helped clear the dishes from the main dining room. But she moved as if she were tied to the ceiling by strings.

The servants in the kitchen were talking. They stopped when they saw Lizzie. Then Clarissa took a look at her and said, "Your friend got caught. They found out where she was hiding."

Lizzie dropped the plates in her hands. By some miracle they didn't break, hitting the floor with a loud noise. "What?" she said.

"The one with the African name."

"They got her?"

That part of her she thought was dead woke back up. She felt her knees give out. It took everything she had to keep standing.

Clarissa nodded.

"How did they find her?"

She shook her shoulders. "Child, I wish I knew. But you know it's a lot of snakes in these here parts."

The other women nodded and continued on with their business. Nobody liked to talk about such things. Only Clarissa stayed, holding on to Lizzie's arm.

Once again, it was Lizzie's fault. She had not been able to make up her mind, and Mawu had obviously tried to wait for her. And the woman had given her the lucky necklace. Lizzie didn't believe in superstitions, but she did wonder if she had taken Mawu's luck. She tried to block out in her mind what Sir would do to her. It hurt too bad to think about. She just hoped Mawu's strength was real.

"They was all after her," Clarissa was whispering as she neared close enough to Lizzie to continue working while she talked. "Her master ain't come back this summer, but he upped the reward money. I suspect it's the highest reward money I seen in these parts in a while."

Lizzie asked one of the young women to help her up the stairs because she didn't think she could make it by herself. Just as they were about to go, an elegant colored woman walked into the kitchen. She was dressed like a white woman, but she was passing through the kitchen door. Her sheer size made her dress seem even grander. There was a man with her who looked just like her. They were both dressed like free colored folks of stature. And from the looks of it, they were brother and sister.

If her mind had not been completely elsewhere, Lizzie might have recognized the face. She might have remembered the girl in the dirty head rag who used to work in the hotel and help her father on occasion when he came to cut the men's hair. But there was something big sitting on top of Lizzie's chest. Too big for her to see past.

The pretty colored woman with the smooth skin came right up to her. Lizzie stepped back.

"Lizzie," she whispered.

Then it came to her. The barber's daughter. Philip's wife.

The woman leaned forward as if to say something in Lizzie's ear. "Philip says for you to meet him by Sweet's grave under the cover of night. He'll be waiting for you."

Then she put a bonnet on her head, her companion took her arm, and they were gone. Lizzie stood there looking after them, turning the words over in her mind.

Did Philip know they were leaving? He knew this was the last summer of the resort. Mawu must have talked to him.

She stood there weighing everything before her: Mawu's capture, Reenie's letter, Sweet's death, Nate and Rabbit, Drayle's touch, Fran's admission. With Mawu gone, little seemed to matter anymore. And yet it did. Did Philip know that Mawu had been caught?

Lizzie put her hand on her belly. She wanted to ride Mr. Goodfellow again. She wanted to go back to the days when Drayle brought her gifts. She missed seeing her children throw horseshoes. She thought of Big Mama and how she had taught her to cook using next to nothing.

She made it to her room and took off her dress. She stretched out in the middle of the bed, naked, her belly poking out just beneath the navel. She put both hands on her middle.

The old me would have cried. The new me is all torn up inside.

How can I still love him?

FORTY-FOUR

Philip had his hat against his chest, and he was kneeling before the grave. Even though his head wasn't bowed Lizzie could tell as she approached that he was praying. It was late, not quite middle of the night, and he was wearing a suit. She had never seen him in a suit before. She touched his elbow, trying to pull him up. She did not want him to get the knee of his pants dirty.

"Lizzie." He hugged her to him.

"Your wife. She told me you would be here." She said the word "wife" with a lilt.

"So glad you came, Miss Lizzie. So glad you came. Come on over here. I got something for you to sit on."

He led her to a tree stump that he had covered with a red cloth. Lizzie did not want to sit on such a cloth. But he guided her onto it, and then stood looking down at her.

"You happy?"

"I sho am. I got a good woman. She come from a good family.

They treat me right. Being free is . . . it's something I can't rightly explain."

"Do you remember the old days?"

"What you mean? It ain't been that long. Course I do." He paused. "I miss my horses. They about the only thing I miss."

Lizzie looked down at her lap.

"And the children. I miss them."

"You ought to see Nate," she said. "He's almost a man."

Philip looked off. She heard the clucking sound in his throat.

"Long as he a slave, he ain't gone never be a man," he said.

"You an abolitionist now?"

He set his hat on the stump beside her. "Ain't no such thing as a colored abolitionist. That's a word for the white folks. We ain't got to distinguish ourselves."

Lizzie nodded. "I guess you're right."

She fingered the edge of her dress. "You heard about Mawu?"

"Yeah. I don't understand why she stayed round here. These is dangerous parts. She should've left long time ago."

Lizzie heard an owl hoot. Owls were such precious birds. Even though she had heard owls plenty of times, she had only seen one once. It had not moved even though she was right near it. It stared at her blankly. She'd wanted to reach out and take it in her hands, stroke its feathers.

"You know why I come to you. I know you believe in Marsuh Drayle. I know you think he different than most white men. But I wants you to know that if you got a mind to leave, I can help you. We can go right now if you wants to. I can point you in the right direction."

Lizzie felt the front of her dress for the drawing Mawu had given her. She had burned Reenie's letter after hearing that Mawu was captured. But she still had the map.

She didn't know how to explain to Philip how she had changed. She didn't know how to explain that if she returned she would not be doing so out of loyalty to Drayle. She would not be returning just for the sake of her children. She would be returning for another reason, a reason she could not quite articulate. It didn't have to do with God, but it did have something to do with the sky.

"Philip, I do appreciate your coming." She stood and cupped his chin in her hand.

He stroked his face against her palm. "I know what that mean. That mean you ain't coming. That mean you still can't bear to leave him."

She took the paper out of her dress. "Mawu gave me this before she got caught. She was waiting for me. She believed in me just like you do. Ain't that something? Everybody seems to think I'm somebody I ain't."

She pressed the paper into his hand. "Take it."

"You know I can't read." He unfolded it and studied it. He slid it into the pocket of his trousers.

"This is what I want you to tell them. Tell Jeremiah that he still owe me from that game of checkers. Tell Young Joe that . . ." He proceeded to give her a litany of messages for the men back on the plantation. Lizzie tried to imprint the messages in her mind, associating them with the faces of the men he mentioned.

" . . . ain't no chance?" he was saying.

If she left, there was no doubt in her mind that Drayle would find her. He would hire every bounty hunter in the country. She would not get far. Even with the speed of not being burdened with a pregnancy, she would have a difficult time outrunning the dogs.

Still, freedom beckoned to her. Even the thought of it made her feel lighter on her feet. It made her want to jump up and down, run screaming through the forest, hug the nearest person to her. If she could do it. If she could win the freedom of her and her children, she could have a real life. She was still young. The children were still young. They had all their adult years to be free.

But there was the sky. And there was no denying it. It had a say in this, too.

Lizzie sat in Drayle's lap. He swung back and forth in the rocker on the porch of the cottage. She placed her toes on top of his. "My Lizzie, do you know why I came this summer?"

"No, I reckon I don't."

He clapped his hands on her thighs. "You are going to be so happy with me!"

She looked at him. Only one thing could make her happy. But Drayle lived in his own world. She had no idea what he thought would make her feel joy.

"They are selling this resort to a group of missionaries. Some holy folks who are going to turn it into a school."

Lizzie nodded. She was still bleeding lightly, but Drayle had taken her on the floor of the cottage just moments before. She had lain there listlessly, thinking about the previous night's meeting with Philip, trying to remember all the messages he had sent to the slaves back home.

"A school for colored."

He stopped rocking and Lizzie turned to look at him. He nuzzled his nose in her neck, clearly looking for appreciation.

"What are you talking about? I can already read."

He shook his head. "No. For Nate. My son. He needs to get his lessons properly. When we return, I'm going to get him a teacher to come to the house and give him his lessons. You've taught him just about everything you can. Now he needs a real education. After that, I'm going to . . ."

The words ran together. She needed to slow him down, but her lips wouldn't move. What was that he was saying? Lessons? School? Education?

"After that you're going to what?" she asked.

"You didn't hear me? I'm going to send him here for school."

She had been waiting so long for this kind of news that she wasn't prepared for it. Her head didn't feel as if it were properly attached to her body. It was as if it would break off and roll across the floor if she moved an inch.

"F-f-free him?"

Drayle chuckled. "I didn't say that. He is still my son, and so still my rightful property. But if he does well in school and doesn't get any notions in his head to run off, I'm going to bring him back south and give him his own plot of land to work. I imagine he could build himself a house and find him a woman to bear his children."

"Oh?"

"My grandchildren. I'm hoping he'll get him a sweet yellow gal."

"Oh." Lizzie felt her eyes begin to moisten. It was too much to take in. Had he told Fran? What did she think? Would she approve?

"But." She was breathing rapidly. "Rabbit."

Drayle shook his head. "Lizzie, you are something else. You know that? You are never satisfied. I give you an inch and you want to take a yard."

Lizzie knew what that meant. There were no such plans for Rabbit. So what did he intend for her? Surely, he had thought of her getting properly married and bearing his grandchildren, too. A scene came into her head of Rabbit playing on the grounds of the nearby colored resort. "But she's smart, Drayle. She needs education, too."

Drayle pulled her to him and closed his eyes. He was ending the conversation.

Lizzie knew him well enough to understand what his silence meant. Rabbit would be the bait that would bring Nate home. Rabbit would bear children that would give him house slaves, while Nate would bear the children that would inherit Drayle's name. He had worked it all out in his mind.

Lizzie knew she should feel excited about one of her children escaping the plantation. And she was. But she wanted more. She felt she deserved more.

FORTY-FIVE

Lizzie had been told they were leaving that very day. Drayle wasn't taking any chances. He'd had Lizzie tied to the front porch of his cottage all morning long. She'd been sitting there all day, lapping up water out of a bowl like a dog. She put her whole face in it trying to cool off. Could she drown in that bowl if she stuck her face in it long enough?

"You ought to be happy about seeing your children," Fran said through the window. "They'll be waiting on you."

My children ain't the only thing I love. If I was allowed, I reckon I'd love myself, too.

It was clear to Lizzie that Drayle had not told Fran about his plan to send Nate to Ohio to be educated. Did Drayle really think Lizzie would try to escape when her son's future rested on her decision to return south with him? She supposed he had her tied up because he did not want to risk having his plan disrupted. Lizzie scoffed at his ignorance. Surely he realized that if she had planned to escape, she would have done so long before then.

Drayle had a cart brought around to carry the trunks up to the hotel. Lizzie wondered about her rag bundle. Her two dresses. The necklace Mawu had given her.

"I need my things," she called out to Fran.

"What things? You act like you own something," Fran said as she came out of the door. She squatted and placed a cracker on Lizzie's tongue. "I put them in my trunk," she added.

Lizzie chewed and looked out over the pond. The cabin that Mawu burned down the summer before was gone. There wasn't anything there now but a square patch of dirt with weeds shooting through. The other cabins looked empty, doors swinging back and forth in the wind. Lizzie was glad the hotel had been sold to a missionary group for a colored school. The land would belong to God now. She looked over at the spot where Tip had beaten Mawu in front of all of them, and she hoped the missionaries could bring some holiness to the place.

The water wheel turned.

She remembered how she used to want to learn to be a lady. To learn to hold her skirt over the ground. It had never worked for her. It seemed like each time she had tried to grab a fistful of fabric, it got caught between her feet and tripped her up.

A thought stopped her. What if he had lied? What if he had told her he was going to educate Nate just to make sure she returned?

She dismissed the thought. Drayle had told the truth. She could feel it.

As she leaned against the porch post, she thought of Rabbit and what she would teach her. This was what she would say: *Don't give in to the white man. And if you have to give in, don't give your soul over to him. Love yourself first. Fix it so you don't give him children. If you ever make it to freedom, remember your mammy who tried to be good to you. Hold fast to your women friends because they are going to be there when ain't nobody else there. If you don't believe in God, it's all right. God believes in you. Never forget your name. Keep track of your*

{288} DOLEN PERKINS-VALDEZ

years and how old you are. Don't be afraid to say how you feel. Learn
a craft so you always have something to barter other than your private
parts.

What kind of craft could Rabbit learn? Big Mama had made soap, but she had lost both eyes because of it. Philip had trained horses. Lizzie could cook. She thought of Sweet and her ability to sew. It had sustained her while she was mourning. Maybe she would make certain that Rabbit knew how to sew. Then she thought of Reenie's ability to birth a baby. That was a skill that could come in handy, for sure.

Drayle climbed the steps of the cottage. He leaned down and kissed Lizzie on the head.

"How is my darling?"

"Not understanding why you tied me up. I ain't going nowhere."

"I know. I just don't want to have to go looking for you. You ready, Francesca?" he called.

"I'll walk on up by myself," she answered.

He smiled at Lizzie. She tried to make sense of it, this smile of his that looked for all the devil like he meant it.

She watched him walk in the direction of the hotel. He disappeared into its crumbling whiteness.

FORTY-SIX

Mawu told her this story the last time she saw her. It was about her name. She said that she was named after an African god who made everything and everyone—man, animal, and plants. She said she didn't believe in Adam and Eve. The old root doctor who lived on her plantation had told her this story and renamed her after an African god named Mawu. He said this Mawu had a twin named Lisa. So when she met Lizzie, Mawu suspected she was her other half because of her name. But then Lizzie told on her and Mawu became doubtful.

When Mawu returned to Louisiana, the doctor told her Lizzie might still be the one. Even if she were a traitor. So she came back to Tawawa and gave Lizzie a second chance. To learn Lizzie's true heart, not the one that had been tainted by slavery. So during the entire second summer of her visit to Tawawa House, Mawu studied Lizzie to see if she had this strength. And she concluded that Lizzie did. She said she recognized it. That's why she waited on her in the end. Because Lizzie's heart was her heart. Her twin. Lizzie was Lisa.

So according to the hoodoo man, these two—except they weren't really two, they were one—made everything in four days. On the first day, they made mankind. They made everyone out of clay and water and gave them features like kinky hair and brown skin. On the second day, they made the earth so mankind had somewhere to reside. They put plants and animals on the earth so the people could eat and live. On the third day, they gave mankind reason, separating them from the animals. They gave the people the power to speak and think. On the fourth day, Mawu-Lisa gave them the tools they needed to farm the land and clear the forests in order to build their houses.

Mawu was the moon and Lisa the sun. Mawu cold, and Lisa hot. Mawu the night and Lisa the day. Mawu the earth and Lisa the sky. Mawu the west, Lisa the east. The rootworker told her that even though Mawu was considered to be the mother and the wise one and the creator, Lisa was the one with the strength. Lisa was as strong as a man!

All Lizzie could say was, *a woman helped create the world?*

The story made Lizzie believe in something. So even though she was going back to Tennessee, she wasn't the same woman. She was something else.

When she thought of her two children, she thought of Mawu-Lisa and she prayed to them that her children could possess the same strength she had gotten on account of her name. All these years, she realized, she had been putting her faith in Drayle to free her children. Now she had to put her faith in herself.

At night, before she went to sleep in her cabin down in the quarters, she remembered Mawu's story and told herself that she was a god, a powerful god. Each and every day, she reminded herself of this so that she wouldn't fall backward. She was more than eyes, ears, lips, and thigh.

She was a heart. She was a mind.

AUTHOR'S NOTE

This is a work of fiction. Tawawa Resort did exist, however. Located near Xenia, Ohio, it opened in 1852 and closed in 1855. It is documented by historians that Southern slaveholders frequented the resort with slave entourages, and that these visits were a reason for the decline of the resort's popularity. The presence of slave concubines is part of local oral history.

The land and surrounding area were sold to the Cincinnati Conference of the Methodist Episcopal Church, and it established the Ohio African University in 1856. With the onset of the Civil War, enrollments declined and the original campus was closed. In 1863, the property was purchased by the African Methodist Episcopal Chuch and was renamed Wilberforce University; it continues to be the nation's oldest, private, predominantly African American university. It is believed that the children of the unions between the slave women and the slaveholders were among the early students at the university.

ACKNOWLEDGMENTS

I did not do this alone. Many people helped. Thank you to those who helped with research: Michaela Hammer, my student research assistant; University of Puget Sound for research funds and the Mellon Sabbatical; Jacqueline Y. Brown at Wilberforce Stokes Library; Elizabeth L. Plummer at Ohio Historical Society; Gwenyth G. Haney at Dayton History; Peggy Burge at Collins Library. Thank you to Bread Loaf and Tin House Writers Conferences. Thank you to my manuscript readers Colleen McElroy, Kathryn Ma, and Kirsten Menger-Anderson. Thank you to my mentors for unflagging support: James A. Miller, Randall Kenan, Richard Yarborough, Tayari Jones, Helena Maria Viramontes, Lawrence Jackson, Hans Ostrom. Thank you to my sister, Jeanna McClure, for inspiration. Thank you to my agent Stephanie Cabot, and her colleague, Sarah Burnes. I am grateful for the opportunity you gave me. Thank you to my editor, Dawn Davis, for patient guidance. Thanks, again, to my parents who always encouraged my love for books.

Finally, thanks to my best friend and husband, David, for sharing me with this book and these characters for these last few years. Your intellect and honest feedback kept me going when I faltered. And for my little Elena, who taught me what Lizzie's love for her children meant to her.

About the author

About the book

Read on

Insights,
Interviews
& More...

Meet Dolen Perkins-Valdez

© Louie Escobar

DOLEN PERKINS-VALDEZ'S FICTION
and essays have appeared in *The Kenyon Review*, *African American Review*, *North Carolina Literary Review*, *Richard Wright Newsletter*, and *Robert Olen Butler Prize Stories*. Born and raised in Memphis, a graduate of Harvard, and a former University of California President's Postdoctoral Fellow, Perkins-Valdez lives in Washington, D.C. This is her first novel. Visit her at www .dolenperkinsvaldez.com. ∾

The Women of Tawawa House

An Interview with Dolen Perkins-Valdez

by Catherine Delors

This interview was originally published on www.catherinedelors.com. Catherine Delors is the author of two novels: Mistress of the Revolution *and* For the King.

Wench *is a powerful, provocative title. How did it come to you? Did you think of alternative titles?*

Excellent question. It's one that I'm sure lots of people have a curiosity about. My original title during the "unpublished manuscript" phase was *The Women of Tawawa House*. I liked that title as well. It was fine. Yet as I continued to think about the novel and tinker with my drafts, I began to think more of this word, particularly as it was applied to African American women during this period. Many of the reward posters seeking runaway slave women referred to the escapees as wenches. There was a terrible stereotype that arose from this period that regarded black women as hypersexualized. This stereotype had an earlier counterpart in the travel journals of Europeans who traveled in Africa and, after observing bare-breasted African women who lived in villages, came to the startling conclusion that Black women were more sexual than White women. ▶

Originally, the word "wench" in the Middle English meant simply a young girl. It evolved to mean a wanton woman. It was only after the word entered American usage that it became specifically attached to Black women. I felt that given the sexual servitude of my female characters, this word would most accurately evoke the set of cultural expectations they were entangled within.

This is your first novel. How did the idea for this book arise?

I was reading a biography of W. E. B. Du Bois and, during a section about his tenure at Wilberforce University, came across a stunning line about the existence of a summer resort in Ohio that was popular among slaveholders and their enslaved mistresses. I could not get this idea out of my head. I had so many questions. I began to delve into the archives and found very little. These women left no record behind. Neither did the men, as far as I could tell. I know that you have read Annette Gordon-Reed's brilliant historical book *The Hemingses of Monticello*, and one factor that allows her to write so vividly about Thomas Jefferson's relationship with Sally Hemings is the fact that Jefferson was a meticulous record-keeper and also that he was such a prominent national figure. Well, there were many instances of relationships between slaveholders and their enslaved women that escaped the public eye. In fact, I would venture so far as to say that

❝ I felt that given the sexual servitude of my female characters, this word ['wench'] would most accurately evoke the set of cultural expectations they were entangled within. ❞

this was not an unusual arrangement, except there are few records because not every slaveholder was a meticulous record-keeper and not every slaveholder was famous. I wanted to write this book to answer my own questions of what it would have been like for these women.

Tawawa, where the story takes place, no longer exists. Yet in this book you manage to bring back to life this odd setting, so close to freedom for Lizzie, your heroine, and her friends, and yet a place of enslavement. How did you recreate it?

There is a sketched broadside of the actual resort that I found at the Ohio Historical Society. It is actually quite large—poster-sized—and very detailed. In the newspaper advertisements for the resort, I was able to determine how people traveled there (via steamboat and railroad), and there are topographical descriptions that helped me to recreate the physical setting. Although there were no personal accounts of slaves who traveled there, there was definitely information about the place itself. I merged that detailed research with my own knowledge of nineteenth-century slave narratives as well as early fictionalized accounts of Black women's experiences such as *Incidents in the Life of a Slave Girl* by Harriet Jacobs. I wanted to provide another account of the Black female slave experience, but I did not want it to be altogether disconnected from earlier accounts. ▶

> " There were many instances of relationships between slaveholders and their enslaved women that escaped the public eye. In fact, I would venture so far as to say that this was not an unusual arrangement. "

The Women of Tawawa House *(continued)*

I am not a slave, not African American, and yet in some ways Lizzie's story felt very close to my own experience. Would you call her relationship with Drayle, her master/owner, love?

I want to mention that Fran, the White wife of Drayle, also finds herself in a delicate situation. I hope that the novel points out the ways in which *all* women in the South were affected by slavery. Many women readers, especially Southern women, may find that this book speaks to their sense of Southern history. As for whether or not Lizzie and Drayle love each other, I am not sure. Certainly, we can say there is genuine affection between them. But was it love? I think this is a great question for book clubs. I can't answer it. If I say to you that the concept of love must be taken in the context of the period, then you could possibly answer that any concept of "love" must be contextualized. So there is no easy answer for that. All I can say is that their relationship is a complicated one. And, believe it or not, as I wrote the novel, I felt sympathy for Drayle as well.

Some of Lizzie's friends and fellow slaves at Tawawa were clearly raped. In the context of master/slave relationships, where does seduction stop and rape begin?

Very good question. I don't know the answer to that. Lizzie is first taken by

66 I hope that the novel points out the ways in which *all* women in the South were affected by slavery. 99

her master when she is thirteen years old, and there is a clear seduction there. These are such imbalanced power dynamics.

What moves you most about Lizzie?

What makes my heart break for her is that, despite her exceptional intelligence, she has such difficulty emotionally extricating herself from her situation.

The story takes place during the 1850s, tantalizingly close to the Civil War. I very much wanted to follow Lizzie and her children further. Will you write a sequel?

I don't think so. I feel that one can take refuge in knowing that the Civil War is coming and that Lizzie and her children may see freedom.

What authors influenced you?

I am influenced by so much more than fiction, but the great novels that changed my life include Toni Morrison's *Beloved*, Gabriel García Márquez's *One Hundred Years of Solitude*, Vladimir Nabokov's *Lolita*, Gayl Jones's *The Healing*, and Edward P. Jones's *All Aunt Hagar's Children*.

What can you tell us about your next projects?

I am working on a new novel. Stay tuned!!! ∾

> " One can take refuge in knowing that the Civil War is coming and that Lizzie and her children may see freedom. "

The Evolution of a Footnote

This article was originally published in January 2010 on BookPage.com: America's Book Review.

I HAVE NEVER BEEN VERY GOOD at coming up with ideas for stories and novels. When I was in graduate school, they encouraged us to scan the obituaries for stories. I could never do this! Aside from the fact that I'm a Southerner and have a deep respect for the deceased, I often take ideas to my desk and find they don't work. I don't know your experience, but I've found that most ideas aren't viable ideas.

So when I came upon this historical footnote about a summer resort that existed near Xenia, Ohio, in the 1850s, notorious for its popularity among slaveholders and their enslaved mistresses, I did not know where this fact would lead me. I began by just digging in the historical archive. I learned that the resort had been established by a lawyer and state legislator named Elias Drake. At the time, it was very popular among the country's elite to travel to areas with natural springs. Hoping to create a successful business, Drake acquired the property in 1851 and opened it in 1852. Eventually, Northern visitors displayed their disdain at the sight of Southern slaveholders and their slave entourages. Ohio was a free state, and many of the Northerners were abolitionists. They did

> 66 When I came upon this historical footnote about a summer resort . . . notorious for its popularity among slaveholders and their enslaved mistresses, I did not know where this fact would lead me. 99

not enjoy vacationing with the Southerners, so they stopped coming and business declined. The place closed in 1855.

This was my first time writing something set in another era. As a result, I had a lot of research to do: What kinds of clothes did slaves wear? What did the men hunt in Ohio? What kinds of flowers and vegetation grew there? Then, when the novel takes the reader back to a plantation in Tennessee, I had to research the daily culture of life on a Southern plantation. After I felt more comfortable with this era, I had to figure out how Southerners would have made it to Ohio in the first place. I learned that advances in transportation, such as the ever-improving steamships that traveled up and down the Mississippi River, or the recently constructed Little Miami Railroad that stretched from Cincinnati to Xenia, made a significant impact on who was able to vacation in this Ohio town known for its mineral baths.

Even with all this fascinating history, I knew that I wanted to complete more than a scholarly essay on this period in history. What I really wanted to find was a record of the women who were alleged to have been the mistresses of their owners. Of course, I found no such records because most slaves left behind very little other than oral remnants. That's when I knew there was a rich fictional landscape waiting to be mined. I understood that I would have to imagine myself into the minds and bodies of these women. It was a task that I undertook with great care. What ▶

66 What would it have been like to be a slave woman at this resort at this particular time? . . . Would the bond with her master be so strong that it would have a hold over her that even the promise of freedom could not overcome? 99

would it have been like to be a slave woman at this resort at this particular time? Would she have considered escaping to freedom? Or would the bond with her master be so strong that it would have a hold over her that even the promise of freedom could not overcome? Ultimately, I discovered there are different kinds of freedoms. I was in the face of something very complex, so complex that it took four years to work through it.

Throughout my drafting period, the novel was titled *The Women of Tawawa House*. Once I entered the contract with Amistad, I shared with my editor Dawn Davis another idea for a title. "Wench," I said. She asked why. I told her that I was interested in this word because it originally meant, in the Middle English, a young girl. As it evolved, it came to mean a "wanton woman." Yet it was only when it entered American usage that it began to be specifically applied to black women. Many reward posters seeking runaway slave women referred to them as "wenches." It was a derogatory term of the period that I wished to highlight, complicate, recast. I wanted to humanize the women to whom this term referred. Give them a chance to tell their own story. To my delight, my editor agreed.

And so my debut novel *Wench* was born. ◌

66 Many reward posters seeking runaway slave women referred to them as 'wenches.' . . . I wanted to humanize the women to whom this term referred. 99

10

Women and Slavery
Imagining the Historical Gaps

FICTIONAL NARRATIVES offer us a unique perspective on the history and legacy of slavery in the United States. This history is so rich, so complex, that one novel can only tell a small part of the story. If you are interested in learning more about how slavery affected women, I highly recommend these books.

Incidents in the Life of a Slave Girl by **Harriet Jacobs:** Published in 1861, this is one of the most important pieces of American literature from the nineteenth century. Widely regarded as an autobiographical novel, this book urges the reader to think about the complex compromises made by black women in slavery. Furthermore, the novel portrays the obstacles one faced as a free woman of color.

Beloved by **Toni Morrison:** This beautifully rendered classic American novel portrays a slave who detests slavery so much that she would rather kill her children than have them thrust back into slavery.

Property by **Valerie Martin:** The main character of this book, Manon, struggles with her husband's affair with their house slave, Sarah. *Property* reveals with extraordinary sensitivity the difficult position of white women in the slave-owning south. ▶

> 66 Fictional narratives offer us a unique perspective on the history and legacy of slavery in the United States. This history is so rich, so complex, that one novel can only tell a small part of the story. 99

Women and Slavery (*continued*)

Dessa Rose **by Sherley Anne Williams:**
In this well-researched novel, Sherley
Anne Williams tells of a slave woman
who helps lead an uprising among a
group of slaves. It also features Rufel,
a white woman who helps harbor
runaway slaves on her plantation
while her husband is away.

Sally Hemings **by Barbara Chase-
Riboud:** Like many Americans, I am
fascinated by the relationship between
Thomas Jefferson and his slave Sally
Hemings. Yet long before DNA evidence
proved that Hemings's descendants
possess Jefferson DNA, Chase-Riboud
penned a controversial novel about the
relationship. Originally published in
1979, this novel is an important link
in this American saga.

Corregidora **by Gayl Jones:** Out of all
the novels mentioned here, only this
stunner by the remarkable Gayl Jones is
set in the contemporary era. This novel
explores the legacy of the relationships
between slave owners and their female
slaves. Ursa, a blues singer, detests the
nineteenth-century slaveowner who
fathered both her grandmother and
mother. The novel suggests there is a
generational impact of such memories
upon families.

Kindred **by Octavia Butler:** In this
imaginative and fantastical novel,
Dana travels back in time to experience
firsthand what it is like to be a black
woman during slavery. ❧

Don't miss the next
book by your favorite
author. Sign up now for
AuthorTracker by visiting
www.AuthorTracker.com.